Praise for the Detective Ga

'Mind blowin

'Keeps you on the edge of your seat'

'A great crime procedural series!'

'An amazing thriller from beginning to end'

'Couldn't ask for a better read'

'This series just keeps getting better.
I was hooked from the first page'

'A five-star read, no question'

Born in Dublin, **JENNY O'BRIEN** moved to Wales and then Guernsey, where she tries to find time to both read and write in between working as a nurse and ferrying around three teenagers.

In her spare time she can be found frowning at her wonky cakes and even wonkier breads. You'll be pleased to note she won't be entering *Bake Off*. She's also an all-year-round sea swimmer.

Also by Jenny O'Brien

The Detective Gaby Darin series
Silent Cry
Darkest Night
Fallen Angel

Lost Souls

JENNY O'BRIEN

ONE PLACE. MANY STORIES

HQ
An imprint of HarperCollins*Publishers* Ltd
1 London Bridge Street
London SE1 9GF

www.harpercollins.co.uk

HarperCollins*Publishers*
1st Floor, Watermarque Building, Ringsend Road
Dublin 4, Ireland

This paperback edition 2021

2

First published in Great Britain by
HQ, an imprint of HarperCollins*Publishers* Ltd 2021

Copyright © Jenny O'Brien 2021

Jenny O'Brien asserts the moral right to be
identified as the author of this work.
A catalogue record for this book is
available from the British Library.

ISBN: 9780008457051

To Joël, Remi and Freya.
You inspire me each and every day.
Be happy, be brave but, most important of all, be kind.

Chapter 1

Elodie

Friday 31 July, 1 p.m. Colwyn Bay

Elodie Fry was bored. It was only two weeks since school had broken up for summer but she had nothing to do and nobody to do it with.

The house was quiet, the only sound to be heard the distant hum of the hoover as her mum vacuumed the stairs. She could of course help but when she'd offered she'd had her head snapped off for her trouble, which was such a rare event that she'd retreated to the lounge in a huff with her library book. That was an hour ago. Her book was long since finished, her water bottle empty and there was nothing on the television that grabbed her attention.

She scrabbled to her feet, her skinny legs almost too long for her body. Her fair hair was still pulled back into the netted bun she had to wear to her ballet lessons, a look that was at war with her pink hoodie and scruffy jeans. She left the lounge and wandered into the kitchen, humming a little tune she'd made up in her head. Her mum's bag was slung around the back of the chair, her half-full mug of cold tea abandoned on the pine table. She could always start on her lunch but she wasn't in the mood for a sandwich. Her normally placid demeanour was disturbed by the bitter taste of annoyance at the way her mother had spoken to her.

While she didn't have a dad, she did have an amazing mum who worked all the hours to ensure that they had enough money to eke out over the month. There was never much left over for treats and a new school uniform was one of the corners that her mother had to cut in favour of second-hand. But she always managed to scrape enough money together for a pair of proper leather school shoes and a decent pair of trainers, even if they weren't as designer as Elodie would like. No, Elodie had a lot to be thankful for. Her lack of a dad was a niggle but there were far worse things than a snappy mum and no dad.

There was nothing in the kitchen that she wanted so, instead of dawdling, she twisted the key to the back door and headed out into the fenced garden, the warm burst of sun on her face causing her to break out into her signature cheeky smile. The garden wasn't big: barely a few metres of grass bordered by a small patio and with a large shed taking up the whole of one corner.

After a few walkovers and handstands she was bored again. Her gaze lingered on the shed. What she needed was a ball, something she could bang against the side of the house until her mother had finished whatever she was doing upstairs.

The shed opened easily under her touch, the bolt sliding back with a slight squeak. She held her breath and her fingers gripped the edge of the door. Her mother had told her on more than one occasion that she had no business going into places that didn't concern her, which meant that the shed was clearly out of bounds. But just like Eve and that apple, Elodie didn't heed the warning. She was still feeling aggrieved at being told off and it wasn't as if she intended to do any damage, she thought, taking in the neat line of old garden tools hanging from bright red hooks beside the freezer.

Continuing to hum her little tune, she rummaged along the shelves in vain for something to play with. There were no toys but the possibility of an ice cream had her walking towards the freezer, her mouth starting to water. The sound of the shed door banging against its hinges caused her to quicken her step. She wasn't doing anything wrong, not really. As she brushed a stray cobweb off her sweatshirt, the hairs on the back of her neck stood to attention, her failsafe warning system finally alerting her to the danger up ahead. She turned and stared, her fingers trembling, closely followed by her arm, her breath heaving as her lungs scrabbled around for enough oxygen to meet the sudden rampant demand placed on it by her galloping heart.

Life paused, then flashed before her in a rapidly blinking strip of images. She couldn't move when she knew she must. One second passed, then two, before her feet found the will to turn and run, the open door of the shed forgotten in her hurry to escape the very worst of nightmares.

Elodie pulled the straps of her rucksack tightly across her shoulders, taking the time to scan the room for any essentials that she might have forgotten. There'd be no coming back, not now. Her gaze dawdled on the pile of teddies that had grown exponentially over the course of her young life. She'd allowed herself only one, Ted, because he was small and she was able to tuck him down the side of her rucksack at the expense of a pair of socks. She'd also allowed herself a book, again only the one. But suddenly she felt an affinity with Harry Potter and his Philosopher's Stone, not that there could ever be a happy resolution to her own personal tale of woe. Unlike Harry there was no Dumbledore to guide her, or Hagrid to protect her from what was coming. She'd poked her nose where she shouldn't and fleeing the security of the only home she'd ever known was the one outcome left to her.

Wiping her sleeve across her eyes, she headed for the door, not bothering to close it behind her. Her mother would know soon enough that she wasn't in the one place she'd expect – bed. With her hand clenched around the banister, she avoided the creaky first and third stairs as she hurried to the bottom, fearful now that her mother might guess that something was up. She'd certainly questioned her at length over the weekend, but what could Ellie tell her? She wasn't prepared to lie and she'd never in a million years believe the truth. Ellie had spent the last two days trying to persuade herself that Friday had never happened, but it was no good. She only had to close her eyes and she was back in that shed ...

The kitchen was next and this was the place that delayed her the most. She had a few quid, not much but enough for a start. However, she needed food – as much as she could carry but not too heavy to weigh her down. Tins of beans came first, luckily with a ring pull as she didn't fancy depriving her mum of the only can opener in the overflowing cutlery drawer. A spoon, a fork and a knife. She paused over the knife, an intense look of concentration pulling at her brow. She hadn't thought of a weapon but what was the likelihood that she might need one? Her hand fingered one of the wooden-handled set of six steak knives that her mother had picked up cheap at some car-boot or other. The knife got placed in the bottom of her bag as did the small wind-up torch that lived in the pot on the kitchen shelf. She also took some matches, bread, cheese and a few other cans before testing the weight of her rucksack and reluctantly pulling the drawstring and lifting it onto her shoulders.

Ellie was small for her age, but wiry. A life spent practising ballet had firmed her muscles and hardened her resolve. She could do this. She had to do this.

There was no note. She wouldn't have known what to write in any case. A solitary tear tracked down her cheek. Instead she picked up a pink Post-it Note and drew a heart before sticking it to the side of the kettle and heading for the door without a backward look.

Chapter 2

Gaby

Monday 3 August, 7.05 a.m. Rhos-on-Sea

'Darin speaking.'

Acting DI Gaby Darin glanced down at the screen of her mobile, a frown firmly in place. With Owen Bates, her DC, still on paternity leave until later today, she was the senior officer on the North Wales Major Incident Team and as such available 24/7 whether she liked it or not. She didn't mind covering but she wondered why they always phoned her when she was about to sit down to eat. Porridge was bad enough but cold it was a thick, unpalatable, paste-like gloop.

'Ma'am, it's Jax Williams. We have a runaway girl.'

Gaby leant back in her chair, breakfast forgotten, her mind full of another missing girl, a mystery they'd solved only a short time ago: twenty-four years too late. There couldn't be a second one surely – not so soon. But, hand resting on her brow, she knew she shouldn't be surprised at the news, only her reaction. Instead of the adrenalin that usually soared through her veins at the thought of a new case, all she could come up with was a deep sense of disappointment. It suddenly felt as if she was losing her identity with each successive crime, as if someone was taking a chisel and chipping away. Gaby Darin: acting DI. Not Gabriella: sister, friend, lover.

Last week had been a good week, the best week in ages. Her relationship with Rusty Mulholland, the resident pathologist, was continuing to blossom. Still only friends, she could see that changing to something more but only if she was allowed the opportunity of cultivating their growing rapport.

'Ma'am, are you there?'

With a huge effort, Gaby pulled herself together. It wasn't like her to wallow in self-pity and it certainly wasn't like her to daydream about red-headed pathologists with startling blue eyes and a temper that was on an even shorter fuse than her own. She was there to fulfil the role she was paid for. If she didn't like it, she could always ... She shook the thought away. No. She couldn't!

'Yes, sorry, Williams. It must be a bad line,' she said, crossing her fingers behind her back as the easy lie slipped through her lips. She wasn't going to tell him the truth. 'Go on, you were saying?'

She grabbed her keys from the centre of the table and, heading into the hall, picked up her bag and jacket from the newel post, careful to avoid the mess that was currently her lounge. Painting the wood panelling that lined the bottom half of the room at the weekend wasn't the greatest of ideas but, with work being quiet, she'd optimistically thought that she'd be able to get it finished in the evenings after work, refusing to dwell on the image of cosy meals for three while she continued getting to know Rusty and his young son, Conor.

'We got the call about thirty minutes ago. Elodie Fry, age ten. Her mother went to wake her this morning only to find that her bed hadn't been s-s-slept in,' he stuttered, heaving air into his lungs. 'After phoning around and a quick search, she rang us. I'm heading over to interview her.'

'I'll meet you there – and, Jax, grab Amy. The sooner we get

6

a FLO involved the better. It's times like this that family liaison officers come into their own.' She pushed against the front door to check the latch had caught, making a mental list, which she started to tick off in the maelstrom that was now her mind. 'And get Márie and Mal involved ASAP. They can get the search underway while we wait for Owen.'

'Did you want me to give him a ring too?'

Owen. Her fingers gripped her keys, the hard, cold metal biting into the soft flesh of her palm. How would he take another missing girl after the recent ordeal that his wife and unborn child had gone through? How would he stand up to the pressure when he'd nearly decided to throw his career away? There was only so much she could do to protect him on a case like this.

'No, let me contact him. You've enough to do. What's the address?'

Ystâd golygfa'r môr, or Sea View estate, was the largest housing development in Colwyn Bay. A mixture of social housing, the sprawling concrete jungle had a reputation that struck fear into the hearts of the coppers who had the misfortune to attend any of the frequent call-outs. But as with most of these estates the inhabitants got on with their own business, the few bad ones spoiling it for everyone.

Number 312 was a narrow, two-bedroomed house with distant views over the Welsh coast and bordered by a wasteland of tarmac littered with potholes and the odd dolls' pram along with the usual detritus of cola cans and sweet wrappings. But the house was different again. While small and cluttered, it was spotlessly clean. The sofa and recliner chair were arranged around a small TV, the mantelpiece over the three-bar electric fire displaying unframed photos, all of the same pretty blonde girl. But Gaby wasn't interested in the girl's appearance, not yet. All her attention was on the faded middle-aged woman currently leaning forward on the sofa, a long, low keening sound coming from her mouth.

Jax dipped his head to whisper in Gaby's ear. 'Ms Anita Fry, ma'am. She's been like that ever since we arrived. I've sent Mal and Marie a copy of the most recent photo for distribution and DS Potter is on her way.' He turned, adding over his shoulder, 'I thought I'd make her a cuppa. S-s-she looks as if she needs it.'

Gaby nodded in agreement, her gaze pinned to the woman in front of her. About forty, and dressed in jeans and a loose top the colour of an overripe avocado, Ms Fry had the complexion of someone who'd had several knocks over the years: her jawline saggy, her skin that pasty tone of too little time spent out of doors. Life was hard for some families, none harder than in this room.

As an experienced detective, it took a lot to engage Gaby's sympathies. She'd seen far too much of the human race to ever believe what was in front of her. She'd been lied to and conned in both her personal and professional life far too many times to take people on trust. But if anyone was going to engage her compassion it was this woman.

'Hello, Ms Fry. My name is DI Gaby Darin.' She dropped into the chair opposite, leaning forward, her clasped hands dangling between her legs, the line of her favourite navy Zara jacket bunching around her shoulders. 'I've already pulled a team of officers together to scour the neighbourhood but I need to ask you some questions that will help us. To begin with is there any reason you can think of that might have made Elodie decide to run away? And are there any friends or family she might have gone to stay with?'

'Ellie.'

'Excuse me?'

'No one calls her Elodie. It's Ellie and she's not like that. She'd have no reason to run away.' Ms Fry raised her head from where she'd been staring down at the floor, her eyes red-rimmed and her skin coated in dark shadows that long predated her missing child. 'We're a team, her and me. A tight little unit. She'd never have just upped and left like that. She'd have had no reason. Yes, money's tight but we still manage to get by.'

'What about school? Is she happy? Friends?'

'Happy enough. She likes it, would you believe? I don't know where she gets it from but she's clever too. There's even talk of trying for a scholarship next year at St Elian's College.'

'And friends?' Gaby reminded her softly. 'Anyone she might have gone to stay with?'

'But why would she? There'd be no need and certainly not in the middle of the night,' she said, her tone taking on the shrill note of someone on the edge. 'There's really no one apart from her best friend, Heather, and even then they don't see much of each other. Only in school and for the occasional playdate. Outside of her ballet lessons – she's mad on ballet – she spends the rest of the time either reading or out with me.'

'I believe you're a cleaner.' Gaby watched her stiffen.

'And what if I am? It's a good, honest job.'

Gaby spread her hands only to clasp them together again. 'It certainly is. An essential one,' she replied, relieved to see Anita visibly relaxing in front of her. An aggressive witness – and witness was what she had to view her as – was the very last thing she wanted. Time was precious. The most precious thing where a missing child was concerned. They needed clear, accurate information and they needed it fast – it was up to Gaby to get it. 'So, what about anyone else she might have decided to slope off to see? Any siblings? What about her father or even a boyfriend?'

'There's no one. No father. He was never on the scene. No siblings, and a boyfriend at ten? Come on. She's not interested in boys and, even if she was, there isn't the time in her day for her to go and chase them.' Her features hardened, frown lines forming deep tracks on either side of her mouth. 'And before you ask, I don't have a boyfriend either. They're far more trouble than they're worth.'

Gaby took a sneaky glance at the plain, black-strapped watch on her wrist, her mind on the investigation. The seconds were ticking by. No one knew more than her what little time they had left if there was to be a happy resolution. But she still had questions that needed to be answered.

'Tell me about yesterday then. Anything that you can think of to spark her running away?'

'I've already told that officer on the phone earlier. Yesterday was a normal day. Nothing happened. We got up. Ellie stayed in her room until lunchtime finishing up a crafting project and reading. After lunch we headed out to the beach for a walk. We came home, had tea and slobbed out in front of the TV. The exact same as every other Sunday.'

No, not the exact same or otherwise your daughter wouldn't be missing. But instead all she said was, 'And there was no trouble at school? No bullying?' Gaby rose to her feet and walked over to the mantelpiece to study the photos: the 'thin as sticks' limbs, and eyes that dominated the girl's heart-shaped face. 'She's very slight. No problems with depression? Eating all right?'

'Ellie eats like a horse, Detective. You probably can't believe it,' Anita said, tugging at the pool of flesh around her middle. 'But I used to be the same.'

Gaby smiled briefly. 'I can well imagine. So …'

But she didn't get to finish her sentence. Anita sprung to her feet, quite unaware of the look of desperation etched across her cheeks. Gaby knew what she was going to ask. Every single relative of a missing person asked the exact same question, their words layered with the same frantic tone. They were asking the one question they knew it was impossible to answer at this stage but still they asked it.

'Will you be able to find her?'

Chapter 3

Ronan

Monday 3 August, 7.05 a.m. The Great Orme

Ronan Stevens wasn't your average rough sleeper, if there is such a thing. A product of middle-class parents, he'd spent most of his life being tutored in the public school system where the size of his parents' wallet was more important to the other boys than the size of his brain. Ronan's mother and father, while wealthy in comparative terms, were veering towards the breadline when compared with the affluent students who attended St Gildas independent boys' school in Beddgelert. The offspring of minor royalty and foreign oligarchs didn't take kindly to fellow pupils who didn't fit their jelly-mould existence and took great pleasure in making his life a daily hell.

All that had changed when Ronan had been pushed up against a wall and held there while he had his clothes stripped off and was given the beating of all beatings. But the two boys had made one crucial mistake. Leaving him collapsed and bleeding, they'd turned their backs – and in a black rage that contained all the injustices of the last five years at the school, Ronan Stevens curled

11

his hands into tight fists and fought for his life. Oscar Hurley-Pride and the Right Honourable Ollie Braden learnt valuable lessons that day on the side of the tennis courts, lessons they'd be forever reminded of each time they took off their shirts and revealed their scars.

Ronan Stevens didn't need to learn any such lessons. He knew that life wasn't fair but what he didn't expect was to be expelled, therefore setting off a train of events that would ultimately lead to him roughing it on a hillside when he should have been awaiting the results of his A levels – exams he'd never got to sit.

He bundled up his sleeping bag into a tight ball and added it to the top of his dad's old rucksack, pulling the toggle tight, the rest of his meagre belongings squashed down flat. He didn't need much. His clothes rolled up in an old jumper acted like a pillow and, as he never bothered to get undressed at night, pyjamas were unnecessary. His most precious possession was something that had once belonged to his father, a Swiss Army knife that was never far from his hand. Not that he'd ever had to use it, apart from the miniature pliers. Sleeping rough at any age was dangerous but for an innocent eighteen-year-old, who would be the first to admit that he was still wet behind the ears, it was often terrifying.

The cave, situated on the headland of the Great Orme in Llandudno, was a cold, dark and isolated place to hide away from the rest of the world. Ronan had always been reclusive, preferring his own company to any other. He'd never been a great one for friends so it wasn't something he could say he missed. He also wouldn't admit to feeling lonely although he was desperately so. There was a wealth of difference between favouring his own company and enforced solitude. He often thought about his life and of how it used to be but that made it worse. Only by keeping active and continually on the go could he pause the relentless shower of self-pity from overwhelming him. At night he was too tired to do anything but sleep.

Ronan weighed decisions calmly in the quiet of his mind prior to taking any steps. The only exception was that seething anger, which had ended up destroying his future prospects. But that was all in the past. So much had happened in the last twelve months or so that it almost felt as if he were a different person to the one that had inhabited his former life. The bullying and expulsion from school seemed minor when sitting alongside his mother's cancer and his dad's arrest. He couldn't pinpoint one solitary reason for running away but, with his mother trying to make a new life for herself along with his two younger brothers, it seemed as if there was no room in her plans for him. Not that she'd told him to leave or anything. But the mess he'd made of things was there in every look and every sentence.

So, one morning, two months ago, he'd put everything he thought he'd need on the top of his bed. Picking up his dad's rucksack – his rucksack now – he'd methodically packed the minimum of belongings and headed out of the house, leaving behind a ripped page from a jotter with a few words penned in his careful hand.

His life wasn't what he'd planned but, until he could puzzle out what he actually wanted, he was content enough to let the days run into each other. He had access to his savings account, which he eked out on yellow-sticker products in the local supermarkets, supplementing his diet with visits to the soup kitchen run by one of the local churches. He even managed to take on some work for the vicar, who'd swiftly realised that Ronan was a touch out of the ordinary compared with his usual lost causes. He didn't drink or smoke for a start and as for doing drugs …

A quick scan of the brightening sky told Ronan that he needed to get a move on. The cave was the safest place he'd found in which to rest his head but only as long as he remained undiscovered. Security had tightened with the warden increasing the patrols now that it was the height of the summer but, for whatever reason, they were yet to discover Ronan's secret resting place. The caves, a favourite with social dropouts, had each been fitted with gates for the very purpose of keeping the likes of him out.

A precocious child, Ronan had decided from an early age that the only barriers were the ones he erected and, with dedication and practice, he'd always solved whatever mental problem he set. He'd astounded his parents when he'd mastered the Rubik's Cube but, for someone like Ronan that was child's play and he rapidly progressed to more complex puzzles. Learning to pick locks was one such skill he'd honed in the quiet of his bedroom. With the help of the little pliers hidden in his dad's Swiss Army knife, and two sturdy paper clips, the padlock was no barrier unless they found him.

Turning to give a final tug on the gate, he nearly jumped out of his skin at the sight of the kid in front of him. His gaze raked over her, taking in the long fair hair, jeans and large rucksack in one glance, while he peered over her shoulder for her parents. Was this it then, his secret out? There was no way he could explain away what he was doing.

'Hello. Shouldn't you be with an adult?' he said, finally deducting that she was on her own.

'Shouldn't you?'

He raised his eyebrows.

Feisty little thing. Perhaps the absent parent wasn't as clear-cut as it seemed but she was so not his problem.

He bent to pick up his rucksack, adjusting the weight on his shoulders and clipping the strap around his waist. Whatever she was doing, the one thing he knew was that he couldn't hang around or they'd find him.

'Well, see you around then.'

'Hold on.' She ran to catch up with him, her legs working overtime to match his long stride.

'What is it?'

She stood there, her eyes starting to fill. 'I-I've run away.'

14

'You've run away,' he repeated, struggling not to let his jaw drop. 'Why?'

But instead of answering, she simply dropped her head.

He stared at her, recalling the determined set of her mouth with a frown. She was only a kid and a little kid at that. She wouldn't last two minutes on her own. He closed his eyes. She'd last less than that if someone didn't watch out for her. He'd learnt far more than he'd expected since running away, much of which he'd never be able to forget despite wishing it otherwise. He knew what happened to the young and uninitiated and it was down to luck and a kindly word in his ear from Reverend Honeybun that his instincts had been sharpened to stiletto thin. A kid her age, pretty too, would be torn to shreds by the sharks that inhabited the streets.

'How old are you?' he continued, slowing his stride to match hers as he made his way down the gentle slope towards the Happy Valley and the road beyond that led to the pier, ignoring the goat that skittered away into the undergrowth ahead.

'Fifteen.'

'Fifteen. If you're fifteen, I'm fifty.'

'You're looking good for your age.'

He found he was hiding a smile at her quick responses. Growing up in a house with two younger brothers, brothers he longed for with an ache that gripped his insides, the banter that peppered their relationship was the thing that he missed the most.

'Ha, very funny, not. If you don't come clean, I'm going to leave you here to fend for yourself.'

He felt a pull on his arm, her finely boned fingers remarkably strong for someone so little.

'I'm ten, all right?'

No, it's not all right. It's far from all right. Ten!

He glowered down at the top of her fair head, struggling not to grab her by the hand and march her to the nearest police station. But he wouldn't do that, not yet. The reason he'd left home was now mangled into a giant tangled mess that he couldn't unravel. His beef wasn't only with his mother, it was with the world in general. A world that had robbed him of his father and turned his mother into a parody of her former self. But he wouldn't have considered leaving at ten, no matter what the issues were within his family. He'd learnt a lot in those first few days huddled in a doorway along Mostyn Street, too scared to close his eyes for even a second. Primarily he'd learnt that for some children a life on the streets, while a tragedy, was the safer option.

The outline of his keyring in his pocket was a sharp reminder that home was only ten minutes away. His mother didn't know he'd taken the spare key that lived under the third plant pot to the left of the back door and he didn't want her to find out. It was his safety net but one he'd never planned on using. But this was an emergency. He couldn't desert the girl, and putting her in the hands of the police might mean returning her to the very situation she was trying to escape from. No. It seemed like he'd have to resign himself to her company until she trusted him enough to confide in him.

Kneeling down on his haunches, he said, 'If you're going to throw your lot in with me you have to promise to do exactly what I say and not ask any questions. In return, I promise to mind you in the same way I would one of my kid brothers.'

'Do we have to spit on it?' She flexed her palm and moved it to her mouth.

Ronan laughed, the first genuine laugh to get past his wall of grief since he'd lost his dad. Instead of replying, he took her hand, her cold fingers curling around his. He had no idea if he was making the right decision but one thing was certain: the loneliness that gripped him from the second he opened his eyes to the moment sleep grabbed him at night seemed suddenly to be a thing of the past.

'Come on, we have a lot to do before it gets dark.'

Chapter 4

Gaby

Monday 3 August, 7.50 a.m. Colwyn Bay

Will you be able to find her?

Gaby dreaded this question more than all of the others put together because she didn't know how to answer. She could quote statistics at Ms Fry but that wouldn't help. They all knew that the first hour was the most precious of the lot. If Ellie wasn't found in that hour – and she hadn't been – the likelihood of her being found alive shrunk from the realms of most likely to hopefully. But the woman in front of her wouldn't be of a mind to accept such lame words and, if their positions were reversed, Gaby wouldn't accept them either.

Instead of replying straight away, she picked up one of the mugs of coffee Jax had produced and, shifting to sit on the sofa beside her, offered it, handle facing outwards.

'Have your drink.' She watched Anita raise the mug and take a tentative sip only to place it on the coffee table and push it away.

'You still haven't answered my question?'

And I'm not going to because I can't. If I tell you the truth you'll never forgive me.

'I think you probably know that it's not a question I can answer right now but please believe me when I tell you that we are going to do everything possible to find her.' She lifted her head at the sound of the front door opening and just managed to suppress a sigh of relief at the sight of Amy Potter, the FLO.

Gaby leant forward and picked up the mug again, placing it in Ms Fry's loose hands. 'Have another sip of your drink. I'd like to ask your permission to search Ellie's bedroom if I may? And while I'm having a scout around, my DS, Amy Potter, will stay with you and fill you in on the steps we're taking.' She tilted her head at Jax to follow her and once back in the hall turned to him.

'Right, any news?'

'Not a peep, ma'am,' he said, phone in his hand. 'Malachy has contacted Dafydd Griffiths, the country park warden, who's rounding up a search party for both Ormes, while Marie is heading up the sea and beach one. I've also taken the liberty of contacting the coastguard. The lifeboat crew has been assembled and are about to launch. They mentioned contacting Caernarfon Search and Rescue in case you want to mobilise the helicopter?'

'Good idea. What else?'

'Well, I thought I'd set about interviewing the neighbours, if that's okay?' he added. 'It's unlikely that they'll have seen anything but we might get lucky.'

'Don't forget CCTV, Jax. There can't be that many ten-year-olds roaming the streets in the middle of the night for her to have gone unnoticed.' She matched his serious look with one of her own, their minds working in tandem. 'Okay, you crack on. I'm heading back to the station after I've finished here. If she doesn't turn up soon, the DCI is going to have to cough up additional coppers to help with the search.'

She watched him turn on his heel and head out the open front door and around to the next house, not that he had to

18

walk far. The houses were terraced, each with an excuse of a front and back garden and little else. It was places like this that often turned up the most interesting facts. The residents, living in such close proximity, often knew more about their neighbours than was healthy. If they knew anything, DC Jax Williams would hopefully weed it out.

Ellie's bedroom was a box of a room with little space to fit anything alongside the small divan and matching wardrobe. There wasn't even room for a chair or a desk but that hadn't stopped her from filling nearly every available space with books. There were shelves piled high, the sight of which struck dread in Gaby as each one would have to be flicked through to see if they held any secrets between their pages. But that wasn't her job, she reminded herself, pulling her mobile from her pocket and placing a quick call to Jason, the senior CSI back at the station. Anita wouldn't thank her for having her home invaded by a team of strangers but if there was one clue here that would lead them to discover the child's whereabouts then they had to find it, and sooner rather than later.

Phone back in her pocket, Gaby turned her attention to the bed, not that she could see much of the plain pink duvet cover, piled high as it was with so many cuddly toys to the extent that there was barely room for a child to sit let alone lie down. Pulling on the pair of disposable gloves that she always carried in her pocket, she opened the wardrobe. Mainly jeans, tops and leotards. The shoes tucked in the bottom were the usual black lace-ups she'd anticipated, along with two pairs of ballet shoes and a pair of wellies. All in all, apart from the books and teddies, there wasn't much but everything was clean and tidy, obviously cared for by a loving hand.

Bending down, Gaby peered under the bed. It was amazing what people hid in the most obvious of places but in this case there was only a shoebox stuffed with what were presumably Ellie's precious belongings. A broken silver bracelet with a dangling star.

A pile of shells and another of stones. A feather. A photo of an elderly couple, probably grandparents. She removed the picture before returning the lid to the box and pushing it back out of sight with the tip of her shoe.

Ms Fry was sitting where she'd left her, Amy by her side. Gaby retook her seat, keeping her voice soft as she held out the photo.

'I have a couple more questions, if I may. Firstly this couple. I take it they're known to Ellie?'

'My parents.'

'And are they close? Would they be people she'd run to?'

'Hardly.' She pressed a tissue to her face, mopping up the tears. 'My parents are both dead, Detective. It's only Ellie and me. No one else.'

'Okay.' Gaby laid the picture on the table with a steady hand though she felt far from steady. She'd had a premonition when she'd taken the call earlier that this wasn't going to be a straight-forward case. Finding Ellie holed up around at her gran's after a row with her mum was a scenario that wasn't going to be played out. Ellie had run away for reasons unknown and currently there were no clues as to her whereabouts.

'And the other thing?'

'Pardon?' Gaby looked up from where she'd been studying the photo, meeting Ms Fry's red-rimmed stare head on.

'You said there were two things?'

'Ah, yes. Of course,' she said after a moment, managing a smile of sorts. 'You said in your initial phone call that your daughter had run away as opposed to gone missing. How did you make that distinction? It's not always an obvious one to—'

'Because she planned it. She must have, to know what to take.'

'And what did she take?'

'I've just been telling her everything that's missing,' she said, jerking her head in Amy's direction. 'A rucksack for starters and—'

Amy patted Ms Fry on the shoulder. 'It's okay, Anita. I'll take it from here. Ms Fry did a quick recce of what was missing while

20

she waited for the police to arrive, ma'am. Really it was to prove to herself that something untoward hadn't happened. So, apart from a pink rucksack, one that Ellie normally uses as a school bag, there's a sleeping bag. A few clothes but not much. There's also a torch and a few tins of food. She's also taken her birthday money; it was in a tin in her room.'

Gaby's look of concern mirrored that of her friend. Ellie Fry had taken all the things necessary to start a new life, except the most important. The common sense needed to realise how vulnerable a ten-year-old was out on the streets by herself.

21

Chapter 5

Ronan

Monday 3 August, 7.50 a.m. Church Walk, Llandudno

It didn't take long for Ronan to make his way to the large, detached property situated on a small *clos* off Church Walk. But he didn't rush. He didn't rush at anything these days. Much to the annoyance of the girl by his side, he slowed his pace to that of a laborious walk and waited, every so often telling her to shush and be patient.

There was a reason for Ronan's caution, not that he was going to tell her. The less she knew about him the better as far as he was concerned. If he was being totally honest, he'd have left her to her own devices had she not been quite so young or innocent. But now that he was lumbered, he had to make sure that he protected himself. He knew his mum, after all he'd had the pleasure of living with her for eighteen years, and the one thing she wasn't was stupid. Like him, she had a fierce intelligence and used every one of her brain cells to analyse each and every situation prior to making a decision as to how best to act. He was well aware that she'd do everything possible to make him return and that there was a good chance she'd succeed.

This was the primary reason he'd decided to avoid the family home, suppressing a laugh at the thought, a laugh without even a glimmer of humour. They were far from a family now, their little unit smashed into smithereens by the crimes of one man.

The car pulling out of the drive was his dad's, something he wasn't prepared to think about. As the grey Saab approached, he suddenly grabbed the girl by the shoulders and, bending down, started messing with her shoelaces, his face turned away. But he managed to catch a glimpse of his mother, the grim set of her lips, the grey hair that had started to drift past the collar of her pristine navy-blue dress. The word *forgiveness* popped into his mind out of nowhere, stopping his restless fingers as he tightened the knot on her laces. He knew it was unfair to blame his mother for what had happened but some part of him couldn't help himself.

'Hey, what do you think you're doing?'

The sound of the girl's voice punctured his thoughts but instead of replying, he jumped to his feet, grabbed her hand and started pulling her in the direction of the house. 'Preventing my mother from spotting us – that's her house up ahead. Now hurry up; we don't have much time.'

'Much time for what?'

'Enough already.' The only thing that prevented him from shouting was the knowledge that the neighbours might hear and call the police. 'You said you'd do as I asked and I'm asking you to hurry up and shut up.'

'You're worse than my mother,' she grumbled, increasing her footsteps to match his.

'And don't you forget it. Remember this was your idea and not mine.'

Heading around the side of the property, he slipped through the gate at the back and made his way to the kitchen door. He knew he was taking a risk but he didn't have any choice. They wouldn't have a chance with her slowing him down, especially if the police became involved. He'd just have to skew the odds in their favour.

He ignored the kitchen and all of the downstairs rooms instead racing up the stairs to his parents' bedroom and the bathroom beyond, the girl's hand still glued to his. The house held too many memories for them to be anything but painful. The kitchen, one of his favourite rooms, was littered with the remnants of a hasty breakfast, the plates piled up haphazardly beside the sink, the cupboards bearing the artwork from both his brothers. It was like a physical pain to be back remembering how it once was. But there was nothing for him here.

The bathroom was different again. His parents' en suite wasn't a room he'd frequented often. The black tiles and white bath with its fancy gold-plated taps and coordinating black and beige towels held no memories that he couldn't cope with. Once inside, he crouched down until he was eye level, suddenly remembering something he should have asked. 'What's your name, by the way?'

'Elodie, but everybody calls me Ellie.'

'I'm Ronan. If you want to come with me, Ellie, we're going to have to do something about your appearance,' he said, flicking a finger at her blonde hair. 'So have you ever thought about becoming a boy, Lee?'

'I'm going to be a boy?' she repeated, parrot fashion, her mouth rounded. 'How?'

'With this.' He opened the mirrored cabinet above the sink and withdrew a pair of scissors in addition to a pair of clippers. 'And before you go all tearful on me, it's the only way. That hair of yours is too much of a giveaway. You'll have us caught within seconds if anybody spots it.' He took a step back. 'So, Lee,' he said, elongating the syllable, 'there's still time to change your mind. I'm more than happy to drop you off at the nearest police station if you like?'

Pale to begin with, Ellie's skin tone lost what little colour it had and Ronan was hard pushed not to put out his hand to her.

She didn't speak but by the frightened expression stamping her features he guessed that speaking wasn't something she could do right now. Instead she surprised him yet again by plucking the scissors from his hand and immediately starting to cut away huge hanks of her hair.

'Hey, go easy a minute or you'll—' But he was too late or she was too quick as the sharp edge of the scissors pierced the tender flesh on the back of her hand, and the cut started to gush with blood.

'Ouch.' Her hand automatically lifted to her mouth.

'No, don't do that.' He took hold of her wrist and led her to the sink. 'Shush, it's better than it probably feels. Little more than a scratch really,' he said, deliberately playing down the sight of her tear-streaked cheeks while he ran cold water over the cut and patted it dry with some toilet paper, pressing down hard. 'It'll stop bleeding in a minute and Mum has a first-aid box here somewhere. Hold that for a second while I find it.'

After a moment of rummaging in the same cabinet, he managed to produce a handful of plasters. He stuck one in place, the others he tucked away in his pocket. He had a premonition he was going to need them.

'Right then, stay still a minute while I finish off your hair.' With two snips he removed the longer bits, leaving Ellie looking as if she'd come off worse in an argument with a lawnmower.

'Number one?' she said, fiddling with the settings on the clippers, all trace of her earlier bravado masked under an expression that declared her acceptance of what was to come.

'Perhaps you could get away with a number four.' He hovered, unsure of quite what to do. He'd never had to clip hair before, but then again neither had she.

Chapter 6

Janice

Monday 3 August, 7.50 a.m. Church Walk, Llandudno

Janice Stevens's immaculate appearance was hardly in keeping with the thoughts scattering through her mind. But then she was never one to allow her inner turmoil to impact on the mask of indifference she presented to the world. As a lawyer, she'd learnt the hard way to screen her feelings with a calm smile, something that had proved invaluable when her husband had turned from the man she'd married into one of Britain's worst monsters.

Rounding the corner out of the *clos*, the only indication that she wasn't her usual self was a slight tightening of her hands gripping the steering wheel. The two boys squabbling gently in the back would have no idea that she'd just spotted their brother loitering by the lamp post near their home. It had been nearly a year since her world had descended into a tragedy but only a couple of months since her rocky relationship with Ronan had dismantled completely. To wake up and find him gone with only a scrappy letter telling her not to search for him was worse somehow than all the months gone previously.

She flicked on the indicator before turning left onto the dual carriageway. She looked at the entrance to the sports centre up ahead, her mind for once not on the usual list of lunch boxes and school bags that had to be remembered before the boys could jump out of the car and join their friends. Instead she dipped into the past, a place drenched with sorrow. Casper, currently on remand awaiting trial, couldn't hurt her now but Ronan's problems and life choices were a constant source of worry and pain. Along with the additional stress of having to wind up Casper's shop and go back to work in order to pay the bills, there was also the constant fear about her own health. She was only managing to keep the family together by a thread. If her cancer returned ...

Janice was brought back to the present by the sound of Jacob and Caleb's voices as they scrabbled around the back seat collecting their belongings.

'Bye, Mum, love you,' they flung in her direction before slamming the doors; words that, for once, stabbed like a knife as she remembered other similar words before Ronan had disappeared.

Like an automaton, she reversed before performing a neat three-point turn, the powered steering wheel of the Saab taking the weight off her shoulders. She knew she should get rid of the car. Three cars in the driveway was two too many but a trip to the garage had decided her that the pittance they were offering wasn't worth the effort. There was always the hope that Ronan would come to his senses and pick up the driving lessons he'd abandoned along with all links to his past.

With her foot hard on the accelerator, she decided to do the one thing she'd been told not to by Reverend Honeybun – to speak to her son. Oh yes, she'd traced Ronan's movements almost as soon as he'd left the family home. He was an intelligent lad, far more intelligent than either Casper or herself; that's why they'd taken the decision to move him to St Gildas instead of keeping him at the local secondary school. She'd visited the vicar in desperation over those first few days, when the police had reminded her that, as an adult, Ronan was free to make his own choices. Reverend Honeybun, with his soft voice and wispy grey hair, had gone out of his way to both settle her mind and arrange her thoughts. Ronan needed to have a reason to come home and no amount of badgering on her part could change that.

She pulled into the drive a little less than thirty minutes after leaving it, ignoring any thoughts of the nine o'clock meeting she had lined up. Ronan back home was all she could think about. Closing the front door, she leant back against it, her palms flat against the wood and listened. But all was quiet apart from the ticking of her father's mahogany clock, which sat next to the Portmeirion vase on the hall table.

It only took her a few seconds to see that the rooms looked exactly as she'd left them. The boys' cereal bowls and spoons were piled beside the dishwasher for later. The study, Casper's domain, was a room she hadn't entered in weeks and, pushing open the door, she held her breath in case any trace of his aftershave lingered. Just like she now avoided the lounge, this room – his room – was a no-go area unless she desperately needed to check one of the many household documents that resided in the steel filing cabinet under the window.

His study was decorated in uncompromising shades of dark grey, a large antique wooden desk taking up much of the floor space, the walls lined with bookshelves. But this wasn't where her gaze rested. It was on the partly open filing cabinet that she knew she'd slammed shut only days before when she'd had to check something on their household insurance policy.

She walked over to the drawer and closed it with a snap, regretting with a sighing breath her decision to protect Caleb and Jacob from finding out about their brother. If she'd only stopped the car ...

She left the room. Regrets wouldn't get her anywhere. The stark truth was that Ronan would have waited if he'd been ready to speak to her.

Chapter 7

Monday 3 August, 9.45 a.m. St Asaph

It was nearer ten than nine by the time Gaby walked into her office. She slipped off her jacket and, after placing it on the back of her chair, headed to the kettle situated on the ledge beneath the bookshelves and shook it. Her luck was in for once and with a flick of her finger, she set it to boil while automatically spooning coffee into two clean mugs. The role of acting detective inspector had many advantages. Firstly an office but secondly, and far more important as far as she was concerned, clean mugs and a half-litre of milk supplied daily by one of the invaluable station cleaners.

She'd texted Owen Bates, her senior DC, to join her for a quick catch-up and with the sound of the heavy tread of his footsteps on the laminate flooring outside her office, she knew he was going to be on time as usual.

As soon as he knocked on the open door, she handed him a mug and gestured for him to take a seat. The last time she'd seen him was when she'd visited him and his wife, Kate, in hospital following the birth of their daughter. It was amazing what a week away from the office could do to someone, she mused, taking in his relaxed demeanour and broad smile. He seemed like a different man, which made her pause as she wondered how long it would last in light of the news that she was about to share with him. As a copper, Gaby had never been one to withhold information, and always insisted on sharing knowledge as soon as she was privy to it. But now she decided to delay telling Owen about the missing girl until they got the pleasantries out of the way. She owed him that much. In truth she owed him a whole lot more.

'It's good to see you back, my friend.'

'I wish I could say the same but …'

'But?' she prompted.

'But I hated having to leave Kate and the kids.'

'That's perfectly understandable. I'd have been disappointed if you didn't. Work is work after all and only to be tolerated as something that pays the bills.'

'Easy for you to say. I'm sure you'd be quite happy to work for nothing if you could.'

'Ha. I'm far from a charity, Owen.'

'Talking of which, how's the delectable—?'

'Right. Back to work.' She changed the subject neatly to one where she had an element of control. Her relationship with Doctor Rusty Mulholland was in its infancy and not something she was prepared to discuss with anyone yet. They hadn't even kissed, apart from a peck on the cheek, which didn't count. Suppressing a blush at where her thoughts were taking her, she said, 'I'm sorry to say we have a missing girl, Owen. I know, right? It's only been a week since we wrapped up that problem on the Great Orme.'

'That's life, isn't it? We tootle along trying to keep busy in case Sherlock decides to cut our numbers along with our budget only to have a flurry of serious investigations come in back to back.'

'God, don't chance fate like that. I don't think I could cope with any more.' She propped open her leather briefcase and placed

30

Ellie's photo face up, pushing it across the clear expanse of desk, her attention on his compressed lips and unflinching gaze.

'Elodie Fry,' she said, getting right to the point. It was easier that way. Less messy in the long run to deal in only the facts. 'Ellie for short. Last seen yesterday evening when her mother went in to turn off her light, a regular occurrence as the girl is a voracious reader. Sometime after, she packed her school bag with all the rudiments of a runaway. She hasn't been seen since.' She stopped a moment, expecting him to interrupt with his usual insightful stream of questions but all she got was silence, a silence she finally broke. 'I've left Amy holding the mother's hand. She's also in the ideal position if the CSIs turn up anything. In addition, Jax has started a door-to-door and Marie and Malachy are coordinating the sea and land searches respectively. I've asked them all to be on hand to give us an update at one o'clock if nothing's turned up by then,' she added, taking note of the time on the silver-finished clock that hung on the wall above the door.

'What would you like me to do in the meantime? You seem to have all the bases covered—'

'Accompany me when I interview the headmistress over at Ysgol Ger y Môr primary school. She's made herself available to meet us even though it's closed – I'm expected in thirty minutes, which doesn't give us much time.' She pushed back from her chair and picked up her mug. 'Come on. I don't want to be late. We have a lot to get through.'

'Hold on a mo.'

Gaby watched him withdraw a folded sheet of paper from his inside jacket pocket and gritted her teeth in anticipation of what he was about to tell her. She remembered back a week and the vow he'd made about not handing in his notice. But lots had happened in the last seven days. If he'd decided to rescind his promise there wasn't a thing that she could do about it after what had so nearly happened to his wife.

'God, Gaby. You need to lighten up.' He opened the page

31

and held it out to her. 'You should see yourself – you look as if someone has died.'

'That will be you, if that's what I think it is?' she said, eyeing the sheet with an expression that was all too easy to read.

'Ha, as if.' He gave a deep chuckle before letting the paper float down between them. 'I don't change my mind that easily. I'm here to stay, for the time being anyway. No. Sherlock collared me as soon as I came through the door. He's disappointed not to have received your application for DI and, with the interviews arranged for tomorrow, he's pretty livid that you haven't bothered to apply.'

'Ah. Yes. Well. I um haven't quite made my mind up about—'

'Perhaps this will help.' He scooped up the sheet and held it out a second time. 'Apparently there was a lot of interest in the position but only one candidate shortlisted.'

She glanced up from where she'd been toying with her pen, the inflection in his voice the only indication that he was about to tell her something she wasn't going to like.

'He also said that, as he's out of the office later, he'd like you to take his place and show the candidate around.'

'And?'

Owen picked up his empty mug and dangled it from one finger.

'It's that tosser you were telling me about back in Swansea. DS Bill Davis. If Sherlock doesn't have your application in by midnight there's a very good chance that Davis will be our new boss.'

Chapter 8

Owen

Monday 3 August, 10 a.m. St Asaph

Owen and Gaby didn't waste any time. They were soon striding down the corridor and towards the main entrance, only to stop at the sound of the desk sergeant's urgent tone.

'I was about to phone, ma'am.'

'Yes, what is it?'

He lowered his voice to such a level that they both had to lean forward across the desk to hear him.

'There's a problem that I can't deal with,' Clancy said, shifting his attention briefly to the other side of the room. 'It looks as if a serious crime may have been committed.'

Owen's attention flickered to the man sitting next to the fire extinguisher, a plastic bag resting across his knees. They got all sorts through the door and the man occupying the chair was only a variation. Dressed in stained jeans and a chequered shirt, he was obviously someone who worked with his hands, his fingernails blunt-cut and ingrained with dirt. The weather-beaten hue of his skin had Owen immediately jump to gardener, his curiosity piqued at the thought of what the man might have to tell them.

'I think you'd be better to get the story first-hand,' Clancy continued, his next words pulling him back into the conversation with a jolt. 'I don't think I've ever heard the like.'

Owen drew his brows into a frown, trying to imagine what could have popped through the door in the few minutes he'd been hiding away in Gaby's office, but it was impossible. There was only one way to find out.

He walked across the floor, a ready smile on his lips. 'Good morning, sir. I believe you have something to show us?'

As an experienced officer, Owen would never dream of shirking his duty but if he could find something to keep him away from thoughts of that missing girl, he'd grab it. He'd also worked with Gaby long enough to know that she'd let him. The interview at the school only needed one detective, which meant that she must be concerned as to how he'd cope. He wasn't about to confirm those fears.

The man stood, his fingers curled around what appeared to be a sandwich bag, the crumbs clinging to the sides a clear indication of what it used to contain.

'Yes. Although it would probably be best if I showed you in private?'

Owen took a moment to sum up the level of the problem, his gaze lingering on the dark shapes visible through the plastic as he tried to guess what they might be and knowing full well that the reception area wasn't the place in which to discuss it. Coming to a snap decision, he turned to Gaby.

'I think I should probably deal with this, ma'am. I'll try and follow on in a few minutes.' He didn't wait for her frown. Instead he gestured for the man to follow him into interview room four, which he'd walked past on his way down the corridor and knew to be empty.

'Right then. What can I help you with, Mr ... er ...?' Owen asked as soon as they'd settled in their chairs.

'Penrose. Martin Penrose. I work over at the Welsh Hills Memorial Gardens in Colwyn Bay.' He placed the bag on the table, starting to pull at the neck. 'I'd like to show you something.'

'Wait a minute. If it's evidence in there we need to …' Owen dug around in his pocket and pulled out a pair of disposable gloves.

Martin grinned, revealing a mouthful of yellow teeth. 'What, try and preserve it? I've watched a fair few crime dramas in my time but there's no way you're going to get any clues from this lot. The cremator can reach temperatures of 1,800 degrees Fahrenheit so any evidence is dust by now.' He paused a moment, waiting for permission to continue. 'Right then, just in case you don't know what these are … prosthetic hips,' he said, placing the three long objects on the table, quickly followed by three marble-sized balls, before tapping each one with a grubby fingertip. 'Looks like something from an alien spaceship, doesn't it? This here ball fits into the hip while the pointed bit is rammed into the top of the leg bone. Sometimes the long bone is still attached but not in this case.'

Owen sat there, wishing he hadn't accepted that coffee from Gaby, the rush of hot acid up the back of his throat almost making him gag at the sight of the blackened lumps of metal. He reached out a hand before he could stop himself, the feel of the cold hard surface holding some kind of a morbid fascination. He didn't know what he'd been expecting but certainly not something like this. Martin had leant back in his chair, his arms folded across his broad chest while he waited for him to speak – what could he say?

'Okay. So you've brought us these because …'

'Because how many people do you know with three legs?'

'Excuse me?'

Martin let out a low gravelly laugh. 'I said, how many people do you know with three legs?' He unfolded his arms and tapped each of the joints with his knuckle. 'One. Two. Three. That's how many hip joints I removed from the cremator on Saturday evening when there should only have been one, or two at the very most.'

'Right.' Owen removed his gloves and lurched out of the chair, the noise of the legs scraping against the floor causing him to wince. 'I'd like to take it right back to the beginning but, as we might be here a while, would you like a cuppa?'

Martin nodded. 'Is it okay if I have a smoke?'

'I'm afraid not,' he said, gesturing towards the iconic red and white sign pinned to the wall below the window. 'I won't be long.'

Owen couldn't wait to get out of the room, his mind still trying to shift back into gear after a week of baby duties. He'd been hoping for a few quiet days where he'd be able to adjust to the changes in his home life. Now thoughts of even one normal shift flew out of the window as he worked the drinks machine, situated on the opposite end of the corridor, before grabbing a handful of sugar sachets.

'Sorry, not sure if you take any?' He dropped the packets on the table and sat back in his seat, his hand hovering over the switch on the wall-mounted microphone. 'Now, I'd like you to confirm your full name and address and that you currently work at the Welsh Hills Memorial Gardens?'

It didn't take long for Owen to deal with the formalities using his customary efficiency and leanness for words. He never used two words when one was more than sufficient.

'What exactly happened, sir, for you to think that a crime may have been committed?'

'Well, cleaning out the cremator after use is normally Barry Salt's job but he's been off sick the last couple of days.' Martin took a sip from his mug, grimaced and added another sachet of sugar. 'Do you know anything about cremations?'

'No, absolutely nothing.'

'The fact is that, while the hot temperatures will burn most things, there's always a residual. Bones and metal don't burn. So, in the same way you clear out your grate after a fire, someone has to clear out the bottom of the cremator. The bones get crushed while the metal gets discarded. You understand?'

Owen pulled a face. 'Pretty gruesome but I get the picture. Carry on, you're doing fine.'

'We had a cremation on Friday and again on Saturday morning,' Martin said, pointing to the hip prosthetics. 'And it was my job to clean out the ash afterwards.'

'So, with two bodies surely finding three metal hips isn't out of the ordinary?'

'You don't understand, Detective. We have to clean out the cremator after each service and, as it was me doing the cleaning, there is no way any of the hips came from the first cremation.'

Owen leant back in his chair, one hand on his beard. 'And I take it that no one else could have added one? You know, as a joke?'

Martin's eyes widened. 'A funny type of joke that would be! At weekends, apart from cremations, the whole place is closed up and there wasn't any sign of a break-in.'

'So, putting two and two together, it looks as if someone must have added something into the last coffin before it arrived at the crematorium?'

'I can see that's what it looks like,' Martin said, his eyes narrowing into thin slits. 'But I'm telling you, here and now, that that's not what happened.'

Chapter 9

Gaby

Monday 3 August, 10.30 a.m. Colwyn Bay

Ysgol Ger y Môr primary school was situated along the thin ribbon of road that skirted the North Wales coast as far as the eye could see. After pulling into a parking space, Gaby grabbed her phone off the passenger seat and slipped out of the car, her shoes taking a second to get used to the loose grey gravel underfoot. She studied the building with interest as she headed for the main entrance, noting the dull grey frontage and the effort taken to make it less utilitarian with large tubs of annuals flanking either side of the door. There were hundreds of similar buildings dotted around the UK. The only thing setting it apart was the signage in two languages.

As with most non-Welsh-speaking people living in Wales, Gaby was reliant on the street signs and notices that included an English translation. Welsh was such a melodious language and something that she'd added to her bucket list to learn after she'd transferred from Liverpool to Cardiff. But as with most things, her busy lifestyle meant that she'd had to shift it to something that she'd like to do as opposed to needing to. With her current crazy workload the likelihood of her ever finding the time wasn't something she was prepared to dwell on.

Miss Garland, the headmistress, was a thin, pale woman who wore her grey-streaked brown hair pulled back off her face in a French pleat. Dressed in tailored trousers and a cream silk blouse, she made Gaby feel scruffy. But there was nothing she could do about that apart from scheduling in a trip to Marks and Spencer for a new suit.

'Take a seat, Detective. Is there anything I can get you? Tea? Coffee? A glass of water?'

'No, I'm good, thanks,' Gaby said, crossing one leg over the other and resting her phone on her knee. 'And thank you again for coming in during your holidays. I'll try not to take up too much of your time.' She paused a moment to open up the notebook App on her mobile. 'As you're already aware, Elodie Fry has gone missing so anything you can tell me that you think might be of use would be helpful.'

Miss Garland stared across her empty desk, toying with a thin gold bracelet on her wrist. 'I really don't know what to say. It's the first time that anything like this has happened at the school.'

'What's she like as a pupil? That will do for a start.'

'A quiet child, studious even.' She continued playing with the bracelet, her attention fixed on the small gold heart charm dangling from the clasp. 'You have to remember I've been a teacher for a very long time, the last fifteen years as headmistress of the school. I've seen all sorts of pupils over the years but Ellie is different.'

'In what way?'

'In every way, Detective Darin,' she said, finally raising her head. 'Oh, she looks normal enough with her long blonde hair and love of all things pink. She even likes some of the things that the rest of the girls in her year are mad about such as ballet. She's obsessed with ballet but that's where the similarity ends. In your job you must know what it's like to be different, Detective? Different children, just like different adults, end up being picked on and that's no reflection on the teachers. That's just how it is. Outside of her lessons, she spends her time holed up in the library, reading. I'm not about to decry the advantages that come with an inquiring mind. There is more research than I can quote on the benefits of children who read but Ellie isn't just stimulating her mind through the pages of a book, she's hiding from her peers.'

Gaby's heart sank at the words, which dragged her back twenty years to her own experiences of bullying. Growing up the youngest of first-generation Italian parents she was well versed in the devious ways of children who were determined to make the lives of others a misery. The only thing that had saved her was the strength of her mother and the support of her brothers. Ellie obviously wasn't so lucky.

'What about her background? I'm assuming that you've dealt with the mother on occasion?'

'Ms Fry is pleasant enough. I've observed her with her daughter at school pick-up and parent–teacher meetings and they seem to have a good rapport, if that's what you're getting at? She has never given me any reason to think that she's anything other than a loving parent and there have certainly been no concerns expressed by the teachers as to any safeguarding issues in respect to Ellie's home life.'

'What about men?' Gaby asked, making a couple of entries in her phone and raising her head. 'Any sign that Ms Fry had a boyfriend?'

'Teachers aren't usually privy to that kind of personal information but she always attended school meetings either by herself or with her daughter.'

'Okay. One final thing.' Gaby tapped her forefinger against the side of her phone case. 'What about any friends?'

'I thought that was something you might ask,' Miss Garland said, sliding back in her chair. 'I managed to track down her teacher, who's camping up in Scotland for the next couple of weeks, and she reminded me about Heather Powell. If I'm honest I think that it's a friendship born out of necessity as opposed to anything that they might have in common. Heather is from quite a well-to-do family of hoteliers over in Rhyl but she's different again and in need of careful handling.'

She rose from her chair, her hands pressed flat against the top of the desk. 'I wouldn't like you to get the wrong idea about us. But with such a large catchment area it's a challenge to meet the individual needs of all of the children. The teachers do their best given the circumstances, but some children slip through the net. The likes of Ellie Fry and Heather Powell are what keep me up at night. Now, unless there's anything else?' she said, turning and walking through the door, her expression carefully tailored to reveal little of the inner woman.

Gaby filed away the conversation to puzzle over later, her footsteps slowing to a near stop as the memories of her own disappointing childhood flooded back. While she'd managed to erect a steel wall around her emotions, she'd still ended up carrying her poor self-esteem into adulthood. Something that had affected her relationships with men, she brooded, her mind swinging briefly to thoughts of Rusty. She'd like to tell each and every one of Ellie's peers the damage they were causing with their behaviour but she wouldn't. She knew that some of the children would be intrinsically good just as she knew that the home lives of some of them would drive weaker personalities off the rails. The teachers had impossible jobs and it was left to the parents to pick up the pieces. Those children who evaded help usually ended up coming to the notice of her team.

So, what had Ellie Fry done or not done to think that running away was the only option open to her and why was it that her mother had no knowledge of her being bullied?

Chapter 10

Owen

Monday 3 August, 11.30 a.m. St Asaph

Owen stifled the yawn that had been trying to work its way up his chest ever since he'd crawled out of bed. It was all very well having had a week's paternity leave but it wasn't in any way a break. Not that he minded in the slightest. While there was very little he could do to help Kate with feeding their newborn daughter, he'd strengthened his nappy-changing skills and taken over the mountain of washing that had invaded every surface of the house. Had it been the same with Pip, their soon-to-be three-year-old? It seemed so long ago now that he could barely remember.

All he could think about was trying to keep busy, and awake, until the hands of his watch shifted to five. Being stuck in the office meant that he'd have to catch up with Ellie's disappearance when Gaby got back but there was little he could do about that. Her terse reply to the quick phone call he'd made to her was warning enough of the pressure they were under to find her.

With every available team member taking part in the search, he had the incident room to himself and the temptation was to rest his head in his arms and take a quick forty winks. Instead he took a detour to the most important piece of equipment in the office, the cafetiere, and poured himself a mug, adding a heaped spoonful of sugar for good measure. He didn't have a sweet tooth but caffeine and sugar were the next best things to the solid seven hours' sleep that he wouldn't be getting anytime soon.

He felt guilty at not being involved in the hunt for the girl but, with a dearth of clues, the rest of the team was as stumped as he was as to what could have happened to her. He was partly placated by the fact that a detective had to hang around within shouting distance of the station – it might as well be him and, in the meantime, he could continue working on what was going on at the crematorium.

There were only two secretaries for the whole building to type up victim witness statements and reports but Owen's near one hundred per cent recall meant that he didn't have to wait. Opening up the lid of his laptop, he cleaned the dust off the screen with his sleeve and logged on to the system. It didn't take him more than a few seconds to create a new spreadsheet, his mind working through everything that Martin had told him, fact by gruesome fact.

The obvious answer was that Martin hadn't cleaned the cremator properly between funerals but that was also the most convenient and Owen had been around too long to settle for the convenient answer. The direction he was leaning towards was murder. What if someone had hit upon a cremator being the ideal method of body disposal? He had to admit that it was a pretty spectacular way of getting rid of clues. They could have been doing it for years. In fact, apart from that slip, it could be viewed as the perfect crime.

Killers usually got caught by being sloppy. They were either seen entering or leaving the scene of the crime or traced because of clues left on or near to the body. If the murderer had found a foolproof way of beating the system, they'd markedly reduce the risk of getting caught. His fingers hovered over the keyboard, his eyes trained on the screen, while he read back over what he'd typed, his mind going off on a tangent. If they'd found the perfect formula for murder, why stop at one victim?

He picked up his mug and, after draining it in one, pushed it to the side. He'd get in touch with the undertaker in charge of yesterday's cremation and take it from there.

H Prince and Sons funeral directors was situated only a five-minute drive away in a small lane behind Chester Street, which was as good an excuse as any for Owen to shift his bottom off his chair and visit them in person. His reasoning was twofold: the sensitive nature of the inquiry and the lack of impact the caffeine and sugar combo was having on his ability to keep his eyes open. Sitting behind the wheel of his car, he spent a minute to check in with Kate but, apart from a request to pop into the supermarket for a few things on the way home, everything was running as well as could be expected under the circumstances.

H Prince turned out to be Hayley, a diminutive brunette with an attractive face and an overexuberance when it came to the application of make-up. In her mid-to-late thirties or so, Owen could only assume that the sons were a work in progress.

After enduring the heat of the mid-morning sun from inside a stifling car, he welcomed the cool interior of the funeral home and the offer of another coffee, in the vague hope that an extra shot of caffeine was what he needed.

'Do take a seat, Detective Bates. I'll be back with you shortly,' she said, directing him into her office, a room dominated by a large mahogany desk, a couple of easy chairs and a squidgy sofa pushed up against one wall. The thick, mushroom-coloured carpet muffled the sound of her heels as she strolled towards the door, leaving a lingering trace of some perfume he didn't recognise but thought Kate might like. He hadn't gotten around to buying her a gift yet but perhaps a bottle of scent might be a nice gesture until he could take her to help him choose something special. He'd learnt the hard way how fussy she was with regards to jewellery. He couldn't remember the last time he'd seen the necklace he'd bought her, to commemorate the birth of Pip, anywhere apart from in the bottom of her jewellery box.

He was pulled out of his musings by the sight of Mrs Prince pushing the door open with her elbow and, leaping to his feet, he divested her of the tray, which held white bone china cups and saucers and a plate of biscuits.

'This is very kind of you, Mrs Prince. I've never met a detective yet who's turned down an offer of coffee.'

'You're very welcome. My brother's a copper in Whitstable and I've heard, on more than one occasion, what a tough gig it is.'

She joined him on the plain, mushroom-coloured sofa and crossed one ankle over the other, her slim hands neatly folded, a thin yellow band the only jewellery on display apart from discreet diamond studs in her earlobes.

'Go on, help yourself.' She pushed the plate of biscuits in his direction.

'Thank you.'

'Now, how can I be of help?'

'I'm afraid this is a little delicate, Mrs Prince.'

'Well, Detective, we're used to dealing with delicate situations within these walls. You'd be surprised by the requests from some of the relatives and that's not even touching on the family dynamics that get revealed.'

'I can imagine. We have a situation going on with regards to one of your recent clients, shall we say?'

'I'm listening.'

'There was a ceremony on Saturday over at the Welsh Hills Memorial Gardens that I believe you arranged?'

'Saturday, you say? The one just gone?' She rose and made her way across the room to the desk before flipping through the large black leather-bound diary. 'It's just that, despite our size, we're a very busy firm. Last Saturday we had one interment of ashes and one cremation?' she continued, the inflection in her soft voice matching her raised eyebrows.

'The cremation. A Mr Broome, I believe.'

'Ah yes. Mr Duncan Broome – Broome with an E. His family were very particular about us not forgetting to leave out the E on his headstone,' she confirmed, one hand resting against the polished surface of the desktop.

Owen started, nearly spilling his tea. 'But I thought that he was cremated?'

'He was, but his two daughters particularly specified that his wishes were for his ashes to be interred along with his wife, who's buried in Llanrhos Cemetery.'

'Okay. You'll have to excuse me. I'm not that *au fait* with what goes on with regards to burials and the like.'

'No need to apologise, Detective. It's not something people need to know about until it happens to a family member.'

'Indeed.' He gave an embarrassed laugh. It wasn't the time to think about his parents, happily living out their retirement in Llandudno. 'So, getting back to Mr Broome, what else can you tell me?'

'Hold on a minute while I check.' She settled into her chair and, reaching out a manicured fingertip, flipped open her laptop. It didn't take her long to bring up the correct file. 'Here it is. Mr Duncan Broome, aged eighty-five, died on July 1st. His daughter contacted us by phone on the same day but we had to wait a few days for the body to be released. We picked him up from St Asaph's on the 5th.'

'And it's taken all this time for him to be cremated?'

'Well yes. I did say that we were very busy. It's not like the old days where you could get buried within the same week, sadly.'

'And why the delay at the hospital?'

'Oh, that's easy. Mr Broome was an in-patient at St Asaph's and, as the verifying doctor was unable to confirm the cause of death, his family agreed to an autopsy.'

Owen turned away from the already depleted pile of ginger nuts, lifting a hand to wipe the crumbs from his beard. 'And that's usual practice, is it?'

'It's a regular occurrence, sadly, although relatives can argue against the importance of knowing the exact cause of death – an autopsy is distressing for everyone concerned.' She lifted a hand to tuck a stray tendril of hair behind her ear. 'Is there anything else I can help you with?'

'Going back to the funeral and his interment ...' He paused. 'How does that even happen?'

'It's a very simple process, Detective. Usually the family have a member of the clergy attending the graveside to say a few words. Then the ashes, contained within an urn, are placed in a specially dug hole.'

'Okay. So, getting back to Mr Broome, was there anything else unusual in the instructions?'

'In what way?'

'I'm not really sure,' he said, with a disarming expression. 'In any way?'

She returned to the computer screen. 'Nothing. He had a pacemaker but that was removed by the hospital.'

'And why was that?'

'Because they explode when the cremator reaches temperature, Detective,' she replied, her eyes twinkling.

'Really? Not something I've ever heard about.'

'Probably on a need-to-know basis. There's nothing else. He was a nice old boy. We did our best to follow both his wishes and that of his family.'

He met her gaze over the rim of his cup. 'You didn't say that you knew him?'

'Does that make a difference?' She closed the lid of her laptop and returned to the sofa, picking up her cup, which must have been cold by then. 'He signed up to one of our PAYG schemes following the death of his wife. Funerals can place a huge financial burden on families so he decided to spread the cost of his own by paying a little each month.'

'Oh, I see. What an amazing thing.'

'Isn't it just? We're so pleased that we're able to offer it.' She placed her barely touched drink back on the tray, her intention obvious. 'Well, if you have everything you came for, Detective, I've a few things I need to be getting on with.'

'Yes. Thank you. Oh, there is just one thing. Nothing to do with the case or anything,' he added, feeling a flush creep up to warm his neck. 'That scent you're wearing. I think it's something my wife might enjoy.'

'I'm sure she would.' She smiled. 'It's d'Orage by Chanel. My husband lacks imagination in the present-giving department so he keeps to a few set gifts, this perfume being one of them.'

'I'd better write that down.' Owen had an encyclopaedic brain full of all sorts but there was very little hope of him remembering the name of some random perfume. Removing his diary from his pocket, he frowned down at the blunt end of the attached pencil, another of the little tasks that had evaded his memory with his recent disturbed nights.

'Here, take mine,' she said, sliding her pen across. 'They stock the scent in Boots. A little pricey but then I'm sure that she's worth it.'

Chapter 11

Gaby

Monday 3 August, 12.45 p.m. St Asaph

Gaby watched her team walk through the door of the incident room in dribs and drabs, their body language telling her more than her silent phone that there was no news. Owen appeared the most upbeat but that was hardly surprising considering his recent family news. But Malachy Devine and Marie Morgan's downcast heads and an absence of their usual banter echoed her own low mood. Time was running away from them and, with nothing to follow other than the standard protocols written by police experts on what to do in the case of a missing child, it was all becoming a bit desperate. There was no sign of Jax Williams so, in the interim, Gaby pointed to the sandwiches she'd arranged to be delivered from the station canteen.

'Sorry, it's going to be a working lunch but we have a lot to get through. While we're waiting for Jax to arrive has anyone got anything pressing to say about the case?'

'Only that I'm surprised a ten-year-old can disappear so completely,' Owen said into the lengthening silence, a cheese sandwich in his hand. 'There's usually someone who's seen something or knows something in cases like this, surely? For a girl of her age to go wandering off beggars belief.'

'But that's what appears to have happened,' Gaby said, selecting a ham and tomato on brown and lifting her head in the direction of the door. 'Ah good. Shut the door, Jax, and grab a sandwich. I take it there's no news from the park warden?'

'Not a dickybird. Dafydd's got a team of volunteers scouring the Great Orme and is having the caves and old mines searched as we speak.'

Gaby set her, as yet untouched, sandwich to one side and headed for the first of the three whiteboards that took up the whole length of one wall. Choosing the black marker, she started to scribble in her neatest handwriting, which was far from neat.

'So, Elodie Fry, aged ten, suddenly decides one morning to up and leave. To all intents and purposes her home life is a happy one. It's her school life that's more worrying.' She recapped the marker, placed it on the table and turned back to face the room. 'You don't need me to tell you that when a person runs away they are either driven to it by circumstance or made to because it's the only option open to them. In Ellie's case that's not clear-cut as yet.' She picked up her sandwich and took a quick bite, her attention back on the whiteboard and Ellie's most recent photo. 'I'm not even going to touch on what could have possibly happened to her once she decided to leave home. What we need to concentrate on is the reason for her disappearance.'

'Who knows what kind of rubbish goes on in a ten-year-old's head?' Malachy said through a mouthful of sandwich.

'Exactly, but we have to start somewhere, Mal, and any ideas would be welcome.'

Gaby switched her attention between Jax and Malachy, the younger members of the team. While they might be of a similar age, they couldn't be more different in both their looks and outlook. Jax Williams was tall and blond with the body of a runner

50

and a cheeky smile to match his bright blue eyes. Malachy Devine was also tall but that's where any similarity ended. Brooding was the best term she could find for the large handsome man with a physique only to be found in the most determined of gym aficionados. If truth be told, not that she'd admit it to anyone, up until recently she'd preferred Jax. But during the course of the last case, Mal had proved himself a worthy member of the team – even if his mouth still had a tendency to get him into trouble at every opportunity.

'What about fear?' Marie said, picking up her mug and cradling it between her fingers, ignoring the sandwiches.

'What about it? What would a ten-year-old have to be frightened of?'

'More than you know, Mal. She's a pretty thing, isn't she?' Marie continued. 'What if the fear was closer to home? A man? A family friend? The mother's partner? Even a teacher at the school? And it doesn't have to be a man. There's just as many female weirdos running around.'

'Okay, good point. Let's continue in that vein.' Gaby started to make a list on the whiteboard. 'I've met the mother in addition to the head teacher. On the face of it there's nothing untoward and Ms Fry comes across as being devastated. She says there's no father on the scene but that's something we can easily confirm. There'll be Ellie's birth certificate to start with. Also we can pull up the tenant agreement she would have had to sign with the housing association. Marie, I'll put you on to it as there's probably not a lot of coordinating to do now that the air and sea searches are underway. You're far more use to the investigation working from your desk than chasing around Wales.'

'Yes, ma'am.'

'You can also make tentative inquiries at the school. I've already primed the head teacher so a list of employees should be winging its way over anytime soon. They should all have had an enhanced DBS check but, as we're aware, some people always manage to slip through the net.' She lifted her hand, smoothing her hair back off her forehead. 'The same goes for the ballet class she attended.'

Gaby returned her attention to Malachy, noting his smart silver-grey suit without a change in her expression. He looked like a male model and, for the thousandth time, she wondered what he was doing working on the MIT. Amy had told her the rumour going around the office that Marie was staying with him since the break-up of her marriage. She only hoped it wasn't going to affect their working relationship.

Gaby was broad-minded enough to know that unforeseen events happened between colleagues and that she was only privy to a small portion of what went on between the members of her team. By the same token that was the reason she hadn't told anyone about the change in her relationship with Rusty. She'd have to tell Amy sooner rather than later but they hadn't managed to catch up for a proper chat in what seemed like ages, and conversations about their personal lives were best left to when they were off the premises.

Reining in her thoughts, she shifted her attention over to Jax who, with his boyish good looks and lopsided grin was as easy to read as a comic. 'Tell me about your morning, Jax. Any luck with the neighbours?'

'Not a huge amount, I'm afraid. The neighbours in the houses bordering the Frys didn't see anything. In a way I'm quite surprised. An estate like that with so many residents – you'd think they'd be in and out of each other's doors borrowing sugar, but not a bit of it. They gave me the impression that everyone keeps to themselves, the few bad ones ruining it for everyone.'

'Isn't that the usual way?'

'Probably. The drug problem on the estate is common knowledge and something that may hamper the investigation if people are reluctant to talk. Obviously there's s-s-still some out at work so I was going to drop in again this evening.'

'Good plan. Don't forget to add it to your timesheet and that goes for the rest of you,' she said, with a tilt of her head. 'I'm sure DCI Sherlock will be quite happy to pay overtime rates for something as important as this. So that's Jax and Marie sorted. Malachy, I want you to go through our list of undesirables. Loath as I am to admit it, we can't ignore the possibility that someone might have picked her up on the off-chance and, as Marie has quite rightly reminded us, we have our fair share of weirdos on our patch. That's it for now unless anyone has anything to add?'

Owen placed his sandwich back down on his folded paper serviette and swallowed hard. 'I know it's not the time but if I could fill you in on the issue that arose this morning, ma'am?'

'I'm all ears, Detective,' Gaby said, her smile lessening the impact of her tone.

'There's a problem over at the Welsh Hills Memorial Gardens.'

'What, that funeral place behind the Welsh Zoo?' Marie interrupted.

'You know it?'

'Not well or anything. It's where my grandfather was cremated a while back.'

Owen stared at her. 'It seems as if there's a bit of a mystery, which will need further investigation. It's a little difficult to get your head around but basically one of the groundsmen found something unexplainable when he was cleaning out the cremator.'

'Hold on a minute. The cremator. I take it that's where they burn …?' Gaby asked.

'Exactly. Another word for furnace,' he said, again glancing in Marie's direction. 'A bony residual is left following cremation, which has to be crushed down into a powder but not before all the metal parts have been removed and disposed of separately.'

'Gruesome but fascinating. Everyone okay with this?' This time they both glanced towards Marie, who was now examining her black, low-heeled slip-ons as if they were the most significant thing in the room. Since the recent failure of her marriage Marie had been holding on to her emotions by a thread of steely resolve.

Neither of them wanted to be the one to cause her to snap. Owen only continued after a slight nod from Gaby.

'Well, anyway, to cut a very long story short, yesterday evening, when the handyman was cleaning out the cremator, he found three metal hip replacements and, as he said himself, unless someone has been going around North Wales on three legs, we have a problem on our hands.'

'Okay, but surely not an urgent one? It's not as if the corpse is going anywhere.'

'I'm not so sure about that.'

Gaby watched as Owen stood and made his way across to the window, his hands dug deep in his pockets in what she'd come to term his thinking pose. Over the last few months, the stocky Welsh detective had become more of a friend than a colleague but that friendship didn't in any way influence the contribution he made to the Major Incident Team. Owen was a complex individual with rigid principles and the darkest sense of humour but no one could match his insight into the criminal mind. There was something bothering him. Something that he had to work out first. Despite the urgency, he'd only speak when he was ready.

He turned finally, his hands still entrenched in his pockets, his habitual twinkling eyes for once serious.

'There's been a smattering of elderly people who have gone missing. Not many but always disappearing without a trace. Remember the one last year that we ended up putting down to a suicide, for want of a better explanation?'

'Miss Jane,' Jax interrupted.

'Yes, that's her. It was before your time, ma'am.' Owen sent Gaby a brief look. 'I remember because of the unusual surname, kept thinking I was forgetting to add something at the end like Smith or Jones.'

'Same here,' Jax said. 'Apparently it's common enough in Cornwall. Anyway that's by the by. We all assumed that her body would turn up eventually – it hasn't yet. The case felt as if she'd upped and disappeared into thin air. The thing that worried us the most, at the time, was the full washing machine in addition to the packed fridge. Who goes to all that trouble if they're going to top themselves and, if it was an accident it's likely that the body would have been found by now.'

'As we've already said, there were no clues. We've been waiting for a body – it's very difficult to forge a crime out of her disappearance without either a body or a motive.' Owen met Gaby's gaze. 'But it's not only that. How did the additional prosthetics get into the coffin? I had a chat with the funeral director over at Prince and Sons and she was as flummoxed as me. She even knew the man cremated, a Duncan Broome, which was slightly worrying until she informed me about the PAYG funeral he'd bought into.'

'The PAY what?' Malachy interrupted.

'Pay As You Go, Mal. It's a way of spreading the cost of funeral expenses to minimise the financial burden on your next of kin. Nothing for you to worry about quite yet,' Owen added, managing to squeeze out a laugh.

'Oh, right!'

'Owen, you do realise that we don't have the time to investigate this until we've found the girl, but we'll get to it as soon as we can.' Gaby tapped the pile of photos of Ellie that were ready for distribution. 'It's not as if it could be Ellie and she's my main concern for now. If there's a free window this afternoon, we might be able to arrange a visit to the Memorial Gardens but I'm not promising anything.'

Chapter 12

Barbara

Monday 3 August, 12.45 p.m. Wisteria Cottage

Barbara Matthews was running late due to an unfortunate set of circumstances that included a build-up of traffic along the A55 and a longer than usual queue at the butcher's. It had been a busy day for the soon-to-be eighty-one-year-old but hell would have to freeze over before she missed her weekly appointment for a wash and set at her usual hairdresser in Craig-y-Don.

Unloading the boot of her Toyota hatchback took seconds and, with one hand full of shopping, she made her way up to the front door. She paused to pass a couple of words with her next-door neighbour, a woman she couldn't stand, before sliding her key into the lock.

The feel of the cool air rushing out to greet her had her heave a sigh of relief. While she'd enjoyed her morning, returning to the sanctuary of her own home was the best feeling of all. She pursed her lips, remembering the recent conversation she'd had with her GP about starting to wind it down a little. It was all very well for him to say, with his smart suit and even smarter wife. Golf was her life, closely followed by her weekly bridge party. So what if she consumed more than her recommended units a week or had a fondness for cream buns from that nice little bakery beside St John's Methodist Church along Mostyn Street. She didn't owe anybody anything and was prepared to meet her maker as and when he invited her.

The downstairs of the bright and airy dormer bungalow was open plan and painted in rich creams to maximise the light streaming through the floor-to-ceiling windows with views out over Conwy Castle. When she'd originally chosen to renovate the property, following the death of her father, she'd decided there and then that it was the ideal opportunity to turn their former family home into the house of her dreams. With no siblings or children to look out for, she could spend her money how she liked and if it did mean that there was less to leave to the RSPCA then so be it. The kitchen, only ten years old, retained the feel of an old country farmhouse with its hand-worked oak units and wrought-iron handles, while the tall American fridge was a little piece of extravagance she was yet to regret.

With the kettle on, she unloaded her shopping and, with two lamb chops on a covered plate in the fridge for her supper later, set about making herself a quick coffee.

The doorbell rang to interrupt her peace.

One hand massaging the ache in her lower back, she walked to the door making sure to secure the dainty gold-plated security chain. Deganwy Quay was one of the quieter parts of North Wales but one couldn't be too careful these days. She only had to open the paper to appreciate that things weren't what they used to be, far from it.

There were few people that Barbara Matthews could say she genuinely liked. The new vicar was one, even if she was convinced his wife cheated at golf. But, as her mother used to say, there was a woman who was no better than she ought to be. Barbara had never been quite sure what her mother had meant until she'd met

Reverend Honeybun's wife, with her blood-red nails and carefully teased blonde curls. But the person on the doorstep wasn't anything like Della Honeybun. The person on the doorstep was her kind of person, right down to their discreet choice of grey pinstripe suit, polished shoes and black leather briefcase. Turning her back, she was already planning on stretching out their visit with a glass or two of wine. It would be the perfect way to shorten the time between her solitary meal and her bridge party.

Barbara Matthews wasn't what you could call a nice woman. She had an ingrained dislike of anything that didn't match her own personal ideals. She was also a very stupid woman. Once you understood that she valued breeding and social standing almost higher than oxygen it was easy to fool her into believing that you were exactly what you appeared. Turning her back on her impromptu visitor was the last mistake she'd ever make.

Chapter 13

Gaby

Monday 3 August, 2.40 p.m. St Asaph

'Detective Darin, I'd like a quick word.'

Gaby stopped at one end of the counter while she waited for Clancy to finish tying a green luggage label on the bunch of keys that had been dropped off by a middle-aged man, who was examining his every move from under the security of a fine pair of bushy brows. The truth was most of their front-of-desk work was mundane and their back room was littered with boxes full of sundry items that, like missing socks, were destined to never be matched up with their erstwhile owners.

'Thank you again, sir. Good day to you,' Clancy said, his tight muscles bunching under his uniform in frustration as he propelled the man outside with the force of his intransient stance and professional glare.

'Having problems with the public again, Clancy?'

'Not half! They do keep expecting to be in the middle of an *NCIS* episode when the reality is that missing keys is as exciting as it gets. That's the third bunch dropped off today already.'

Gaby waited a moment for Clancy to get to the point, ensuring that her expression showed no trace of the impatience building up under her calm demeanour. She always had a ready smile and a few words to say to the middle-aged policeman who'd been the first one she'd met when she'd trekked across Wales for her interview with DCI Sherlock. He'd taken her under his wing with a protective fatherly manner and had been looking out for her ever since.

'I've just had a call from a member of the public who's reported one of their old cronies as missing.'

'God, not another one. What's going on with the world?'

'The thing is,' he said, leaning across the desk, 'she's only just gone missing. In fact, I'd nearly go so far as to say she's most likely late and not missing at all.'

Gaby tried not to fidget but she was desperate to get back to the office and catch up with the team about Ellie. Missing persons were all very well but there was a hell of a difference between a missing ten-year-old and this.

'There's four of them that meet up every Monday to play bridge,' Clancy continued finally, glancing down at the report in front of him. 'They take it in turns to visit each other's houses. When they met up earlier, outside Barbara Matthews' house, they found her car in the driveway but no answer when they rang the bell. They also tried her mobile in case there'd been an accident or she'd been delayed for some reason – they heard it ringing out in the hall.'

'Well, all I can say is they must have remarkable hearing for their age.'

'I believe one of them was peering through the letter box at the time. Looking for a dead body, no doubt.'

'No doubt.' She managed to restrain a smile at the image popping into her head, tweed skirt and all. 'So, there is a possibility that she's collapsed then? Perhaps we should send around an ambulance?'

'And a squad car, in case they have to break in? They're quite posh houses along that stretch. Probably security systems up to their bright shiny gutters and soffits.'

'Go on then,' Gaby conceded, picking up the pile of post he'd pushed across the counter, her mind already back on Ellie's disappearance. 'Let me know as soon as you have anything concrete. I'm planning on heading over to the Welsh Hills Memorial Gardens with Owen, after I've checked in with the team,' she added, almost as an afterthought.

Gaby didn't have the time to worry about some old woman with both a missing child and the problem over at the crematorium to deal with. While puzzling, there was very little they could do until they knew that a crime had been committed.

Despite having lived in the area since the start of the year, Gaby had never visited the Welsh Mountain Zoo and she'd certainly never visited the Welsh Hills Memorial Gardens. Perched on a hillside overlooking Colwyn Bay, the crematorium was squeezed in behind the zoo and as such shared the same panoramic view of both land and sea. The sweeping vista made her swiftly add a trip to the zoo, one of the top tourist attractions in North Wales, to the list of family-friendly places she could visit with Rusty and his son during the summer holidays – that is if they were still on speaking terms. She never knew from one minute to the next with the taciturn pathologist.

With the sun beating down on their heads, she thought at least she'd be able to wear something a little more suitable than her trouser suit and plain white work shirt as she pulled a grimace at the feel of the fabric sticking to her skin. The weather had been variable over the last few weeks but it finally seemed as if summer had arrived with a vengeance. With her heavy workload she loved nothing better than spending her free time lazing in her back garden under the shade of the large pear tree, a book in her hand and a glass of iced tea by her side. But with a missing child to find that wasn't going to happen anytime soon.

'Let's get a move on. What I wouldn't give for a nice cold drink at the moment, but it will have to wait.'

'Preferably beer,' Owen said, slamming his car door shut and locking it. 'The front office, do you reckon?' he asked, pointing to the flat-roofed building up ahead with the word *Reception* picked out in gold lettering.

'I think. I'd like to have a quick recce to see the set-up first. Penrose can wait half an hour or so. You were born and bred around here. What can you tell me about the place?'

'Not a lot, I'm afraid. Up to now my family have opted for burial.'

'If I'd thought we wouldn't upset Marie further, I'd have taken her aside to pick her brains,' she said, walking beside him across the block-paved pathway and towards the highly polished front door. 'How do you think she's coping?'

'In what way exactly? The break-up of her marriage or moving in with Devine?'

There was a sharpness to his words that Gaby didn't like and couldn't account for. He should know her better than to think that she hadn't asked out of anything but concern. Never one to let things go, she put a hand on his arm, pulling him to a stop.

'Come on, Owen. Don't be like that. I shouldn't have to tell you that I only have her interests at heart. She's a good copper and doesn't deserve the half of what she's been dished out.'

'That's not the part that concerns me.'

'Excuse me?' she replied, her voice dropping.

'It's Mal.'

'Why Mal? He proved himself a huge asset to the team during the last case even if he puts us all to shame with his dress sense and clothing allowance.'

'He could dress like the Queen of Sheba for all I care. You haven't been here long, Gaby, certainly not long enough to see the way Marie has changed. She's far better without that git of a husband but that's something she has to learn for herself. Shacking up with a player like Devine isn't going to help and it could very possibly make it worse but that's not what concerns me.'

'I'm listening,' Gaby said, reaching for the brass door handle, her head tilted in his direction.

'What's in it for him? Because I can't think of one thing apart from the obvious and if that's the case, Marie is completely out of her depth. Yes, she's a good-looking woman but there's the age difference for one and, from what I hear, she's pretty much dependent on him for everything from the roof over her head to the sheets on her bed.' He placed his hand on the side of the door and, pulling it open, gestured for her to precede him. 'I wonder what his price will be and whether she can afford to refuse to pay it?'

Gaby walked into the plush surroundings, her feet starting to skid on the highly polished wooden floor as she tried to switch her thoughts from concerns about her staff and back to the investigation. Managing her team was the one part of her promotion to DS and then acting DI that she didn't relish. She knew where she was with the dead. While they couldn't speak, there were other ways for them to share their secrets. But people management was like finding an unexpected trunk poking out of that proverbial can of worms. She could cope with the day-to-day detritus that accompanied office life but the unexpected elephant popping up in the corner was something she wasn't equipped for. Gaby would be the first person to admit that she was crap at relationships. Her mind dipped back to Cardiff and her entanglement with Leigh Clark, which had ended in his heavily pregnant wife exposing her for the fool that she was. If she could make such a catastrophic mess of her own life, what were the odds that she'd be just as likely to mess up someone else's?

No. She was going to leave Marie and Malachy to their own devices. All she asked was that any relationship issues they might have didn't impact on their work.

Her thoughts shifted to Rusty but, approaching the wide expanse of desk, she forced them to shrivel and die, leaving only withered remains. Her relationship with the man was far too new to be allowed room during the middle of an investigation. She was meant to be seeing him later – only time would tell if she was able to honour that plan. She had the hurdle of dealing with Bill Davis to face first, a man who would do anything to see her fall flat on her face.

Gaby had had such high hopes when she'd been transferred from Cardiff to Swansea but she'd only worked there a day when she'd had her first run-in with the DS and, as his junior, she'd had to take everything he'd dished out. The worst of it was he still blamed her for the untimely death of her former boss, Rhys Walker. And sadly, part of her agreed with him. The only saving grace was that she'd managed to save the life of Izzy Grant in the process, in a case that was also about a missing child, she remembered – an investigation into the disappearance of Izzy's newborn baby daughter.

She wouldn't last five minutes if Bill got the job of DI but the only way she could prevent it was to apply for the post herself, therefore leaving her even less time for any sort of a personal life. Catch 22.

Gaby paused her musings to take in the quiet, ambient surroundings that featured lots of highly polished glass and subtle furnishings. It took both time and effort to create such a calm, stress-free environment, one which was at odds with the hustle and bustle she was used to. The person standing up to shake their hands matched the environment exactly.

Trevor Beeton was firmly in the grasp of middle age, his thick, brushed-back grey hair a perfect foil for his heavy jaw and deep-set eyes. The suit he wore was dark and formal, the shirt pristine white, the tie dark grey instead of the black she'd been expecting. The shoes were buffed to a high sheen. There was no jewellery apart from a thick wedding band and a steel watch, which looked like it needed a pilot's licence to operate it. He appeared exactly what he was: affluent and opinionated.

'How can I be of help, officers?' he said, sitting back in his chair. He picked up a gold-lidded fountain pen and swirled it through his fingers. 'It's not often we get a visit from the police. In fact, I can't remember the last time.'

'No, well, when they get to you it's usually a little too late for us to intervene,' Gaby replied, angling her head in Owen's direction. This was his party and she was quite happy for him to take the lead.

'I'm not sure whether you know but one of your staff came to see us at the station earlier. A Mr Martin Penrose?'

There was no change in Trevor Beeton's expression but for some reason Gaby sensed that he was annoyed. It made her think that he wouldn't be the most compassionate of men, which was interesting when taking into account his career choice.

'Really? I am surprised. I'm sure that the police have a lot more important things to concentrate on than a little problem of sloppy housekeeping.'

'But Mr Penrose is adamant that he cleaned the cremator thoroughly on both occasions?'

'And why wouldn't he – be adamant that is?' he said, his grey eyes narrowing with a steely determination. 'You obviously don't know Martin as well as I do but he's on his final warning. The truth is I should never have employed him. He hasn't got the wherewithal for the job but he gave me some sob story about not being able to make ends meet.'

'That's beside the point,' Owen said. 'Mr Penrose came to see us about his discovery and, however unlikely his story might be, we are duty-bound to investigate.'

'Of course you are, officers. So, I repeat, how can I be of help? It's not as if I can produce a body,' he added with a laugh, a laugh that didn't make his eyes.

Gaby watched Owen stiffen. As interviews went this one wasn't going to plan. She couldn't actually say that Trevor Beeton was hostile but he wasn't the usual cooperative member of the public they were used to.

'As you can't produce a body, we need details of the cremations performed over the weekend. In particular, Duncan Broome's. Obviously this is only an informal chat but we can easily obtain a warrant for something that is, after all, a matter of public record.'

Gaby hid a smile at the corner Owen had neatly propelled him into, her attention on Trevor as he considered his options. There weren't any. If he made them get a search warrant it would only delay the inevitable and, with death notices freely available online, there was no reason for his objection except perhaps bloody awkwardness.

With a loud sigh, he heaved to his feet and made his way to the filing cabinet positioned to the right of the window. Maintaining a heavy silence, he searched through the files, withdrew two and dropped them neatly onto his desk. Apart from the squeak from his chair when he retook his seat, the silence persisted as he searched through the top folder.

'As the nearest cremator for hundreds of miles, in addition to arranging funerals, we also allow other firms to use our very extensive facilities and that's the case with Mr Broome. Apart from his details, there's very little to add. You'd need to speak to Hayley Prince, over at Prince and Sons ...'

'I've just come from there,' Owen said, leaning forward in his chair. 'Mrs Prince was very helpful,' he continued, the stress being on the *very*, in contrast to Mr Beeton's lacklustre efforts so far. 'So there's nothing to add,' he repeated. 'Nothing odd about the cremation?'

'Not a thing.' Trevor withdrew a piece of paper and, after glancing at it briefly, slid it across the desk. 'We made our usual record of the funeral timings, a list of attendees and who made floral contributions. I'm happy to email you a copy for your records?'

'Thank you. What about the previous cremation? It's something we need to look into if, as you've suggested, the problem is down to "sloppy housekeeping" rather than anything nefarious.'

Trevor opened up the second folder without a word. Removing the contents, he spread them out, his expression impossible to read as he quickly scanned the sheets for the relevant page before handing it across to Owen.

Gaby felt a clinical detachment at odds with their current situation. She hated funerals almost as much as Marie but, after a life well lived, she could rationalise that they had to be viewed as a celebration more than anything. The truth was people died. There was nothing she or anyone else could do to change that.

The silence extended, both Trevor and Owen reluctant to speak first. Owen cleared his throat, his gaze fixed on the sheet in his hand, his knuckles blanching through the skin, even as Gaby glanced down at the name typed in capitals at the top of the page.

MISS OLIVE JOHNSON, AGED TEN.

Chapter 14

Ronan

Monday 3 August, 2.40 p.m. Llandudno

For once Ronan was in a pickle not of his own making. With two younger brothers, he no more knew how to act around a ten-year-old girl than he did a stranger in the street, and strangers were the people he was most wary of. If a pair of supposed schoolmates could assault him on school premises, how was he meant to trust someone he'd only just met?

He couldn't remember a time when he'd had the ability to trust anyone apart from himself. Perhaps when he was younger but since then the world had let him down in such a spectacular fashion as to make a mockery of his previous dependence on others. It wasn't his mother's fault that she'd developed cancer but he could certainly blame her for the way it had changed her. He gripped Ellie's hand firmly within his, pulling her away from Mostyn Street and down one of the side streets towards the train station. No, for all his mother's faults, she couldn't be held responsible for her illness or the changes it ultimately wrought on his family.

'Hey, where are we going?' Ellie said, interrupting his thoughts, her voice the gruff squeak he'd told her to adopt.

He dropped her hand now that they were out of sight of the main artery of the town but instead of answering, he carried on walking, ignoring the sound of her feet racing to catch up with him.

'Hey, I asked you where we were going,' she said again, her voice breaking into a sob.

He halted in his tracks and turned, staring down at her upturned face. It was hard to remember the girl she'd been before the haircut. All trace of her long hair was gone, the boyish crop just about concealed by one of his brother's baseball caps. He'd expected hysterics when she'd first caught sight of herself in the mirror but instead he'd got silence. He'd been proud of her then, this slight girl with eyes so large they nearly filled her face. She still hadn't told him why she was on the run and, despite everything, he'd let her be. She'd tell him in her own time but, by the mulish pull of her bottom lip, nothing he could say would make her divulge anything she didn't want him to know. Glancing down, he took in his younger brother's jeans and old trainers, which at least added to the illusion of her being a boy, all trace of pink expunged from her wardrobe even down to her rucksack. It would be disastrous if someone recognised her before he'd managed to wriggle out of her why she'd run away. Only then would he decide what was best for her because wandering the streets with him certainly wasn't it.

'Come on,' he said, dropping his voice, a smile edging his lips at the sight of her stubborn bottom lip starting to wobble. He was probably being too hard on her; she was only ten after all and she'd barely said a word since leaving his mother's house. The reality was that she was a very scared little girl. For some reason she'd picked him for the role of her guardian angel, which was the biggest joke of all. He was barely able to mind himself let alone have responsibility for anyone else.

'I thought we'd be going back to the Orme?'

'Did you now? The Orme will be the first place they search so we need to go somewhere that they won't think of.' He stopped again, placing the plastic bag he'd been clutching between his feet while he rearranged the position of his rucksack on his shoulders, which had grown heavier from the tins he'd pilfered from his mother's larder cupboard. He hadn't been back to the house since he'd made the decision to run away and stealing from his family wasn't something he'd ever wanted to do. But there wouldn't be any friendly vicar to turn to where they were going and, without a source of income, his money supply wouldn't last for ever.

'So, where are you taking me?' she said, rubbing the back of her hand across her eyes.

Crouching down, he noted the threat of tears hovering on her lashes and tried to think of how Caleb, his eleven-year-old brother, would cope in a similar situation. He wouldn't. He'd be terrified. But then he couldn't think of a reason for him to desert the family home except possibly their perpetually poor internet speed, which had once been the main cause of the arguments between them. The truth was that Ellie was desperate and Ronan too much of a coward to ask her why she'd run; he wasn't sure if he could cope with the answer. She appeared to be holding it together by a slender thread of bravado. At some point that would snap, leaving him to pick up the pieces. He'd rather that wasn't until after they'd reached their final destination.

His free hand curled around the hard outline of the keys he'd taken from the top drawer of his mother's filing cabinet.

'We're going somewhere they won't find you unless you want them to. You do still want to run away, don't you? Because now's the time to say if not.' He answered her slight nod with another brief smile. 'Okay then. We need to get cracking or we'll miss the train. Watch out for a bin, would you?' He lifted up the carrier bag. 'No point in taking this with us.'

Chapter 15

Gaby

Monday 3 August, 3.20 p.m. Welsh Hills Memorial Gardens

No cost had been spared to furnish the light, bright and airy chapel. The rectangular room was filled with pew-like wooden benches fitted with thick, soft, red velour cushions. The white walls were draped with a variety of tapestry scenes, which added a richness to what would have otherwise been a spartan room. There was a small plain lectern at the front in the same wood used on the benches and a plinth off to one side with a large copper basin arranged with an assortment of flowers, none of which Gaby could put a name to apart from the dahlias. The red curtains on the back wall hung from a thick brass pole and matched the fabric of the seat cushions. She didn't want to think about what they were concealing.

Like many of the places that Gaby visited in her work as a police officer, the room at the back of the chapel, which housed the cremator, was very different to the showy front. Instead of the same grey flooring as in the reception and office areas there was bare concrete. Instead of plastered walls there was bare brick.

The steel cremator was a large square box with a small door fitted into one side and a range of dials, which were all pointing at zero. Apart from the cremator, there was a long bench, which held a small steel unit along with a metal brush, a small rake and what looked like an oversized magnet. There was also a large apron, reminiscent of the one Rusty used during his autopsies, in addition to a pair of industrial gloves hanging from a hook in the corner.

They'd asked to meet with Martin Penrose, much to the displeasure of Trevor Beeton, but that couldn't be helped. They weren't in the business of pleasing members of the public, only in finding out the answers to the questions that were starting to build around the echo of a crime. An extra body. Whose? Why? And finally, to Gaby's confused mind, how?

She turned her attention away from the room, focusing instead on the man propping up the wall nearest the door, his forearms folded across his chest. She'd barely noticed him back at the station. Now she took in his old jeans, baggy around the knees and frayed at the hem where they met his heavy-duty boots, an expression of distrust marking his weather-beaten face. The unexpected expression was one she'd have to think about later but, in the short term, it made her restructure the questions flitting around her mind.

There was no offering to shake hands, something she was thankful for as she took in his work-roughened fingers, the nails split and ingrained. Instead she stepped back and let Owen take the lead. Her thoughts returned to the hunt for Ellie Fry and her phone's disappointing silence.

'Mr Penrose, this is DI Darin,' Owen said, flicking his head in Gaby's direction. 'If you could repeat what you told me earlier so that we can visualise it for ourselves?'

She watched Martin lever himself from the wall and make his way across to the cremator, his hand working the handle that barricaded the metal door. 'Like I said earlier, this is the

72

business end of cremations. After the ashes have cooled, they have to be raked out. There's never much apart from the bones but occasionally we get some metal fragments like gold fillings and if the person had a joint replacement.' He crossed back to the bench and tapped the edge of the metal tray. 'This is where the bits and pieces get sorted. The bone fragments then go into the crusher while the metal parts get separated for disposal later. That's it. The whole process in a nutshell. There's nothing else to tell except that yesterday instead of finding the maximum of two artificial hips there were three.'

'And there's no way there could have been a mix-up?' Owen said, catching Gaby's frown. 'Maybe from a cremation a few days ago?'

'None whatsoever. I had sole responsibility over the weekend and I can assure you that the three hips were from the last service.'

'Okay, let's move on a little, Mr Penrose. Do you have any suggestions as to what might have happened? Perhaps someone slipped a second body into the coffin or even had one already in the cremator when Mr Broome joined it?'

Mr Penrose shook his head in utter disbelief, reinforcing Gaby's view as to his innocence. Even his look of distrust earlier led her to believe that he was nothing if not genuine. There would be no reason for him to go to the police with some jumped-up story that was far too strange to be immediately believable.

'I've no idea how they got there – that's the thing that's worrying me the most,' he said, a nervous tick appearing in his cheek. 'That and the boss using it as an excuse to get rid of me.' He rubbed his hand across the back of his neck. 'I always double-check that I've cleaned the cremator. It's only fair for relatives to know that all of their loved ones' remains are returned to them,' he said, his voice cracking.

'You sound as if you're speaking from experience?'

'I am.' He shook his head and Gaby knew that he wouldn't answer any further questions on that score.

'Okay, let's back up a little. You said that the part that's worrying you the most is how the extra hip joint got into the coffin. What do you mean by that?'

'The problem is that it's impossible. Crematoriums already know how easy it would be for people to use the furnace to dispose of bodies. That's why they've set up precautions like the furnace only taking one coffin.'

'And what about when it's up to temperature? Couldn't somebody have added a second body then?'

He laughed, his head shaking a second time. 'Not if they were interested in living. The cremator runs at around 1,800 degrees Fahrenheit, but not only that – there's a safety mechanism, which means that the door is clamped shut until the unit has cooled down to a safe temperature.'

'But the fact remains that three hip prosthetics were found following one cremation?'

'And no bloody way of explaining it. I've checked with the boss. Mr Broome had what we term an open casket, which means that it wasn't sealed until right up to him being placed into the cremator.' He raised his head from where he'd been staring down at his hands, working away at trying to remove the dirt from under his fingernails. 'I saw the body and I can tell you there is no way that anything could have been hidden.' Pulling back his sleeve, he glanced at his watch. 'Is there anything else? I really do have to get on or it will be another black mark against me.'

'You seem to have a difficult relationship with Mr Beeton?' Gaby said, her voice soft.

'You could say that. He demands absolute commitment and doesn't like that I have to leave early in order to pick up my daughter from school on the odd occasion she's unable to take the bus. He doesn't seem to get that as a single dad I don't have a choice in the matter.'

'He doesn't appear to be the most sympathetic of individuals.'

'You're telling me! The things I could tell you ...'

Chapter 16

Owen

Monday 3 August, 4.05 p.m. St Asaph Hospital

'Ah, Owen, it's grand to see you. Do take a seat – and you've brought coffee too. Thank you,' Rusty Mulholland said, peeling back the lid of the cup set in front of him and taking a long sip. 'I was only thinking what I'd give for a decent drink right now. I believe that congratulations are in order, by the way? You must be over the moon.'

Owen had entered Rusty's office after a brief knock, a large brown envelope clutched under his arm and a couple of take-outs in his hands. While he felt he had a good relationship with the often taciturn senior pathologist, interrupting him without warning wasn't his normal way of working, hence the coffee pacifier.

'Indeed. Although I do seem to be hitting the caffeine rather hard. My daughter certainly has a fine pair of lungs.'

'She's in practice for when she's in a relationship, no doubt,' he replied, his voice taking on a dry note. 'I hear you've called her after Kate's sister. I always thought Angelica a beautiful name.'

'Yes, well. It was the right thing to do,' Owen said, flipping open the envelope and shuffling through the pages to select the one he wanted. It was still far too early for him to talk about – let alone think about – his wife's sister. Angelica's birth was their way of drawing their line through that unhappiest of times. 'I know you're a busy man but something's cropped up with one of your recent autopsies that I'd like to run by you, if I may?'

'Really. One of mine, you say.' Rusty shifted his glasses into place from where they'd been perched on his forehead, his long slender fingers reaching for the top document. 'Duncan Broome. That wasn't too long ago, only a few weeks if I remember rightly,' he said, turning to his computer and logging on to the system. After a moment he added, 'Here it is. Died on the 1st of July here in St Asaph's. There was some question as to the cause of death as, apart from bilateral hip replacements and a pacemaker insertion, he was fit and well.'

'And anything suspicious with your findings?'

'Not a thing. Cerebral haemorrhage, which links to a fall he'd suffered a few days previously. So, all very straightforward. I met with the daughters. Nice women. Clearly devastated.' He twisted back in his seat, his expression frank. 'Is there anything else I can help you with or …?'

'I'm not sure if I'm honest.'

'I'm happy to be used as a sounding board. Sometimes a different viewpoint is all that's needed.'

The problem was that Owen didn't have a clue what he was looking for, if anything. The likelihood was that Martin Penrose was telling them complete porkies but that was far from the impression he'd given them. The other thing of course was that information was always on a need-to-know basis in police work but what the hell. If you couldn't trust a doctor then you couldn't trust anyone.

He placed his already half-empty cup back on the desk and withdrew the second sheet of paper. 'Before we go into that can

I ask if there's anything you can tell me about an Olive Johnson, aged ten?'

Rusty steepled his fingers, his blue eyes suddenly sharp behind his lens. 'Another one of mine, I believe. This investigation wouldn't have anything to do with the department, would it, because if so I'm not sure if I should be—?'

'No. Nothing like that or, at least I don't think so. In fact, most unlikely. I only need to ask if she'd ever had a hip replacement?'

'A hip replacement? Improbable in a ten-year-old but not impossible if she'd been suffering from something like juvenile arthritis,' he said. 'But in Olive's case, no. I'm certain that her problems, while diverse, didn't include damage to her joints. You're intriguing me with this line of questioning, Owen.'

'More like puzzling myself,' he replied. 'So, what would you say to three prosthetic hip replacements being found in a cremator when the last two bodies to be cremated were Olive Johnson and Duncan Broome?'

Rusty sat back in his chair, peering at him over the top of his cup, a thoughtful expression now in place. 'I can see your difficulty due to the rarity of three-legged corpses,' he said, the hint of a smile on his lips. 'You're sure it's not a mistake with the cleaning out of the cremator between … er … guests? As I've said, Duncan Broome is known to have had two hip replacements and, no matter how incompetent his surgeon might have been, it's unlikely a spare hip would have gone unnoticed during the routine post-op X-ray they all have to undergo. The odd watch maybe but—'

Owen joined Rusty in a brief chuckle. 'As sure as I can be, bearing in mind that the person responsible for cleaning it out was the one who came to us in the first place.'

'Good point. So either someone with a prosthetic hip was placed in the coffin along with Duncan Broome or somehow slipped into the cremator after his coffin? An interesting, rather unique method of body disposal.'

Owen shook his head. 'Not possible, I'm afraid. With the temperature safety mechanism, there's no way of opening the door until the cremator has cooled. Also the groundsman told me that Mr Broome had a morbid fear of being buried alive and specifically requested an open coffin right up to just before he was cremated. There's some story about his mother in the Eighties being verified as dead by some junior doctor or other. The nurses were washing the body when they noticed her chest rising. Scared the bejesus out of them, apparently.'

'I'm not bloody surprised.'

'You can appreciate my confusion. If there's no possibility of an additional body hidden in the coffin and we've ruled out Olive Johnson as ever having had a prosthesis then it's right back to the drawing board.'

'Not quite. You're further on than you think, Owen.' Rusty picked up the empty cups and, after throwing them in the bin, rested back in his chair, his hands clasped behind his head. 'Somewhere along the way a spare metal hip has found its way into the crematorium. What we need to do is to find the owner.'

'Easier said than done. It's not as if it's likely to have any evidence attached to it after the temperatures they've been exposed to.'

'No. Not at all,' he said, unclasping his hands and leaning across the desk. 'You wouldn't happen to have brought them with you by any chance? There's a huge amount to tell from the prostheses themselves by someone like me just examining them,' he continued, his gaze resting on the bulky envelope sat between them on the desk.

Owen returned his look. 'Yes, in the faint hope you might have any ideas. It's unlikely there'll be any forensics but—'

'Noted.' Rusty removed a pair of gloves from the box behind his desk and slipped them on before reaching inside the envelope.

Each artificial hip was in its own clear plastic bag, the metal now black and marked instead of smooth and shiny. Rusty removed them, examining each in turn, running his index finger over the surface. 'What do you know about hip replacements, Owen?'

'A lot more than I did this morning,' he said with a grimace. 'But I'm far from an expert.'

'Okay, I promise I'll keep it simple. Basically, a total hip replacement is made up of three parts. A metal shaft that's pointed at one end. The opposite end is flat and smooth, which allows it to work with the head,' he added, pointing to the separate metal sphere about the size of a large marble. 'This ball is normally covered in a polyethylene cap but obviously, as a plastic, its melting power isn't like that of the stainless steel or cobalt chrome, which are the metals of choice for the primary parts.' He lifted his head. 'Are you still following me or ...?'

'Just! So, what about the differences in the sizes and the reason I asked about Olive Johnson?' Owen said, pointing to the much smaller third prosthesis.

'That's a grand question, Owen, but one that's easy to answer. Different-sized people need different-sized prosthetics. Here we have two prostheses belonging to a large male,' he said, pointing to the shoulder of the implant and placing the two side by side. 'While it's not conclusive that they were taken from the same person, there is a strong possibility. The one on the right is much smaller. It's very easy to see why it might have led you astray but I'd hazard a guess that it's been taken from the body of a very small adult female, maybe even of Asian ethnicity simply because it's well known that they need smaller prosthetics.'

'Okay, so how do we go about finding out one way or the other? It's not as if they're going to have their name and address carved into the metal now, is it?'

Rusty threw back his head and laughed. 'Actually you're not too far off the mark, Owen.'

'I'm sorry, you've lost me completely now.'

Rusty grinned. 'With the huge upsurge in medical litigation and the like, particularly around the region of prosthetics, I thought it would be obvious but perhaps not.' He opened one of the bags and, dropping the artificial joint into his gloved palm, held it out for Owen to see. 'There, on the shaft right below where it meets the shoulder. The unique serial number.'

Owen's eyes widened. 'How do you know all this stuff?'

'Because I'm a genius,' he said, his shoulders shaking. 'The part about the serial number is really only common sense – there needs to be a way of keeping track of all implants in case there's a problem and they have to be recalled, although once in situ it's usually too late to do anything about them. The National Joint Registry has a log of all artificial joints inserted in the British Isles over the last eighteen years.' He pushed over the plastic bags, topping them off with a pair of gloves. 'I have a meeting shortly but if you call out the numbers – your eyesight is better than mine – I promise to get back to you with the recipients' names later.'

Chapter 17

Gaby

Monday 3 August, 4.10 p.m. St Asaph Police Station

Gaby arrived back at the station after a brief stop to pick up a bottle of ice-cold water, her mind on the hundred and one things she needed to achieve by the end of her shift and not on Clancy who had to repeat her name for her to take any notice.

'Detective Darin, DS Davis is upstairs waiting in your office as per DCI Sherlock's wishes. He had planned for you to take him on a tour of the station but, with the girl still missing, thought better of it. Instead he's to shadow you for the remainder of your shift.'

Really! But all Gaby did was wave her hand in acknowledgement, when she'd much prefer to bang her head against the nearest wall. Her thoughts dragged her against her will back to Swansea and the DS that had made her life a misery. She hadn't done any more about applying for the job but, if she didn't want to be managed out of the door by Bill Davis, she'd better start thinking about it.

She'd only taken a step away from the desk and towards the flight of stairs that led to her office before her mobile kicked into action but her groan of annoyance quickly disappeared when she realised that it was Rusty.

'Owen has just left. I take it things are busy back at the station and I wanted to check that you're all right for this evening, Gabriella?'

She loved the way he pronounced her name – the soft burr of his Irish accent elongating the sound. It was a name she rarely heard except on the lips of her mother when she was shouting at her. The world was full of strong women but none stronger than her Italian mama who was determined that she was always in the right. Gaby's brothers often teased her that the family resemblance she shared with her went a lot deeper than their hair, skin and eyes. She couldn't see it herself.

'Can I be a pain and push it back to seven instead of six? I was going to make pizza,' she said, recalling her plan to drop into the local supermarket in her break instead of the working lunch she'd exchanged it for. Now she'd have to do her shopping on the way home and in the middle of rush hour too, which was all very stressful and exactly the reason why she hadn't jumped back into the dating game after Leigh Clark.

'How about you forget making dinner and I'll bring something with me instead? After all there's two of us to your one.'

'Only if you're sure?'

'Perfectly. If you're good enough to have my son along on a date then the very least I can do is to be flexible when your plans go awry. And anyway, I wouldn't be offering if I wasn't.'

Yes, she knew that only too well. Rusty would be the first to speak his mind and, with her mother's genes flooding her veins, that wasn't necessarily a good thing. Finishing the call with instructions about where to find the spare key, she sent off a quick text to Owen to be back at the station for a catch-up and headed for the stairs.

Bill Davis was just how she remembered, his receding hairline combed over to make the most of the wispy strands on show.

His expression was dour but then she couldn't remember having ever seen him smile. Sitting behind her desk with his fat fingers laced around the handle of her favourite mug, he looked as if he was making himself comfortable.

Gaby didn't do the usual things she was meant to. The ready smile and welcoming babble were missing, as was the extended hand. Instead she hung up her bag on the hook behind the door and tilted her head in the direction of the corridor.

'The grand tour will have to wait, Bill. We have an ongoing situation here.'

'That would be DS Davis to you, Gaby.'

'Well in that case, DS Davis, as the senior ranking officer in the room, I'm acting DI Darin to you.' She framed the door, her hand on her hip. 'And, unlike you, I don't have all day to sit around drinking coffee,' she added, staring pointedly at her mug. 'I need to catch up with the team and it's the ideal opportunity for you to see them in action.'

On pushing open the door to the incident room the first thing that hit her was the smell. The office was hot with sun streaming in through the one window which, in line with station regulations, was only able to open a few inches in case someone tried to either enter or leave the building unexpectedly. It wasn't an unpleasant odour, more a mingling of stale coffee with an undertone of hot bodies layered with an assortment of perfume and aftershave – after all her years on the force, she'd come up against a lot worse. But she decided to leave the door open in the unlikely event that she could conjure up a through-draught of air.

It didn't take her long to place her phone on her desk, her gaze taking in Malachy and Marie, who barely lifted their heads to acknowledge her return. She shoved all thoughts of Bill aside. The focus of her attention was Ellie's disappearance and where the hell she could have got to.

After walking over to the first whiteboard, she stopped in front of Ellie's photo, concentrating on the heart-shaped face surrounded by a cloud of pale blonde hair. Gaby didn't know what she hoped to find as she studied the girl's translucent skin, stretched over finely etched cheekbones. There were no shadows under her eyes, nothing to indicate that she wasn't exactly what she appeared. A perfectly happy and healthy ten-year-old. But clearly she wasn't – something must have happened to make her world fall apart. The only problem was that Gaby and her team had no idea what. The school hadn't been of any help but then she hadn't really expected them to be. Young girls were very good at keeping secrets and if Ellie was being bullied … Gaby's own personal experience was that her mother would have been the last person to know if she'd decided to keep it from her. It certainly wasn't something that Anita had mentioned.

Gaby did her best thinking with a pen in her hand, in this case a black marker. Removing the lid, she started to add Ellie's personal details under the photo. Her full name. Her age and other random information like a list of the clothes that she was thought to be wearing in addition to a description of the rucksack. She got as far as adding the colour and make of her trainers before the sound of Owen and Jax's voices made her recap the pen and wait, her hip propped against the corner of the table as she stole a glance at her watch. Still a couple of minutes to go but with everybody in the room, she might as well get the meeting underway.

'Okay, everyone. I'm going to start a little early. There's a lot to get through and not all of it in relation to Ellie Fry but she's obviously our biggest concern. But before we begin, I'd like to introduce you to DS Bill Davis who's up from Swansea for a few days.' She only continued after she'd spent a moment to introduce the team and give a brief precis of the disappearance. 'Okay then. I presume I'm right in saying that there've been no further sightings?'

'No, m-m-ma'am,' Jax said, his phone on the desk in front of him, his stutter more pronounced now that there was a stranger in the room. 'The trail is cold apart from a sighting by a dog walker on the Great Orme earlier on this morning. As you'll remember, we did think that the Orme was the most likely place for her to head and that's why we got Dafydd Griffiths on to it straight away.'

'And what has he come up with?'

'Not a huge amount apart from his obvious suggestion about the old mining tunnels and caves.'

'But they're locked up, aren't they?'

'Yes, but as we're all aware, people have ways and means of getting into places they're not meant to.'

'Back up a step, Jax, and tell me again about the sighting?'

'There's not a lot to say – only that the man thought he saw someone matching her description but she was in the company of another teenager. He assumed that they were siblings out for an early morning hike.'

'Because they were wearing rucksacks no doubt. Presumably it also didn't strike him as odd that it was early on a Monday morning and there wasn't a parent in sight,' she added almost to herself. 'When will I stop being amazed at the stupidity of others? I want a police presence on the Orme until she's found.'

'Yes, ma'am.'

'And how have you been getting on at the housing estate? What's the word on the street about Ellie and her mother?'

'Again there's not a lot to say. I spent a few hours going from door to door. Most of the residents recognise them on s-s-sight but, apart from the odd hello, only a few knew them to speak to. As a family the Frys stuck to themselves. Outside of work, school and the daughter's ballet lessons they were rarely seen and certainly never in the evenings. We know that money's tight so they wouldn't have had the disposable income to go out eating and the like.'

'No skeletons then? Not even a miserly bone or two in the back of the wardrobe?'

'Not a thing. They were liked well enough but that doesn't help us.'

85

'Oh, I wouldn't say that. I much prefer that Ellie had a good home life than the alternative. It just makes our jobs ten times more difficult in trying to discover what's going on.'

Gaby stood from her perch and walked across to the window, staring at the deep blue sky over the rooftops with not a hint of a cloud to mar the cerulean backdrop. She knew that she'd been hoping for some kind of a reason to present itself for Ellie running away, some secret that only the most diligent of nosy neighbours could have spotted. But they weren't going to be lucky. It was back to the drawing board.

Instead of heading to the front of the room, she pulled out a chair and settled back, tapping the end of the marker pen between her teeth. 'Remind me who was on CCTV duty?'

'That would also be me, ma'am,' Jax said, sending an anxious look in Bill's direction. 'B-b-but I didn't think you'd mind if I got PC D-D-Diane Carbone on to it. You remember how helpful she was during the last case?'

'Indeed. And has she found anything?'

'Not yet but she's far from f-f-finished.'

'Well, tell her to shift herself from where she's hiding. She needs to base herself here if she's on the team. There's a space free.' She nodded her head at the spare desk next to Mal.

'Y-y-yes, ma'am.'

Gaby hid a frown at Jax's worsening speech, well aware that the cause was the man sitting on her left, the snide expression stamped across his features destroying all the good work she'd achieved over recent months. With careful nurturing on her part, in addition to a romantic entanglement with a local nurse that was starting to look serious, Jax was a new man. His stutter was greatly improved and only showed itself when his stress levels peaked, like now. But Bill had never been one for the soft side of management. As a DS it had taken a strong boss like Rhys Walker to direct him. As a DI, with no one to moderate his behaviour, he'd be a complete disaster. So far, Gaby had been in two minds whether to apply for the job, her skewed work-life balance the biggest deterrent. Now she knew she didn't have an alternative.

Clamping down on the thought, she turned her head towards Marie. 'What about you? Any joy?'

'I don't know whether you'll think it's good news or not that I haven't really turned up anything that we can get our teeth into,' she said, pushing her hair back from her face, the slight sheen on her forehead the only indication that she was suffering from the hot humidity as much as everyone else. Both Mal and Jax had discarded their ties and undone their top button while Owen appeared ready to drop on his feet. Gaby was avoiding mirrors – she didn't need to be told she looked as limp as she felt.

'So far there's nothing in Ms Fry's background to indicate that she's anything other than a hard-working single mum,' Marie continued, taking a swig from her water bottle. 'I've also done checks on all the employees at the school but nothing strikes me as worrying. The same goes for the teacher of Ellie's ballet class, which she takes three times a week at the centre in Eirias Park.'

'What about Anita's job then?' Gaby said, her tone measured while she worked out what to do next. The problem was that police guidelines were only helpful up to a point. While criminal profilers led the way in identifying patterns and predicting how a criminal's mind might work, none of it helped when a crime had yet to be committed. The *yet* was the thing that was worrying her the most.

'There's not a lot to go on. As we know, she's a self-employed cleaner, working around Ellie's school pick-ups mainly.'

'We'll need a list of her employers if only to cross them off our list.'

'Yes, ma'am.'

'We also need to send someone over to Rhyl to interview Ellie's best friend as a matter of urgency.' Gaby pulled her cuff back, hiding a grimace when she saw the time. She still had to speak to Bill and at least make a passing attempt at maintaining a professional front while she tried to shift all the elements of the case into some sort of a pattern. What she'd really like was five minutes to herself with a cold drink and a blank sheet of paper to make sure she wasn't missing anything vital but that wasn't going to happen anytime soon. She'd sort Bill out before heading over to Rhyl – if she left the office by midnight she'd be lucky.

'Thank you, everyone. Before you all disappear the bad news is that we also have the ongoing situation over at the Welsh Hills Memorial Gardens, where three prosthetic hips were found instead of the expected two.' She added the last part for Bill's benefit. 'I'll let Owen explain.'

Owen pushed up from his chair and wandered to the front of the room. 'I've just come back from a meeting with Dr Mulholland. All being well, we should have the names of the people assigned the prosthetic hips by the end of the day.' He ran his hand over his beard, a deep frown in evidence. 'Instead of hanging around, I'd be happy to interview that friend of Ellie's and save you a job? It's only ten minutes away or so.'

Gaby bit down on her lower lip, well aware of the time and the likelihood of rush-hour traffic along the A525. But Owen was a grown-up and one who didn't take too kindly to her interfering in his home life. So, instead of saying what she thought, all she said was, 'It's probably a good idea if you take Amy with you. Phone me if you have anything, and that goes for the rest of you.' She turned to face them. 'I appreciate the stress you're all under but we have to keep on top of the workload. Remember it's a big bad world out there and Elodie Fry is only ten.' Gaby headed for the door. 'DS Davis, my office, if you please.' She knew it was churlish but there was no way she was giving him the opportunity of either sitting behind her desk or drinking out of her mug again.

Chapter 18

Owen

Monday 3 August, 4.55 p.m. Rhyl

Heather Powell lived with her parents in a spacious apartment tagged on to the side of their sea-fronted hotel in Rhyl. No cost had been spared to fit out the accommodation and Owen was hard-pressed not to slip off his shoes at the entrance, the hole in his sock the only thing stopping him. Like everything else in his life at present, the mundane minutiae of his day, like sock buying, was put on hold until Angelica's sleeping pattern was such to guarantee more than a couple of hours' sleep at one stretch.

After a few minutes of word-wrangling with Heather's parents, they were shown into a large family room situated at the back of the apartment. No one liked the police turning up on their doorstep unannounced and Owen and Amy had their work cut out trying to convince them that they only had Ellie and Heather's best interests at heart.

Heather turned out to be a round-faced, chubby girl with long dark hair straggling her back, and unfortunate teeth – Owen's thoughts contracted at the sight. There were so many things about the child sitting in front of him, with her hands clasped tightly on her lap, that could cause her to be bullied and it didn't take a genius to see the truth in Gaby's words by the way Heather was careful to avoid his gaze. The worst of it was that there was very little he could do to help. Their priority must be finding out what had happened to Ellie.

'Hi there. My name is Owen Bates and this is Amy Potter, but you can call us Owen and Amy. We're trying to find out about Ellie. I believe you're her friend?'

'We hang out a bit, if that's what you mean.'

'That's exactly what I mean. So, when did you last see her?'

She wrinkled her nose. 'That would've been Friday at about seven around at hers. Her mum asked me over for tea.'

'Your dad collected you?'

'Yes. Saturdays are busy at the hotel otherwise I could have had a sleepover.'

'Do you often have sleepovers with her then?'

'All the time but usually here instead of—' She stopped, her finger in her mouth as she bit on the skin around her thumb.

'Instead of …?' Amy asked softly.

The expression on Heather's face told Owen that she wasn't going to answer. Instead of pursuing it, Amy asked another. 'So, can you tell me what Ellie was like when you last saw her? You know, was she happy? Sad? Did she seem worried about anything? There must be a reason why she decided to leave home. Is there anything you can tell me that might help us find her?'

Heather shrugged. 'I don't know. She did seem a bit quiet. Not her usual self. She's normally full of talk about her ballet lessons but on Friday she barely said a thing. Her and me, we're good mates. We stick together. I was worried I'd maybe done something to annoy her.' She raised her head again, the downward pull of her mouth an indication of her mood. 'You will find her, won't you?'

'We're doing our very best,' Amy said, leaning forward in her chair. 'So, she didn't say anything then? Anything that might make you think there was a reason behind her running away?'

'She didn't say much at all. In school, she's quiet but then so am I. But outside she never shuts up. Friday, she was different. I don't think she wants to be my friend anymore otherwise she'd have told me what was worrying her.'

'She was worried?'

'I think so. We've been trying to grow our nails.' Heather spread her fingers, displaying ten nails painted in a rainbow of colours. 'She was beating me by a mile. Friday she'd bitten them right down to the bottom.'

'That girl has the weight of the world on her shoulders,' Amy said, after the door had closed behind Heather's back. 'Do you think she'll be all right without Ellie around to support her?'

'I'll have a word with her parents on the way out. We also need to ask them why they were reluctant for her to sleep over at Ellie's. It's probably the snob factor but there could be something that we're missing.'

'While you're at it, I'll phone Gaby and give her an update. Oh, I nearly forgot. She said to tell you not to bother to go back to the office. If she sees you before eight tomorrow there'll be ructions.' Amy raised her hands in a defensive position at his murderous expression. 'Don't shoot the messenger. Those were her words not mine.'

Chapter 19

Ronan

Monday 3 August, 4.55 p.m. Caernarfon

With his baseball cap pulled low, Ronan helped Ellie off the train, his hand firm around her wrist as they made their way to the exit, their heads tilted away from the CCTV cameras pinned high against the wall. To be discovered after coming so far would be the kind of rookie mistake he wasn't prepared to make – not after the trouble he'd already taken to ensure her safety. He didn't release his grip until they were down the road and out of sight of the rush-hour milieu that circled the station entrance.

As he stopped at the end of the road, the sight of the large imposing Caernarfon Castle rising up in the background caused him a stab of grief. Ronan had liked nothing better than a trip to the castle followed by a special treat of fish and chips eaten sitting on the harbour wall while him and his brothers watched the boats tracing their way along the River Seiont and out towards the Menai Strait. But memories were painful. They reminded him of exactly what he'd lost and that there was no going back to those happier times.

With a little shake of his head, he pushed the hazy images away only to replace them with the sight of Ellie's downcast head and determined chin. One hand on her shoulder, he pulled her to a stop, his attention drawn to the small newspaper shop opposite. They had a long walk ahead of them simply because he wasn't prepared to risk a taxi even though there was money enough in his pockets for such an emergency. The sooner they were off the streets and away from the threat of the ever-curious passers-by, the better.

'I'm going to pop over there,' he said, pointing a finger at the shop. 'I want you to wait outside and not speak to anyone,' he added, lowering his voice to a whisper. 'Got it?'

She didn't bother to reply.

Within minutes he was back, his arms full of chocolate bars, sweets, bottles of water and a carefully rolled-up newspaper. Reading the paper had never been on the top of his list of life's essentials and he'd often groaned at his mother's obsession with the news. In fact, much to the displeasure of both his parents, Ronan wasn't a great one for reading novels. He quite liked searching up facts but usually on the internet instead of turning the pages of a book. But the newspaper was impossible to ignore, the headlines screaming out in their blackest print about the disappearance of local girl Elodie Fry. He'd barely glanced at it before adding it to his pile of goodies and paying at the till. The man behind the counter didn't bother to lift his head as he scanned the items into a tidy pile.

'Here, kid. Take a water and whichever sweets and chocolate you want. I'll pack what's left in my bag.' Ronan crouched down on his haunches and opened his rucksack, rearranging what few clothes he had to make room for the additional items.

'But the money?' she asked, the frown marks wrinkling her smooth brow, making him struggle not to laugh out loud.

'You sound like my ...' He stopped, his attention back on his bag as he stuffed his purchases in any old how, the paper folded into four and squashed down on top before he pulled the strap tight. As always, thoughts of his mother, even innocent fleeting ones like this, made his insides creak in agony.

'I wouldn't have bought them if we didn't have the money,' he said finally, his cheeks deathly pale against the stark relief of his navy cap. 'We have a bit of a walk ahead of us and, if you're anything like my younger brothers, sweets and chocolate are bound to help.' He paused, his skin taking on a deep red colour. 'Did you need the loo or …?'

'No, I went on the train.'

'So you did. Anything else you need before we head off?'

But instead of responding, she stuffed the packets of sweets in the top of her rucksack and stood waiting.

'You're not going to eat those? That's why I bought them.'

'Not hungry.'

'I thought kids were always hungry for sweets,' he said, examining her averted gaze and downturned mouth.

She'd only made monosyllabic replies to his careful questioning on the train, spending most of the time curled into a ball, her head resting against her bag, which she'd propped up against the window. He hadn't minded then. The less the other passengers noticed her the better. But now he was worried. He wouldn't get very far if she was sickening for something. The brave girl who had followed him off the Great Orme and let him cut her hair was missing, replaced by a vision of despair decked out in his brother's old clothes. He shook his head. There was nothing he could do about it, or about her until they got to the farmhouse – if they made it that far.

Instead of worrying, Ronan forced himself to calculate how long it would take them to travel what used to only be fifteen minutes by car. They'd have to take the coastal path simply because it was less likely that they'd be spotted. He grabbed her hand again and squeezed it gently, the only thing he could think of to reassure her.

'How do you fancy crossing a swing bridge?'

Her eyes widened. 'A swing bridge?'

'It swings back and forth to let boats through. It's that or adding an extra two miles on to the walk. Your call, kid,' he said, staring down at his younger brother's scruffy trainers, which must be a good two or three sizes too big. They were obviously going to be difficult to walk in, even after taking into account the extra pair of socks he'd made her wear. Hot and uncomfortable too. He spared a thought for Caleb and the note he'd left him, folded up into a small square and carefully positioned under his desktop mouse – a place his mother would never think to look. There was no point in arousing suspicion when a few words would ease any concerns his brother might have about his missing clothes. Although, if he knew Caleb as well as he thought he did, it would probably take him months to notice their loss.

Chapter 20

Gaby

Monday 3 August, 4.55 p.m. St Asaph Police Station

'If you're trying to make me believe that I'm bad at my job ...'

'Oh no, Detective. You've managed that without any help from me. The mammoth cock-up in Swansea should have told you that as a copper you suck. You couldn't find your way out of a paper bag let alone find the missing girl. Enough already! When I get the job, you'll find yourself at the end of a very long dole queue, which is only what you deserve,' Bill said, lumbering to his feet.

'Only time will tell, or do you include crystal ball gazing and palm reading on your short list of attributes?'

Gaby had never felt more like thumping someone than she did Bill Davis. She'd spent the last twenty minutes or so listening to him slating off the members of her team while her fingernails dug deep crescents into her palms. And yet as soon as the clock ticked its way to five, he lurched to his feet and headed for the door, all the while talking about the leisurely meal and early night he intended in preparation for his interview in the morning. He was just the man they didn't want in charge of the MIT but the only way she could block him was by finding the time to submit her own application.

She made a mental note to download the job application form before turning her attention back to her phone. The longer the silence around Ellie's disappearance hovered, the increased likelihood of an unsavoury result and there wasn't a thing that she could do to change that statistical inevitability. They'd pulled in extra police from across the Welsh network, teams of highly trained professionals who were currently walking side by side as they searched the numerous green fields and beaches that flourished in the area. She'd even managed to secure a sniffer dog and all they'd got for their efforts was a possible hit on the Great Orme, a trail than ran cold as soon as her handler had followed her to the traffic-filled street of North Parade.

PC Diane Carbone had been given a desk and access to the CCTV camera footage in and around Colwyn Bay and Llandudno, a herculean task that she embraced with a large steel coffee mug at her elbow. There was a lot of hope residing in these images but apart from a single shot of Ellie Fry's blurred outline as she'd walked along Greenfield Road at 3.01 a.m. there'd been no other sightings. The thought was that she'd headed for Colwyn Bay beach, a CCTV camera black spot. From there, if the dog handler was right, she must have followed the shoreline around to Llandudno, a huge ask for an adult let alone a ten-year-old. Doable if she was desperate enough and that's where Gaby's thoughts were leading her, a pencil in her hand as she worked out the average walking speed on the top of her A4 pad.

Gaby dropped her pencil on her desk and placed her hands on either side of her head, staring at the numbers in front of her. With sunrise not till 5.30 it would have still been dark, a daunting prospect at the best of times but a young child must have been scared witless. If Gaby had been in her position she'd have run most of the way, not that her fitness levels were up to it. But Ellie was reed-slim in her photos and used to running about at school not to mention undertaking all those ballet lessons. No, she'd have arrived at her destination before most of North Wales had even filled their kettle for their morning cuppa. And that's where Gaby's thoughts stopped because she couldn't for the life of her think of what her plan had been. To hole up in the Great Orme with a rucksack stuffed full with tins of baked beans. What then?

Pushing back from her desk, she crossed over to the window to stretch her legs. She'd been thinking about the problem on and off all day but was no further forward. But then again she wasn't a scared ten-year-old, which was probably the main difficulty.

Gaby had a tendency to place herself in the shoes of whichever person she was investigating. It was a trick she'd learnt during her job as a PC in Liverpool and something that had stood her in good stead over the years. But now the common-sense application of standard principles behind human behaviour didn't apply. She could rationalise that Ellie must have been scared but after that? Nothing.

Instead of returning to her desk, she looked up at the sound of knuckle against wood.

'Come in.'

'Hi, Gaby, sorry to interrupt you but it's those old women again about their missing friend, Barbara Matthews,' Clancy said, propping up the doorway. 'They're not prepared to let it rest and are even threatening to take it to the media.'

'Are they now?' Gaby's eyes glittered. 'Look, Sergeant, I have too much on my plate already. The only way I could possibly squeeze even a modicum of interest, this early in her disappearance, would be if it turns out she's had a hip replacement.'

'Ma'am?'

'Just ignore me, Clancy.' She lifted a hand to her neck briefly to try and stem the building tension. 'For one thing the timing is out. What was that about the media?'

'Apparently one of them knows the editor of the *Llandudno Chronicle*.'

'Really. How interesting.' Gaby might sound offhand but the very last thing she wanted was some nosy journo upsetting Sherlock not to mention Chief Superintendent Murdock Winters, who prided himself on his long association with the press. It would also be a black mark if she ever found the time to complete that blasted job application form. She heaved her shoulders in annoyance as she plucked her jacket from the back of the chair. With a bit of luck she'd alleviate their fears and avoid a media storm into the bargain.

'Show them into interview room two, would you please, Clancy, and teas all round. By the sound of things they're the sort that demand the little extras.'

In the time it took for her to pop into the incident room to check that, as she suspected, there was no news about Ellie, Clancy had worked his magic with a tray of tea presented in matching china mugs, which he must have had stashed away in one of the cupboards in the back room for just such an eventuality. But it only took Gaby one glance at the ramrod-straight spines and identikit purse-string lips of the trio in front of her to realise that it would take a lot more than a mug of Tetley's finest to get the three pensioners to agree to any solution apart from the one that demanded maximum effort on her part.

After the usual introductions, she settled down in her chair and set an A4 notepad in front of her, instinctively focusing her attention on the thinnest, for no other reason than the woman acted as if she was in charge.

'I believe you're concerned as to the whereabouts of your friend? Mrs ... er?' Her pen was poised over her pad.

'I'm Mildred Pennyworth,' she said, her voice as sour as the resident expression on her face. 'To put it bluntly, our dear friend, Barbara Matthews, is missing and we want to know what you intend to do about it.'

'I'm not sure quite what you want from us? We've already sent a car around to check on the property, in addition to an ambulance in the unlikely event that she's been taken unwell. There was no sign of any disturbance. They've checked all the rooms, including the grounds and didn't find anything suspicious. Surely it's not outside the realms of possibility that your friend forgot about the arrangements or indeed that something else cropped up? After all, no time has passed.' She sat back in her chair, more determined than ever to send this lot on their way in time to catch the six o'clock news, which was due to feature an appeal for Ellie Fry.

'Absolutely no chance of that,' Mildred Pennyworth said, hugging her bag tightly, the skin on the back of her hands mottled and thin, the only jewellery a fragile thread of gold on her wedding finger. 'Barbara would have been very keen to recoup last week's losses.'

'Losses?' Gaby laid her pen across her pad, her polite smile frozen in place. 'I thought you played bridge?'

'And what of it? A little bet on the side doesn't do anyone any harm. It's not as if we were playing for anything big. The odd fiver here and there. It's fun, especially as Barbara hates to lose.' She relaxed her lips to allow a glimmer of grey teeth. 'No. There'd be no way on earth she wouldn't be there to meet us in her second-best skirt – she saves her best for church on Sunday – and a plate of designer nibbles. She even phoned yesterday, bragging that she'd managed to get some of that Castell Gwyn cracked black pepper cream cheese that we're all so fond of. Her way of rubbing it in that she's far better than the rest of us at preparing a spread. Isn't that right, Doreen and Iris?'

The sight of both women nodding their heads in unison did little to calm Gaby's mind. All she wanted was to send them on their way but that was looking increasingly unlikely. The three of them, with their matching salon-set hairdos and determined expressions meant business and any palming off on her part would probably lead to her photo on the front of tomorrow morning's *Chronicle* – exactly the type of negative media attention that would skew her chances of getting the job.

Picking up her pen again, she turned over to a fresh page and jotted down the date and time in her illegible scrawl, resigned to her fate. If she got home at all tonight she'd be lucky. The thought that she'd need to text Rusty about being late perversely elevated her mood. For the first time in what felt like ages it was nice to have someone on her side, someone who would be waiting with the kettle on standby.

'Right then, ladies. Let's take it from the beginning. Tell me everything you know about Barbara Matthews and what makes you so determined that something awful has befallen her. But before you start ...' She looked up. 'Tell me if your friend ever had any kind of joint surgery. A hip replacement for instance?'

Chapter 21

Ronan

Monday 3 August, 6.15 p.m. Caernarfon

The walk from Caernarfon to Dinas Dinlle was very different to the short car journey he used to take with his grandparents. Then there'd been laughter and little games like I-spy to pass the time. But the stress of the train ride compounded by his silent companion made any form of communication an effort Ronan wasn't prepared to make. He knew it was the ideal opportunity to get her to open up about why she'd left home. Having a child in tow with no idea as to what desperation had driven her to such an extreme act was stupid. She could be anyone and not only that. After the experience they'd been through with his father, Ronan knew more than most the darkness that some people hid under the cover of normality. There was so much he wanted to ask her but, with the sun beaming down and the weight of their rucksacks increasing with each step, he felt instinctively that now wasn't the time. She probably wouldn't tell him the truth but that wasn't his main reason for staying silent. There was a gentle trust building, something he was loath to damage. She'd already run away once. She might not be so lucky the next time with who she bumped into.

He decided to stop off for a quick rest at Foryd Bay, one of the beaches nearest to the farmhouse and a great favourite with the family. The place was deserted apart from a bunch of teenagers throwing stones into the sea. The crystal-clear water was inviting but he turned away, having to drag a reluctant Ellie with him. She was tired, visibly dropping in front of his eyes. With the unexpected activity of the last few hours, he'd have liked nothing better than to curl up on the warm sand for a snooze. But safety was paramount. He had a feeling that he wouldn't feel secure until he had a roof over their heads and a front door to bolt behind them. While north-west Wales was a world away from his isolated hideaway up the Great Orme, it would only take one stranger to change all that.

Keeping the Menai Strait, and the Isle of Anglesey on the right and Caernarfon Airport up ahead, this was the most anxious time for Ronan. The screaming roar of aeroplanes taking off and landing was a constant threat and once he even had to pull Ellie to one side, trying to hide her among the tangled mess of greenery that lined the route. He heaved a sigh of relief when he spotted the tiny hamlet of Saron, the landmark he'd been hoping for. From there it was another half-hour walk following the coastal path until they came to a bridge he recognised.

With Dinas Dinlle beach in the distance, he could finally start to relax and funnily enough so did Ellie. Now instead of silence there was nervous chatter as if she had too much to say and not enough time in which to say it. He learnt lots but nothing of any importance, mainly about her hope to train in London as a ballerina when she left school and her love of reading. He even learnt about her best friend, Heather, and the difficulties they were having at school, their friendship forged by the unkindness of their classmates. He could tell her a lot about bullying but instead he let her continue in case she let something slip that would reveal her reason for running away. But her chatter stopped as quickly as it had started, the sugar rush, from the chocolate he'd plied her with during their short break only a distant memory as she faded into complete silence.

'It won't be long, kid. Another five or ten minutes and then it's straight to bed.'

There was no reply.

The dirt track up to his grandparents' property was starting to show signs of neglect with weeds poking their way through the narrow sloping driveway. The long low farmhouse was just how he remembered, the stone-fronted building as familiar to him as his own home. With the memory of how it had once been pushing through the layers of his mind, the sight of the empty planters that straddled the doorway was a physical stabbing pain as reality hit. To lose both grandparents and his father in the course of a year right on the back of his expulsion from school and his mother's cancer diagnosis was almost too much for him to bear.

His hands laced through the straps of his rucksack and gripped together over his chest, his bitten nails finding purchase on the tender flesh of his palm. The past was best left alone, something he'd been telling himself ever since he'd left his mother's house – he couldn't call it home, not now.

He reached the front door and, fumbling in his pockets, his fingers curled around the hard, cold outline of the keys he'd taken. Ellie waited patiently at his side. The worst of it was that it was all his fault. If he hadn't taken that final stand against those two boys in St Gildas, the cataclysmic chain of events that had led to the destruction of everything he cherished would never have started. There wasn't even anything he could do to make it right. Redemption for him was a never-ending roundabout of what-ifs and maybes, the past something he'd like to change in the hollows of his mind. That was his tragedy and the cause of his recent mental and emotional decay. He needed saving but what was the likelihood with no one around, apart from a ten-year-old girl?

With the Yale key in the lock, he lifted his arm, holding it out to prevent Ellie from entering as he finally examined the wisdom in bringing her here. He'd heard the rumours of what had happened at the isolated farmhouse. He'd have had to be living in Timbuktu not to be privy to the story that had filled the front pages of every paper. Now that they'd arrived, he could almost see a high-resolution image of what might be lying in wait in the room at the end of the hall.

'You stay here. I need to check that it's safe.' He swung his rucksack off his shoulders and propped it up against the flocked wallpaper.

The farmhouse was long and low with only attic space above, he recalled, his attention drawn as if by some invisible force to the hatch that punctuated one end of the ceiling. He used to love rummaging among the old tea chests that held everything an imaginative boy could want. The long hours he'd spent with his brothers playing make-believe with the long-discarded and forgotten clothes held an importance far in excess of the reality of mouldy rags and web-strewn rafters.

Ignoring the living space on the right, he walked in the opposite direction to the extension where a master bedroom and en suite had been added sometime in the Seventies, his pace slowing to a stop when he reached the door.

Chapter 22

Gaby

Monday 3 August, 6.30 p.m. Wisteria Cottage

Wisteria Cottage was the last property situated in the highly sought-after area of Deganwy Quay. Edging the waterfront, the bungalow enjoyed the most magnificent views across the Conwy estuary and the castle beyond.

Turning her attention away from the sight of King Edward II's imposing edifice, Gaby pulled into the driveway behind what was presumably Barbara Matthews' dark green Toyota hatchback, more than half annoyed that she'd reluctantly agreed to visit the property. She had far too much on her plate to be bothered with an old biddy who'd decided to go AWOL rather than face up to the fact that her friends were better than her at bridge.

Instead of jumping out of the car, she paused a moment to examine the sharp lines of the stark cream house, which didn't immediately present with any of the usual features she'd come to associate with the term cottage. The front garden was a neat square of green, cut into regimented strips, where no weed would dare to pop up its head. There were no flowers or shrubs, apart from a pair of neatly clipped box hedges heralding the entrance and certainly no sign of wisteria crawling up the brickwork.

It only took a second to select the Yale from the small bunch of keys clutched in her palm that Clancy had passed on earlier. Modern policing meant that the days of entering a property by force were long gone unless it was either a dire emergency or unavoidable. All it had taken was a knock on the next-door neighbour's house, by the paramedics earlier, to ascertain that they had an arrangement to keep an eye on each other's properties – within moments the keys had exchanged hands.

The hall was tiny with barely space for the narrow table, a pair of navy lace-ups carefully positioned beneath. The lace-ups interested Gaby simply because removing her shoes when she came in from the outside was one of the first things she did after dropping her keys into the shallow bowl she'd bought for that express purpose. It was something that her mother had drummed into her along with hanging up her jacket in her bedroom and ensuring that her bags were packed and ready in preparation for the next day. Little routines that she still performed except, instead of a school bag, she now carried around a smart leather briefcase. If Gaby's work shoes weren't neatly placed in the hall there was a very good chance that she was at the office, a fact that was starting to make her feel uneasy about the current location of Barbara Matthews.

She had an idea that she wouldn't find Mrs Matthews at home; after all, the police had already conducted a thorough search. But Gaby was nothing if not exacting in all aspects of her life. She'd be the last person to admit that she was a control freak but checking up was something she did. It wasn't about a lack of trust, far from it. It wasn't even that she thought herself better than anyone else – the reality was she had self-esteem issues, so nothing could be further from the truth. No. Gaby was again attempting to walk in someone else's footsteps even if, in this instance, there was no evidence that a crime had been committed.

The downstairs of the airy dormer bungalow was painted in rich creams to maximise the light streaming through the floor-to-ceiling windows, which framed the most spectacular views out across the marina. In her mind's eye, she closed the hall door behind her and, after slipping off her shoes, padded into the kitchen towards the kettle. With the switch depressed, the next job would've been to gather together a mug before unloading the food into their relevant cupboards …

Giving a little start, Gaby shook her head, returning to the reality of the empty house. She took in the neat pile of side plates and linen napkins placed at one end of the table alongside four cherry-red wine goblets. Her brow pulled into a frown at the sight of the preparations for the bridge party. Careful not to touch anything, she removed a fresh pair of disposable gloves from her pocket and crossed over to the large American-style fridge, her frown deepening when she caught sight of the box of cheeses just like Mildred Pennyworth had suggested. It looked as if the only thing stopping the bridge party from going ahead was the absence of the hostess. And yet, with no evidence to the contrary, she couldn't be sure that Mrs Matthews hadn't been delayed by something unexpected.

For some reason her concern, which had been negligible, had upgraded to alarm in part due to her inability to trace the blasted woman. The hospitals had all come up blank as had the next-door neighbour, who'd seen her return to the property earlier with her hands straining under the weight of her shopping bags. They'd even passed the time of day on their respective doorsteps like they'd done hundreds of times previously. There was nothing unusual or suspect except her failure to be where she was expected. Reports of missing people in and around North Wales were rare. To have two in one day was unheard of.

Walking through the rooms, Gaby pulled open every cupboard and searched under every bed. She only turned her attention to the outside after she'd exhausted every hiding place. The exterior of the bungalow was surrounded on three sides by nicely manicured lawns and a small patio at the back with steps down to the marina. Apart from a shed, which contained the usual gardening tools, there was nowhere for Barbara Matthews to hide and no reason Gaby could think of for her to do so. Wandering back into the kitchen, she walked over to the sink and the full mug of tea resting on the draining board, which added veracity to her earlier thought that the next thing Barbara Matthews would have done after removing her shoes was to make herself a cuppa. But why leave it barely touched? The rest of the room showed the distinct mark of someone that was house proud. It didn't fit that Barbara Matthews would leave a dirty mug on the draining board unless she had to.

Making one of the snap decisions that she was famed for, Gaby pulled out her phone and speed-dialled the station. She had very little to go on, certainly nothing of any substance, but that had never stopped her from calling for help. A pair of shoes. A mug of cold tea. A few dishes piled up neatly at the end of the table and a fridge full of award-winning cheeses. Call it instinct or sheer bloody-mindedness but she knew that something had happened to Barbara Matthews. The only problem was she had no idea what.

The CSIs took half an hour to arrive but within minutes of the plain white van pulling up outside the property, the bungalow was surrounded by an army of paper-suited personnel, with only part of their faces visible under their drawstring hoods.

'Do you ever go home, Jason?' Gaby said, recognising the sparsely framed, senior CSI by his distinctive green eyes and friendly smile.

'Hah, chance would be a fine thing. I've nearly forgotten my address since you joined the team, Gaby,' he replied, his broad grin taking the sting out of his words. 'So, what is it to be this time? Another serial killer or just an isolated dead body?' he said, making reference to the recent cases that had pushed them to the limit.

'I hope neither,' she said with a smile, propping her elbow on the door of the van while she waited for him to hand out the clear plastic boxes that contained their equipment. 'What I really want is for it to be a huge false alarm and for Sherlock to drag me into the office tomorrow and give me a rollicking for wasting police resources on an unwarranted call-out.'

'There's been one or two of these missing old people over the last year or so though. Is that what you're thinking?' he said, falling in beside her as she walked back inside the property.

'To be honest I'm not really thinking anything apart from finding her as quickly as possible so that I don't have to deflect any resources away from Ellie's disappearance.'

'There's no news on that front?'

'Not even a dickie bird. Poor old PC Carbone has been searching through CCTV for most of the day and all she's come up with is an image from near the girl's home. It's as if Ellie has disappeared into thin air.'

'Or something's happened to her?'

She stared across at him. 'Yes, well, obviously we can't rule that out but I'm hoping not. We're exploring all scenarios and sadly that has to be one of them.'

Standing in the small hall, shoulder to shoulder, Gaby watched him scan the area, his team milling about waiting for instructions. There was something in the way he stooped down to stare at the floor and where it met the plain white skirting board that reaffirmed her suspicions.

She'd long suspected that Jason Moore was as intuitive as he was clever. She'd never come across a CSI quite like him despite her varied employment history of appointments in Liverpool, Cardiff, Swansea and now St Asaph. He seemed to spend more time looking than he actually did doing but still managed to find an array of extraordinary evidence that even somebody with Gaby's extensive experience would have missed.

'So, what have you found, if anything?'

'I haven't found anything as such.' He returned to his feet, his gloved hand slipping a clipboard out from under his arm. 'Nothing that will be of any use to you, yet. But what I will say is, it's a good job that it's the end of the day and not the beginning.'

'I'm not with you?'

'Perfume, Gaby. I never wear aftershave at work and any scent that you might have been wearing will have long worn off by now.' He strolled into the lounge, Gaby trailing behind him. 'As you know, one of the prerequisites of this job is having a discerning nose. All I'm prepared to say is that what I smelt when I walked into the hall wasn't what I'd been expecting,' he said, starting to write on his clipboard. 'For an upmarket property such as this there should be an undertone of polish and perhaps a hint of the owner's unique body odour, be that perfume or whichever hygiene products they use like soaps, shampoos, deodorants or even washing powder. But death leaves a scent too, as anyone who's ever had the grim pleasure of attending an autopsy will attest. I'd almost be prepared to swear under oath that blood has been spilt – I'd hazard large volumes of the stuff for it to leave residual particles in the air after, what is it, six hours or so since she was last seen?'

Gaby's lids shuttered closed. She'd never been comfortable when conversations veered towards the gritty reality of blood, and thoughts of the amount Jason was talking about caused her to weaken at the knees. She wasn't a wuss, far from it. But she'd had an early start to the day and not much to eat. She filled her lungs with air and finally met his gaze, her mind returning to the case that Jax had been talking about earlier: the disappearance of Miss Jane. Two missing pensioners and not one clue between them. The only difference being that with Mildred Pennyworth raising the alarm so quickly, the scent of blood hadn't had a chance to dissipate. Any more cases and she'd have to call in additional staff. She might still have to.

Thoughts of the missing girl took precedence but she couldn't ignore the facts. She dug in her pocket, pulled out her mobile and tapped in DCI Sherlock's number. After this call, she'd phone Rusty, deliberately pushing aside all the reasons why she shouldn't be thinking of embarking on a relationship with him. She'd use this as a trial run and see how he measured up in a crisis. Her lips twisted. Welcome to her life.

'Good evening, sir. We have a problem.'

Chapter 23

Marie

Monday 3 August, 7.45 p.m. St Asaph

Marie squinted down at the little clock displayed on her screen. It was well past the time when she should be thinking of going home but with Malachy having volunteered to join the search party along with Jax, she'd offered to stay in the office until eight when the late shift took over the reins. It wasn't fair that Owen should have to stay when there was nothing for her to go home to apart from an empty room. Oh sure, she had the whole of Malachy's apartment to roam, all apart from his bedroom which was out of bounds, but there was still the embarrassment to work through. It had been a very long time since she'd lived with anyone apart from Ivo, her soon-to-be ex-husband, and she was determined not to outstay her welcome.

With the makings of a casserole slow-cooking in the crockpot since first thing this morning, she didn't even have to worry about having to prepare a meal. What spare time she had was her own and she had no better thought of how to spend it than to continue with her search into anyone and everyone who'd ever come into contact with Ellie Fry and her mother.

The array of dirty mugs told their own story as she stood and stretched, her shoulders bunching under the thin fabric of her cream blouse, which was sticking to her skin. Caffeine was the very last thing she wanted but the thing she needed to keep her from flagging. With a flick of her hand, she scrunched the tell-tale KitKat wrapper into a ball, flinging it into the bin under her desk before collecting up all the mugs and heading to the sink, frowning across at Diane Carbone on the way. Not that the middle-aged blonde would notice. Her head was nearly completely masked by two large computer screens, which held all the CCTV footage available within a six-mile radius of Ellie's home.

The policewoman was an unknown entity, someone she'd come across from time to time when she'd had to visit the Llandudno Station but she'd only ever spoken a few words to her that weren't work-related. Now was the time to change all that especially as she'd overheard Gaby speaking to Owen about encouraging her to undertake her sergeant exams.

'Fancy another one?' she said, angling her head in the direction of Diane's mug. 'You must be square-eyed after a day in front of the screens.'

'You're a lifesaver. Milk, no sugar.' Diane lifted up her hand to her smooth chin-length bob, tucking the ends behind her ears. 'Any luck with the school search?'

Marie shook her head. 'Nope but that's what I'd been hoping.' She picked up the glass coffee pot, pleased to see that it was half full. 'A sexual predator is exactly what we don't need right now. Are you going to go on for much longer or—?' Marie handed her back her mug and, propping her hip against Diane's desk, eyed her over the rim.

'For a bit. Since my dear husband ran off with the barmaid from our local, there's nobody to go home to apart from the cat and Delilah is well able to fend for herself for a few hours,' she said, flashing her a brief smile.

'I'm sorry, I didn't know.'

'No reason why you should. It happened while I was still working in Llandudno and was the reason for my transfer. With the kids having deserted the nest and the house sold, the only remaining link is my surname and I'm in the process of changing that. Diane Smith here I come, and not a minute too soon.'

'I never knew that it was so easy?'

'Best eighteen quid I've ever spent. I should have kicked the jerk out years ago.'

Marie couldn't help but admire the strength and confidence exuding from the attractive blonde, so very different to how she'd been feeing since the break-up of her own marriage and she vowed there and then to change both her attitude and her name as soon as possible.

'How are you getting on with the CCTV?' she finally asked, taking a long sip of her drink, trying and failing to ignore the aftertaste that only stewed coffee could give.

'I'm backtracking a bit over some footage taken yesterday to see if I can come up with a better image of the person she's with. They're too grainy to identify them by anything apart from their clothes and rucksacks. If I can just get a decent shot of his face we can show it around – maybe even include it in the media releases. Here, what do you think?' She stretched out a hand, pushing a small pile of printouts across the desk. 'The one on top is the best image by far. It was taken from a camera off the top of Upper Mostyn Street.'

Marie placed her mug down and picked up the photos, shuffling through slowly. CCTV footage was a waste of time mostly, the images too distorted and grainy to be of any use except in giving the briefest idea as to what someone looked like. But they still had to go through them on the off-chance that they recognised someone.

There were four photos that featured the man, more of a lad really, dressed in a padded anorak on what was one of the hottest days of the year. That jacket told her a lot about the kind of person he was as did the large rucksack strapped to his back. But for Marie the most telling part of the sharing exercise wasn't either the clothes or the bag but the lad's face – a face she thought she recognised.

'Be back in a sec.' She hopped off the desk and within seconds was logging in to her laptop but this time instead of accessing the police databanks she pulled up Google, searching for footage from one of the most horrific cases Wales had ever known. It didn't take her long to scroll through the images to find the one she wanted, the last photo of the Stevens family, reproduced over and over again for the eager ghoul-loving gratification of the British public. There wasn't anything exciting about the picture. Millions of similar snaps existed in dusty albums the length and breadth of the country. The bright cheesy smiles. The parents standing at the back, their arms around the two younger boys. The surly-looking teenager standing slightly apart as if he was struggling to feel part of the group. She printed off two copies of the image and, while she waited, scanned the article for a name, slapping her hand against her thigh when she found it.

Ronan Stevens. She knew it was something unusual. But what a lad of eighteen or thereabouts would be doing with Elodie Fry was another thing as she struggled to remember what Darin had said about him at the time. She blinked, her frown lines creasing. Troubled. That was it. A troubled young man tormented by the actions of others.

Chapter 24

Ronan

Monday 3 August, 7.45 p.m. Caernarfon

The bedroom was very different to the last time Ronan had seen it. The antique walnut dressing table and matching wardrobe were nowhere in sight and instead of the large double bed all that remained was a dusty space. There was nothing in this room now. No shadows of the family photos and the cut-crystal perfume bottles that his grandmother used to collect. All that was left of the paintings that had spanned the walls were faded shapes on the wallpaper, a fierce reminder of the changes wrought since their death. He didn't allow himself the luxury of doing more than glancing at the bare floorboards, which had once been topped with a thick pile carpet in a nondescript brown to match the bedspread. His thoughts shut down the image that was threatening to take over his mind.

Touching the brass handle, he pulled the door closed with a gentle but resolute click and hid his trembling fingers deep inside the pockets of his jeans. While he'd had to see the room if only to prove to himself that everything he'd been told was true, there was no way he ever intended to cross the threshold again.

Back in the hall, he was pleased to note that Ellie hadn't moved. He'd only been gone less than a minute but in that time her chin had sunk onto her chest. It looked as if she'd dropped off to sleep. Her eyes were certainly closed and her chest was rising up and down with a regularity that suggested her relaxed state. It seemed a shame to have to move her so he didn't. Instead he stepped around and walked to the other end of the hall and the rooms on the right.

This was the original part of the farmhouse with a large rustic kitchen and earthenware flagstones. Here the oval table took pride of place and he could still see the marks on the surface from where his grandmother had used to prepare their meals. But he didn't linger, instead he metaphorically crossed his fingers inside his pockets and made his way to the room next door.

He hadn't realised he'd been holding his breath until he felt the air rush through his teeth in relief at the sight of the bunk beds pushed up against the wall opposite and the solitary single divan under the window. This had been their domain. The place where he and his brothers had slept all those summers when their parents had shipped them off to stay with their grandparents while they continued working at their respective jobs. It was here that the three of them had collapsed each evening in an untidy heap, dead to the world as soon as their heads had touched the pillow after a day spent either on the beach or roaming the countryside. The farm had been cleared by his father of anything of any importance soon after his grandfather's funeral. It was providential that the bunk beds and old divan held little value to anyone except for a couple of weary travellers in desperate need of a good night's sleep.

Ronan was a realist. He knew that they'd been incredibly lucky with both the train journey and the walk from the station. But he was well aware of the unlikeliness of their luck holding for much longer. All it needed was one nosy neighbour to realise that the farmhouse wasn't deserted and their hiding place would be discovered. For it to work he had to find some way of keeping them both hidden from view and, after years of experience babysitting his brothers, he knew that asking Ellie to hide away was going to be easier said than done.

Removing his hands from his pockets, he dragged the curtains across the window before making his way back to Ellie, who was still sleeping, now with her thumb stuffed in her mouth. He smiled. After the day she'd had he couldn't blame her. Lifting her into his arms, he carried her into the bedroom and placed her on the bottom bunk. He knew he should probably wake her and encourage her to eat something but a few hours without food wouldn't do her any harm, not after all the sweets she'd consumed on the walk. Instead he slipped off her trainers, covered her with a thin blanket taken from the top bunk and headed out of the room.

Back in the hall, her bag was a temptation he couldn't resist. He knew it might be a rotten, underhand thing to do when she was in no fit state to prevent him but he was determined to find out her secret and perhaps this would be the easiest way. He stamped out any thoughts of how it would make him feel if he caught her rummaging through his paltry possessions. Anyway, she wouldn't find much. A photo of the five of them taken only days before their lives had been pulled asunder. His grandfather's watch, which was the last gift from his father, and his Swiss Army knife. That was it. The sum total of his history contained in those three items. Three items he wouldn't part with for the world.

Ronan had seen some of the contents of her rucksack already when he'd made her repack her gear into his brother's less obvious Nike bag. The small cuddly toy that made his heart twist. The pile of neatly folded clothes that had been ironed by a loving hand. A pink toothbrush and small tube of paste. The items of food. The steak knife hidden in one of the side pockets. His brows creased as he stared down at the vicious blade, not quite believing that someone her age would have the wherewithal to take a knife and even think of using it. Instead of doing what he wanted, which was to dispose of it, he returned it to its hiding place and continued searching. There was a book curled up right at the bottom and, pulling it out, he smiled at the cover before returning it and piling the clothes back on top. There was nothing of the essence of the child. No photographs and little money, his gaze resting on the small, dented tin with a pile of two-pence pieces and a few pound coins. No reason that he could think of for her to desert everything she'd ever known for a life of uncertainty on the road. That was the main thing that was worrying him. He'd do what he could for her but the truth was it probably wasn't going to be enough.

He'd decided he wasn't going to lie to her so instead of repacking the food stuff, he collected it in a neat pile and carried it into the kitchen. They were long on baked beans but that wasn't a bad thing as they could be eaten cold from the tin, something he'd gotten used to when hiding in the cave on the Great Orme. If it wasn't for the cooked lunch that he'd had dished out to him at the church each day, he'd have forgotten what a decent meal tasted like. His staple diet consisted of sliced white bread, the cheaper the better, and tins of whatever he could eat straight from the can with a spoon. If there ever came a time when he felt able to return to society, he'd already promised himself that he'd never eat another baked bean again. Ever.

The pile of food on the work surface didn't look much even when he'd added his own supply but he still had a few pounds tucked away and there was always the hope that it wouldn't take long for Ellie to confide in him.

Ronan was far more sensible now he had a couple of months' experience of being homeless under his belt. He'd chosen his current path out of sheer desperation simply because he couldn't cope with the rows. Arguments that had once passed over his head started to trouble his sleep and affect his appetite. His brothers were too young to understand and his mother too wrapped up in her own problems to spare more than a passing thought as to what was going on in her eldest son's life. She'd wanted him to get a job until he'd decided what he was going to do. For some reason, she couldn't understand that the sheer energy it took to lift his head off the pillow in the morning often felt like too much of a struggle. In the weeks leading up to leaving home, he'd taken to his bed and had stayed there apart from coming out for meals. He knew he was depressed but why wouldn't he be? There was no future for him that he could imagine. No happy ever after. No one to save him and he certainly wasn't in a position to save himself.

Now he had a child to care for and a secret to puzzle out. After that? He had no idea.

Chapter 25

Gaby

Monday 3 August, 7.55 p.m. Rhos-on-Sea

Gaby pulled into her drive, taking a moment to switch her mind from detective on duty to … She shook her head, unable to think up an alternative. It had been so long since she'd had anyone waiting for her, anyone to come home to, that she struggled to think of anything outside of work. What she really wanted was a hot shower closely followed by her oldest and comfiest pyjamas. Food wasn't as important as it used to be and oftentimes she found herself snacking on crackers and cheese with a glass of wine on the side instead of bothering to cook. Relaxation was a chapter or two of her latest read instead of reaching for the TV remote. She was never at home long enough to catch up on soaps and if she watched television for more than an hour a week it was a record. Apart from the occasional movie, she watched the news when she could and sometimes not even that if Amy and Tim popped around from their house, only situated a five-minute walk away.

With thoughts of Amy, her mind galloped off the leash and back to work with all the finesse of a thoroughbred racehorse in sight of the finishing line. Amy had sent her a quick text, after they'd interviewed Heather Powell, but it hadn't really added anything to the investigation. They'd already worked out that Ellie must have been worried about something to run away like that. The problem was they had no way of finding out what. If her mother and her best friend didn't know … Gaby paused, her mind taking her into new territory. Unless one, or both of them, were lying? She made a mental note to pick up on the idea of a liar in their midst later.

Gaby had also caught up with Malachy and Jax when she'd been waiting for the CSIs to arrive at Barbara Matthews' house. Both of them had offered to work through the night and she'd had a difficult job persuading them otherwise. But she needed them at the station tomorrow and, as hard as it was for them to accept, there was already a full complement of officers and civilian volunteers scouring the area as part of the search and rescue team. A couple of extras wouldn't make much difference.

She gathered up her bags and slipped out of the car, checking that she'd locked it. While Rhos-on-Sea was a haven with little or no crime to speak of, she always made sure she took the same precautions as she did when she'd lived in a city. The unexpected lay around every corner, something she'd learnt the hard way.

Standing on her doorstep, one hand on the door handle, the other clutching her keys, she barely registered that her grip was fist tight, the metal from both pressing deep into her palms. What was the etiquette for arriving at home with your would-be/maybe boyfriend waiting inside, especially when you were two hours late for the date? Just like Gaby didn't know how to be anything other than a copper, she now questioned her ability to live through the next five minutes without making a complete prat of herself. Clueless and nervous married with near mental and physical exhaustion were unhappy bedfellows in any relationship. Her hand shook as she tried to insert the key into the lock only to have the door wrenched out from her grasp.

There was no hello. No gushing welcome. There was more – so much more: kindness and consideration blended with a little extra sprinkling of something in his twinkling gaze that caused her cheeks to flood with colour.

'You look shattered.' He took her bags off her and, stepping back, waited for her to precede him while he shut the door. 'Why don't you go upstairs and sort yourself out. I'll pour you a glass of wine, or a cup of tea if you'd rather? Conor can take it up to you.'

If she'd been someone who cried easily he'd have had tears with his welcome. She felt an ache at the back of her throat as she slipped off her shoes and padded across to the lounge. The smell of something delicious was coming from the kitchen, drawing her in like a homing signal and reminding her that she still hadn't eaten. Conor was sitting at the table, a bag propped beside his chair, an open laptop in front of him, a scowl she recognised marring his features. She'd seen the same expression all too often on his father's face.

'Tea would be lovely but there's no point in disturbing him.' She turned and almost slammed into Rusty, who must have been standing right behind her.

'I think he'd like the disturbance,' he said, putting his hands on her shoulders to prevent her crashing into him. The intensity of his stare made her blush deepen. 'Apparently he's losing. I haven't quite figured out at what yet.'

'Even so.' She stepped out of his arms, aware that his son had lifted his head to watch the interplay between them, his scowl still in evidence. Developing a new relationship that included an eleven-year-old wasn't what she would have chosen but, on the flip side, there was no way she was prepared to leave him out. Rusty had never made any pretence of the amount of baggage he was juggling but dropping off Conor like an item of lost property wasn't her style. They weren't a family, nowhere near but, by Conor's demeanour, he'd realised that the possibility might be on the horizon sometime in the future.

'Poor lad,' she finally said, referring to far more than the problems he was having with his game. 'He's probably starving,' she added, one hand circling the banister. 'Thank you for all of this by the way. It's not what I'd been planning but ...'

'But work took precedence. I know what it's like. If it's any consolation, I'm only pleased that you didn't have anything for me.'

'No. Well. Never say never.' Her smile was only a memory. 'There's no news about the—'

'And no news is good news, or did your parents not tell you that?'

'They're Italian so no. We were brought up on a completely different collection of sayings.'

'You can tell me all about it later. Tea in fifteen minutes or I won't be responsible for how it tastes.'

'If the aroma coming from the kitchen is any indication, I'm not going to need even half that time.'

Gaby had always been a take it or leave it type and, despite a wardrobe full to overflowing with all sorts, she opted for comfy leggings after her quick shower, albeit in a flattering black, and a well-washed T-shirt in electric-blue – a shade someone had once told her suited her Italian colouring. She hadn't bothered to wash her hair. Instead she'd pulled it out of its braid, massaged her scalp briefly and piled it on top of her head, simply because it was too hot to leave it flowing down her back. If he didn't like her the way she was that was too bad. There were good days, bad days and then there were impossible ones like today. A missing girl. That spooky find at the crematorium. The missing OAP. Conor's expression ...

'Ah good.' Rusty came out of the kitchen, a tea towel flung over one shoulder and a glass of wine in each hand. 'Here.' He passed her a glass and proceeded to toast her. 'Cheers, Gabriella. Here's to not poisoning you as the pathologist is officially off-duty until tomorrow, 9 a.m.'

'Ha, how did you manage that?' She placed her empty mug on the counter and took a long sip from her drink, relishing the flavours as they took hold of her mouth and made the day start to fade under the weight of their magic. She was no wine expert and she certainly wasn't a wine snob. She knew what she liked but tailored that with what she could afford. Her dad had introduced her to the joys of Barolo in her late teens but mostly she bought whatever was on offer in Lidl or Asda.

'Pulled in a favour.' He waved a hand towards the table in the kitchen and where he'd drawn it out from the wall and rounded up three mismatched chairs. 'Take a seat. It's only spaghetti bolognese – one of the few things I can cook apart from pizza, sausages, and mac and cheese.'

'As long as I didn't have to cook it! I'm sure it will be lovely; it certainly smells it.'

'That will be the garlic bread. I hope you like chilli? Come on, Conor. Grub's up!'

Dinner was awkward, punctuated as it was by Conor's scowl and a discussion that skirted around the usual topic about how their respective days had gone. But the food made up for the conversation shortfall, even as Gaby tried to remember if she had any mints left in her glove compartment for the garlic overload.

Entering the lounge afterwards, she made sure to ignore her usual spot on the sofa, leaving Conor to plonk himself down beside his dad. The smile of satisfaction carved on his face caused her to catch Rusty's eye as they both struggled to hide their amusement, although it was far from funny. Gaby's experience of men was limited and she'd never, knowingly, gone out with somebody who'd had a child. Now she knew why. She liked Rusty for a whole gamut of reasons not least because of his frank appraising stare that told her in all the ways possible that he found her attractive despite any effort on her part. The one thing she didn't need was a man who required her to be something that she wasn't. She was far from glamorous and, the truth was, she was a home bird at heart who liked nothing better than curling up on the sofa with a good book. Instead of living the high life, a walk along the Welsh shoreline was as exciting as it got.

But she could well remember the insecurities she'd felt during her own childhood and she didn't need a degree in psychology to realise how anxious his son must be feeling at the sight of the budding relationship between them. If Amy was to be believed, it wasn't that long ago since his mother had absconded with her latest in a long line of boyfriends. But assuming the thoughts that must be rampaging through his skinny body was one thing, knowing how to tackle them as his father's prospective girlfriend was something completely different. She was tempted to leave the boy to himself for now but that wouldn't make the situation any less awkward. The child was bound to resent her inclusion in his father's life and that needed careful handling.

'Conor, I'd like to ask you something, that is, if your father will let me?' she said, after the silence had become uncomfortable instead of relaxing.

'Be my guest. But I'm not guaranteeing that you'll get any kind of a sensible answer, isn't that right, bud?' He ruffled his son's hair, sending her a quick glance over the top of his head, one she returned with a slight wink.

'You know I'm a cop, right?' She controlled her expression at the sight of Conor's sudden interest. 'Well, we have a bit of a puzzle going on back at the station and, as it's to do with someone that's near enough your age, I was wondering if you'd be able to help me solve it?'

'What sort of puzzle?' he said, his eyes bright under his mop of red fringe.

'The puzzling sort. So, my question is, can you think of a reason why someone your age would run away from home without telling their sole parent where they were going?'

There was complete silence for a moment but she could tell by the frown marking his smooth forehead that Conor was taking her question seriously.

'I'm guessing that they've probably run away to find the parent that's missing,' he said finally, returning his attention to his phone.

'Good answer but what if the kid in question doesn't know where to find them or even who they are? Is there any other reason that you can think of? And before you ask, she also doesn't have any grandparents or godparents to run away to.'

She watched his head shoot up, his blue eyes rounded, his freckles in sharp relief against the pallor of his skin. He looked as if he couldn't believe that someone his age would take such a radical step as to run away with no place to go.

'You're talking about this Ellie girl, aren't you? It was on the news in the car on the way over. Dad always makes me listen.'

Gaby nodded, unprepared to expand further. The truth was, she shouldn't have asked. He was a clever lad, a chip off the old block in addition to being in the same age bracket as the girl. She had no idea what she'd been hoping from him but his comment about Ellie's dad had made perfect sense except for the fact that they had no idea who he was.

'There's only one answer then, isn't there?'

It was Gaby's turn to widen her eyes.

'Something or someone must have scared her enough to make her feel unsafe.' He turned to Rusty. 'Dad, can we go now?'

Chapter 26

Gaby

Monday 3 August, 9.05 p.m. Rhos-on-Sea

Gaby hadn't known what to expect when she'd invited Rusty and Conor over for a meal but them departing within minutes of finishing their dinner hadn't been it. She half-heartedly collected up the dishes and carried them into the kitchen, her mind mulling over what she could do to help Conor understand that she was far from a threat to his relationship with his father. Her mobile ringing was a welcome relief from the mishmash of ideas that had her considering whether Dr Mulholland was far more trouble than he was worth.

'Darin speaking.'

'Ma'am, sorry for disturbing your evening but I have something that I need to discuss with you.'

'Marie! What the hell are you doing working this late?' she said, well aware of the snappy timbre of her voice and making a silent promise to moderate her tone for the remainder of the conversation. In her experience, nothing good ever came from a late-night phone call and she wondered what the problem could be.

'It wasn't planned but Diane was keen to finish the CCTV footage so I decided to keep her company. The thing is, I've come across something that may or may not be relevant to Fry's disappearance. Remember the Stevens case?'

The Stevens case. Gaby nearly dropped the phone. How could she ever forget! One of the worst times of her life and the reason why she wasn't up to full fitness after having her spleen sliced in two.

'Ma'am, are you there?'

'Yes, Marie. I haven't gone anywhere.' She slid back down on the sofa, resting her elbow on the arm, her legs tucked underneath her. 'Go on. You were telling me about the links to the Stevens case.'

'Yes, well, it seems as if the man Ellie met might be Ronan Stevens, the son. Diane had a brain wave and decided to check through the footage from the previous day to see if she could find a clearer image and, lo and behold, she found a couple that show his facial features clearly. I've compared them with the ones taken at the time but I can't be sure. I know you've met him so I've just pinged them over.'

'Okay, I'm going to put you on loudspeaker while I boot up my laptop.' She picked up her briefcase from where Rusty had set it on one end of the coffee table and started fiddling with the leather straps. 'I take it that Diane isn't with you?' she said, her voice loud in the empty room.

'No. I told her to go home. I hope you don't mind me saying but, with her skills and attitude, she'd make a fine addition to the team.'

'Yes. I agree. We'll have to work on her when we have these cases out of the way.' She placed the laptop in front of her, propped up the lid and logged on.

Her inbox had a pile of unread messages. It was a mystery how they built up when she'd made sure to clear them before leaving the office. Ignoring them all apart from the final one, she clicked open the attachment and peered down at the screen, shifting her finger to the zoom button. The image had the same fuzzy clarity she'd come to expect from these sorts of pictures but it was still good enough for her to be dragged back three months and the last time she'd seen the boy, standing beside the open door of his parents' lounge, the look of hope and expectation dying under the weight of her words. The same finely etched features. The dark hollows crowding his cheeks. The broad-domed forehead partially concealed by his overlong dark fringe and the only part of him that reminded her of his father. She'd thought him a boy then, young for his years. There was no trace of the child in him now. Instead there was a man and, with that thought, her insides heaved as she struggled to keep the contents of her stomach in place.

'Ma'am?'

'Yes, sorry. Just thinking. You and Diane have done a fabulous job, thank you.'

'So, it's him then?'

'Yes. I'll have a think as to what I'm going to do about it. It's certainly a curve ball I wasn't expecting,' she said, her attention on the empty coffee mugs. It was a good job she'd barely touched the wine, which had more to do with Conor's disapproving stare than any problem with the Italian Shiraz his dad had brought. What she needed was caffeine, and lots of it, as the thought of getting any sleep tonight slipped further into the distance.

131

Chapter 27

Gaby

Monday 3 August, 9.20 p.m. Amy's house

Knocking on Amy's door was the last thing Gaby had envisaged for the end of her evening, not that twenty past nine was anywhere near her bedtime. She'd planned on being tucked up in bed with a cup of cocoa and the latest novel by Victoria Cooke, to bridge the gap between the dream and the reality of her date with Rusty. Now she was huddled in her thin jacket, hoping that Tim hadn't taken Amy out somewhere after what must have been the most stressful of days. Being a detective was nothing to the pressure that her friend faced in the role of family liaison officer and Gaby couldn't begin to understand what motivated her to continue in such a thankless profession. At least she had the joy of seeing the odd criminal banged to rights. All Amy got was a shift into the next emotionally charged situation where there was no rulebook and actions had to be tailored to the unpredictable behaviour of the people involved.

The door opened on the third knock. Gaby lowered her hand and stuffed it into the pocket of her jacket. 'Sorry it's so late and sorry if I'm interrupting anything.'

'Not a thing. Tim's working tonight so there's nothing to interrupt,' Amy said with a mischievous grin as she tugged her ponytail tight and gestured for her to follow her into the lounge. 'I take it there's been a development?'

'You could say that.' Gaby walked over to the large painting above the fireplace, admiring the bold lines and bright colours. 'A new addition?'

'Yes. You know what Tim's like. There's a new art gallery opened up in Caernarfon, which he dragged me to at the weekend.'

'Well, anytime he'd like to drag me,' Gaby said, squinting down at the signature. 'Once I get my lounge finished, I might very well treat myself.'

'I wouldn't leave it too long. Nathan Jones is up and coming. Anyway, I'm sure you didn't pop in to discuss my walls.'

'No.' Gaby headed back into the hall, not bothering to remove her jacket. 'Come on, grab your bag. I'll tell you on the way.'

'On the way to where?' Amy said, not budging from the doorway of the lounge.

'We need to interview a couple of people and I can't do it without you.'

'Ha, as if I thought it could be anything else. You do remember that I'm getting married in three weeks?'

'How could I ever forget! As soon as we've found the girl, I'm all yours. We'll go out, just the two of us, and tighten any loose ends that need tightening. Your wedding is going to be perfect, Amy. As your chief bridesmaid in addition to your boss I'm giving you my personal guarantee.'

'Thank you. I'm holding you to that. So, who are we going to see?' Amy said, slipping on her shoes and grabbing her keys, phone and bag from the table.

'Ms Fry and—'

'She won't thank you for that,' she interrupted with a frown, pulling the front door closed. 'Is it really necessary? She was in bits when I left.'

133

'I can well imagine but it can't be helped. Finding her daughter has never been a greater priority.' Gaby opened her car door and settled behind the steering wheel.

'You said there were two interviews?' Amy twisted in her seat to grab her belt, only to drop it at Gaby's next words.

'Casper Stevens's son and, before you ask me any more questions,' she added, putting up the palm of her hand towards Amy's unguarded expression of shock, 'I'm going to get Jason and his team mobilised to meet us around at the house. We need to go in, all guns blazing.' She dropped her mobile into Amy's lap. 'He's currently on another job but this can't wait. The odds are that Barbara Matthews is already dead but I won't believe the same of Ellie Fry until we find her body.'

It only took ten minutes to travel from Rhos-on-Sea to Colwyn Bay. Not much time to contact the CSIs and plan their strategy but they managed. With Amy's wedding looming there were plenty of non-work-related topics that were high on their list of priorities. They didn't detour the conversation to discuss even one.

It was a warm night with the tail end of a glorious sunset indulging the sky with a faint hint of navy blue instead of the impenetrable black that was to be expected now the nights were closing in. The estate was busy, children playing tag up and down the road on their bicycles, the sound of laughter filling the air as the occupants took advantage of the last few minutes of warmth.

Number 312 was silent, the curtains pulled tight without revealing even a pale glimmer of light to indicate that anyone was at home. But if Gaby knew anything it was that Ellie's mother would still be awake, hunched in the corner of the sofa, a box of tissues by her side, a stream of half-filled mugs lined up on the coffee table in front of her. She would be no different to any of the other victims' families Gaby had gotten to know in her police career. If she was innocent of any crime – and there was no point in Gaby carrying on in the job if, at some level, she believed differently – then she was sitting alone, breaking her heart at the thought of her daughter out in the big wild world with no one to protect her.

Anita opened the door after one knock and, if her look of expectation was anything to go by, Gaby was right in her estimation of her innocence. She was a woman beside herself with worry, the skin pressed deep with dark shadows, her eyelids a pale, translucent, unbecoming red, her hands shaking as she turned away and walked into the lounge, leaving them to shut the door behind them. Now Gaby wished that she'd had the foresight to phone first. A few words on her part would have reduced Anita's expectation of a happy outcome. The truth was she must know that two officers turning up at this time of night, empty-handed, would only be bringing bad news.

'Go on then. Tell me. There's no point in dragging it out. She's dead, isn't she?'

Anita sank down into the sofa, her mobile clutched in her hand, the depressed cushion a telling sign that she probably hadn't moved far away from her seat for most of the day. She'd been waiting for news and all they had were more questions. Sitting back in the same chair as before, Gaby thanked whatever instinct had made her pick up Amy on the way. It was the only part of the visit that she hadn't made a mess of. Family liaison officers were better at this sort of stuff. If she thought she could have gotten away with it, Gaby would have sent her in alone. She'd certainly considered it.

Amy joined Anita on the sofa and, picking up her hand, gave it a gentle squeeze. 'No. And I'm sorry that our unexpected visit has made you feel that way. I'm going to be perfectly honest with you. The truth is we haven't found Ellie but we have found something that we do need to discuss with you, something that might be vital to the search.'

Rather than speaking again, Amy let Anita find her own way back from the emotions ripping through her body and hampering her ability to answer. There was no glancing at her watch, no quick look across the room at Gaby. Anita would only be able to speak when her tongue had repositioned itself in her suddenly dry mouth, her racing heart dropping along with the level of adrenalin coursing through her veins.

Science had an answer for most things but that didn't stop the feeling of compassion that caused Gaby to shift in her seat, her own pulse escalating a notch at the sight of Amy reaching for the folder. Science couldn't give her insight into what was going to happen over the next couple of minutes and it was this that was causing her the greatest difficulty. Anita would either recognise Ronan Stevens or she wouldn't.

Chapter 28

Ronan

Monday 3 August, 9.50 p.m. Caernarfon

Ronan couldn't sleep but that was hardly surprising given the level of stress he was under. But there was nothing else for him to do and certainly nothing he could do in the shadow of darkness. The farmhouse might be isolated and back on to fields but he couldn't turn on the light and risk being discovered by some intrepid rambler taking a shortcut across private land.

He lay there, with the musty-smelling duvet pulled up to his chin, trying to ignore the sounds coming through the gaps in the warped window frame. In the cave it had been deathly quiet – too quiet. Surrounded by limestone on three sides he'd also struggled to sleep. The stone floor had been difficult to get used to after the comfort of a sprung mattress and a fat feather pillow. So why couldn't he sleep here? Okay, so the mattress wasn't a patch on the one he'd had at home but he was both warm and safe, far safer than the last few weeks on that windswept headland. He was also intelligent enough to rationalise that the sounds were non-threatening. The screech of an owl on his way to find a late-night snack. The sway of the trees in the light breeze that had built up over the evening. The creak of the old house as it settled into its footings. There was an explanation for each and every one of the sounds but that did little to stop his escalating fears.

In Llandudno, at least he had the vicar to turn to in an emergency and the reality of his mother only a short distance away. He'd thought he'd been clever in taking Ellie here but there was nothing clever in the way he was feeling. They were isolated and alone, cut off from civilisation and he still didn't have a clue as to the potential terrors that had made her run away from everything and anybody she'd ever known.

He shifted onto his side, burying one ear into the pillow, the duvet pulled up over his head, his mind returning to the girl. Going through her bags was a wasted exercise. It hadn't told him anything he didn't already know. She lived with her mother but the tears sparkling on her eyelashes along with her quivering bottom lip led him to think that it wasn't this nebulous woman who was the problem.

Stretching out to his full length, he curled his toes under the wooden baseboard, amazed at how many questions he'd managed to sneak under her radar after the chocolate rush had kicked in. Her innocent answers had told him far more than she'd probably intended. The relentless ballet training that took up most of her spare time, her mother running her to and from classes in her old Hyundai i10. He'd even discovered that she didn't have a father and had never felt the need to find him. To an outsider, her life was that of a well-adjusted kid. But as soon as he started to scratch the surface to reveal the carefully concealed reality underneath, she shut up quicker than a liar faced with the truth. He frowned at the analogy, for the first time questioning her sincerity. After all, she'd sought him out and had been a constant presence by his side ever since. Did he trust her and if not what did he intend to do about it?

The long walk while carrying the weight of the world on his

back finally caught up with him, his eyelids winning the argument and sweeping him into darkness, his thoughts scattering as dreams pressed.

Ronan wasn't a great dreamer and come morning he could never recall anything useful about his time asleep. Images passed through his mind but gained no purchase, glittering pictures that held no bearing on his current situation. His breathing deepened and his lids flickered as he shed his worries along with his fears. He still had to find out the truth, whatever that might be – there'd be time enough in the morning.

The scream when it came wrenched him from his cocoon of duvet and had him stumbling to his feet. The room was pitch, the sheet of black at the window as telling as the illuminated dial on his watch that he must have drifted off to sleep. Disorientated for a second, he took a moment to gather his thoughts as memories swept in from all sides. The Great Orme. The girl. The train journey. His grandparents' house.

Now instead of the scream, there were panting gasps punctuating the air in a staccato of grief. With a suppressed curse, he switched on his torch and crossed the couple of paces to her bedside, dropping to his knees as he tried to think of the kind of things his mother might say. The kid had obviously had a nightmare, which was hardly surprising after the day she'd had in addition to all that chocolate, he remembered, and then felt guilty at the thought. It was a good job she wasn't throwing up as well. That would be all he needed – having to act as nursemaid to a kid and a girl at that. It wouldn't be so bad if it had been a boy. He was used to having to deal with his brothers. But an all-boys' school and a dearth of sisters added to his current feeling of woeful inadequacy.

'It's all right, Ellie. It's only a dream. You're safe. Completely safe,' he said, his free hand reaching out and patting the top of her head very much in the way he would a dog, not that he'd ever had much to do with animals. Despite the persistent nagging over the years, his parents had always been too busy to allow them to keep pets.

'I'm not safe.' She paused, dragging the back of her hand across her cheeks in an attempt to mop up her tears, her eyes two large pools of dripping sorrow in the dim beam from his torch. 'You don't understand and I can't tell you. It's bad enough that I know. If they ever find out ... It's a secret that I have to keep.'

'What secret? What is it, Ellie? I'll help, I promise.'

But all he got for his troubles was a rod of spine as she turned to face the wall, her slight frame shaking as her tears kept falling. He continued to kneel beside the bed, watching over her as her gulping breaths slowed, the shape beneath the blanket relaxing as her breathing regulated and sleep carried her off into a world where he couldn't protect her.

For the second time in his life Ronan was helpless as to what to do. But there was no running away from the situation. She'd chosen him; he didn't know for what purpose. The only thing he did know was that he wasn't about to let her down. He'd been let down too many times in the past not to have learnt from the experience.

He didn't let his mind wander any further as he maintained his silent vigil, the carpet doing little to prevent the hard floor from piercing his bony knees. He had problems, too numerous to count and none of his own making. Perhaps he'd overreacted in running away because he was quick to realise that leaving home hadn't changed anything. It had only delayed the time when he'd have to make some sort of decision about his future.

A tear fell and then another, tracking down his grubby cheeks but, instead of wiping them away, he let them fall. He hadn't cried when the bullies had done their worst and he certainly hadn't cried when the headmaster had expelled him. He'd felt cold to emotion when his father had been arrested, inured somehow from the horrors that had overtaken his family. Now when he didn't know what to do or who to turn to, he wept.

Chapter 29

Gaby

Monday 3 August, 10 p.m. The Stevens's property

When Gaby and Amy arrived at the house, Jason was hunched over the steering wheel of the CSI van, his eyes glued to his phone.

'Hi there, apologies for keeping you up so late.'

He looked as bad as she felt and her night was far from over, she reflected, stifling a groan at the thought of the job application form lurking in her briefcase. 'I'm hoping it will only take a few minutes for her to agree to the search.' She nodded in Amy's direction. 'Primarily we're interested in finding any trace of Ellie but also anything unusual, as you know.'

'I know only too well, Gaby.' He ran his hand through his hair, making it stand on end. 'You think I'm the only CSI in the whole of North Wales?'

'No, but we think you're the best, don't we, Amy,' she said, sending her a brief grin.

'Flattery will get you everywhere, not. I hope you've checked in with Sherlock because the way I'm feeling this is going to be triple time.'

'You leave Sherlock to me.' She patted his arm briefly, her thoughts turning to the DCI and what he'd think of how she was handling the situation. But the truth of the matter was she didn't give a damn. He wasn't the one still working at 10 p.m. No. He'd be tucked up in bed while she had the pleasure of interviewing one of the toughest women she'd ever met.

Janice Stevens was how she remembered. Perhaps a little thinner and her iron-grey hair a little longer, but to all intents and purposes she seemed the exact same as the woman she'd met earlier in the year, right down to the expression on her face.

'Sorry for bothering you so late, Mrs Stevens, but we'd like a quick word with your eldest son, Ronan.'

'You'd better come in.' She closed the door behind them and directed them into the lounge. With a wave of her hand, she gestured towards the sofa while she perched on the arm of the chair opposite, her fingers laced in her lap.

'Let's not beat around the bush, Detective. What is it that my son is meant to have done?'

'Nothing as yet but, as he is eighteen and an adult in his own right, I'm sure you can appreciate that it's not something we can discuss with you?'

'Oh, come on! You visit my home this late at night, demanding to see my son and then don't tell me any information as to what it's about? How do you reckon that works then? I just roll over and tell you everything you want to know without you giving me anything in return?'

If Gaby thought she was out of her depth before entering the property, now she was in full drowning mode with no sign of a lifebelt in grabbing distance. As acting DI, she had two choices. To blurt out the truth or withhold everything they had. But instead of doing either, she decided to answer Janice's question with one of her own. After all, there was no law against leading a member of the public to reach the right conclusion all by themselves.

'Mrs Stevens, have you heard the news today?'

'Have I heard the news today?' she repeated, her frown deepening. 'In the car after picking the boys up from summer school but there was nothing—' She broke off mid-sentence, the colour leeching from her face although there hadn't been much colour to begin with. 'You can't think for one minute that my son would have anything to do with that missing girl? It's absurd. Ronan would be the very last person to ...' She stopped again, her cheeks flooding red with some emotion Gaby could only guess at.

Janice weaved to the front of the chair to sit down as if her legs were suddenly too weak to take her weight.

'I don't understand,' she said eventually, her voice a thin thread of sound.

'That's why we're here. To try and make sense of it all.' Amy leant forward, her hand clutching on to a brown envelope. 'Where is your son, Mrs Stevens?'

She lifted her head, a very different woman to the one who'd opened the door only a few minutes ago. It was as if all the fight had drained out of her when she allowed the possibility of Ronan doing wrong to sneak over the tender walls she'd encased herself in.

'Somewhere in Llandudno. I have no idea where. After ... after everything that happened, he decided for whatever reason that he needed some space. He left at the start of June and has been living rough ever since.'

'Are you in touch?'

She shook her head. 'Not since he walked out the door.'

'So, if you're not in touch how do you know that he's still in the area?'

'Detective, you must understand something about my son.' She linked her fingers in her lap, the knuckles white against the stark simplicity of her navy shift dress. 'He's intelligent, absurdly intelligent – some would say gifted but that's a label we've ... I've always tried to avoid. Too much to live up to at a young age. But intelligence in his case is coupled with a lack of common sense.

He was fine at home but school was a trial. He doesn't relate well to others and, in a way, I can see that the idea of running away to some utopian place to live a hermit type of existence would have appealed. If I hadn't been so caught up in my own problems, I might have managed to prevent it from happening but it is what it is.' She paused, staring down at her fingers only to spread them flat across her lap. 'While Ronan doesn't want to live at home it doesn't mean that I don't want to protect him in the same way I've always done.'

She tilted her chin, finally meeting their gaze. 'I got in touch with Reverend Honeybun over at St Luke's, almost as soon as Ronan left and he agreed to keep an eye on him. He's even employed him on an ad hoc basis to help clear parish land and in return he provides me with the odd update as to how he's doing.'

'And how is he doing?' Gaby interjected.

'Better, I think. It's taken careful nurturing but he's even starting to talk about the future.'

'But you haven't been in touch with him since?'

'No, although it's more the case that he hasn't been in touch with me.' She wiped her fingers under her eyes. 'I don't know if he blames me for what happened but the truth is we were barely on speaking terms in the days and weeks leading up to him leaving.'

Amy removed a picture from the envelope and, stretching out her hand, said, 'If you could tell us if this is an image of your son or not?'

Janice's jaw dropped. The A4 piece of paper barely touched her fingers. It fluttered to the floor by her feet, as her fist pressed into her mouth.

Gaby looked across at Amy, the reality of the situation slamming home to them both the seriousness of what they were about to ask her next but they had little choice.

'Mrs Stevens, in light of you not being able to inform us as to the whereabouts of your son and, taking into account that he was spotted on a CCTV camera very close to your home earlier on today in the company of Elodie Fry, I'd like your permission to search the house?'

'You'll need a warrant for that,' she said, a glimmer of her sparky personality finally reasserting itself.

'Yes, and, as a lawyer, you'll know that it will be easily obtained under the circumstances.'

Janice Stevens stood, taking a moment to smooth her hands down the front of her dress. 'Get it over with then. I'll be in the kitchen if you need me and' – she raised her head, her eyes lifting to meet Gaby's full on – 'I'd appreciate it if you wouldn't disturb my boys. They're asleep upstairs and, as they've either been here with me or at summer school, I doubt they'll have anything that they can tell you.'

Chapter 30

Gaby

Monday 3 August, 11.10 p.m. Rhos-on-Sea

Gaby dropped Amy off before returning home to a kitchen full of dirty plates but, instead of tackling them, she pushed them to one side of the worktop and poured herself a glass of water. She'd have much preferred a glass of the wine Rusty had brought but not until she'd cobbled together the sort of CV that DCI Sherlock would be expecting.

With a box of assorted papers in front of her, she was soon up to her neck in trying to find details of courses and copies of past appraisals. Gaby wasn't the most organised of individuals when it came to keeping up with her personal documents and, like most people, became easily distracted by old school reports and the odd photo that had crept into the box, which added little help but lots of reminiscing. She finally pressed send, seconds before the midnight deadline she'd been given, with a renewed promise to take the time to sort out her affairs once and for all. A promise she was destined to break.

Resting back against the sofa, she was trying to pluck up the energy from somewhere to climb the stairs when her phone rang. She muttered a curse under her breath. It could only mean one thing. More trouble.

'Darin speaking.'

'How did I know that you'd still be awake, Gabriella?'

Gaby curled her feet underneath her and, grabbing the throw from off the back of the sofa, wrapped it across her legs. Her frown lines smoothed as a smile appeared – a smile that was reflected in her voice but not her words.

'You didn't. I'd have been mightily hacked off if I had been asleep!'

'I'll have to remember that. Gets grumpy late at night. Is there anything else I should know before we continue our relationship?'

Gaby's smile widened. 'Lots but it's a bit late – or should that be early? – to discuss it.' She shifted her position along with the conversation, addressing the one thing about their relationship that was worrying her. 'How's Conor?'

'Ah. He's fast asleep but not before he gave me a piece of his very young and immature mind.'

'Ah,' she echoed. 'He's not a happy bunny.'

'That's putting it lightly. The thing you need to remember is that when his mother left, she dragged me through the courts for sole custody, something I battled all the way. She only changed her mind when her new boyfriend came on the scene. To put it bluntly, she dropped him off at the hospital with his belongings stuffed into a couple of suitcases and drove into the sunset.'

'Poor mite.'

'Exactly. I told you at the very start that he was my priority and that still stands.'

'You know I'd never—'

'But, Gabriella, it's not what I know that's relevant,' he interrupted. 'It's what Conor thinks and currently you're the devil incarnate trying to steal his dad out from under his nose.'

Gaby dragged her hand across her eyes, too tired and stressed to puzzle out how to answer. What did he expect her to say? That they should stop seeing each other for the sake of his son? She opened her mouth to tell him exactly that only to close it again at his next words.

'I think we have the makings of something good between us but only if we can come to some sort of consensus. I'm not prepared to compromise my relationship with Conor but there's nothing wrong in trying to make a new family for him out of the dregs of the old.'

'So, what do you suggest we do?'

'Continue including Conor in our plans. It means no intimate dinners for two, but it will provide an opportunity for him to realise that things aren't going to change overnight.'

'If that's the way it has to be.'

'I was hoping you'd say that. We'll get there eventually and, in the meantime, continue cementing our friendship.'

'But not right now,' she interrupted, struggling to squash down a yawn. 'I don't mean to be rude but it's been a very long day and with the possibility of exactly the same tomorrow.'

Chapter 31

Gaby

Tuesday 4 August, 8.15 a.m. St Asaph Police Station

Gaby was late and feeling the impact of forgetting to set the alarm on her phone, something she blamed Rusty for. If she hadn't heard next door's car revving up, she'd probably still be in bed. Her forgetfulness had dictated that she'd rushed out of the house, barely taking the time to brush her teeth or check that her hair was restrained in its usual braid. She'd ignored the kettle just as she'd ignored the bread bin, instead opting to stop off at the garage to pick up a sandwich along with the morning newspapers.

All of the dailies carried the story of Ellie Fry's disappearance on their front pages, for once ignoring the petty government wranglings that normally took up valuable front-page space. After a cursory glance, she threw them on the passenger seat along with her cheese-and-tomato bap and, fastening her seatbelt, put her foot down. There had been no news overnight. It had been the first thing she'd checked, after she'd wiped the sleep from her eyes and realised the time. The old adage that no news was good news was far from reassuring and didn't reflect her current state of anxiety as to the whereabouts of the little girl.

The station at 8.15 was busier than normal, which was hardly surprising given their current workload. After collecting her post from the desk sergeant, she raced up to her office to deposit her bag under the desk and head for the incident room. They were all there and by the looks of it had experienced just as unsettling a night. Even Owen had put in an early appearance, she noticed, guilt expanding in her chest at the thought of his wife being left to sort out their son in addition to their week-old baby. Jax and Malachy were dressed in jeans and T-shirts, the sight of stubble on their chins a clear sign that they'd decided, against her advice, to join in with the search. She couldn't blame them and she certainly wasn't going to call them out over it when it was something she'd done herself when she'd been in uniform.

'Here you go, ma'am.' Marie held out a mug for her to take. Gaby couldn't begin to guess at what time she'd got in but, by the sight of her desk littered with paperwork, a lot earlier than her.

'Thanks, just what I needed,' she said, her attention shifting to Amy, who was firmly entrenched behind her laptop, her phone clutched to her ear, only acknowledging Gaby's entrance with a brief lift of her hand.

Gaby took a moment to take a deep sip, the feel of hot tea against her lips doing little to dim the sudden glow of pride she felt for her team. But being Gaby, she didn't say anything. They had a job to do, only that. The time to thank them would be when Ellie was safely back at home with her mother. She barely spared a thought for Barbara Matthews except to pick up her phone and invite Jason downstairs to share what he'd told her last night with the rest of the room.

The whiteboard had taken a hit yesterday, scribbled notes marking most of its surface. Gaby spent a moment reading through her previous comments in case there was anything that she wanted to add or change. Her gaze was drawn to Ellie's photo as she reached for a black marker pen.

'Right then, thanks to Diane's efforts yesterday we now have a suspect in addition to someone in custody ...' She twisted her head, glancing around the room. 'Where is PC Carbone? She should be here. She's as much a part of this team as the rest of us.'

'She was earlier,' Malachy said, his hand rasping over his stubbly chin. 'She probably thought she was surplus to requirements now that she's been through all of the CCTV footage.'

Gaby's sigh was audible across the room, causing the team to eye her in amusement. 'Go and find her, Mal, as quick as you can,' she added, her voice sharpening to a stiletto point when he didn't immediately shift from his chair. 'While we're waiting, I can fill you in on Ellie's disappearance. There is news but I have no idea what to make of it. Marie and Diane have identified the lad on the Great Orme with Ellie as Ronan Stevens.'

Gaby didn't have to qualify who that was, their expressions said it all. 'Quite! Until we speak to the two of them, there's no way of knowing if their meeting was purely coincidental or not, but it's certainly a worrying development. I can't help that old adage *like father like son* repeating like the aftereffects of a dodgy prawn. Amy and I interviewed Ms Fry again last night and she has no recollection of having ever met the boy so, at this stage, there's no evidence that it's anything but a chance encounter. But it does mean that we have to change our strategy. With this in mind, last night, Amy and I paid a visit to Janice Stevens and, following the discovery of a quantity of fresh blood in her bathroom, blood with the same group as Ellie Fry's, she is currently in custody. Yes, that's right. What was a missing persons' case is now a possible murder inquiry, despite the lack of a body, so we're going in all guns blazing on this one.'

The sound of feet in the corridor outside had Gaby tilting her head, no trace of a smile at the sight of Malachy hurrying into the room, Diane following behind. 'While we have to keep an open mind, I don't need to remind you of the antics Casper Stevens got up to. It could even be a case of dear old mum trying to protect one of her brood. It's not as if she wouldn't know how.' She stared across at Marie. 'You and I are going to interview her and make sure we tick all the boxes we're meant to, bearing in mind that she's a lawyer! Jax, I'd like you to continue being the main liaison person for the search and rescue team. We need to make sure that it's a coordinated effort and that we're looking in all the right places. On the same theme, I need you to revisit both the train and bus station. I know we were there yesterday but we didn't have Ronan Stevens's picture to flash around – it might be the break we need. Malachy, you've drawn the short straw.' She recapped the marker and placed it in the little wooden rack underneath the whiteboard, setting it between its best friends; the red and the green. 'We still need to link in the reason for Ellie absconding because, as yet, we haven't come up with anything plausible.'

She looked across at him, her thoughts filled with the stark image of Rusty's son and the comment he'd made. 'The general feeling is that something scared her but we have no idea what. So, I want you to flesh out what we already know about her last few days and follow up on any leads that it may generate. Yesterday we checked in with the train and bus stations but we need to expand on that. It's pretty obvious that she's not going to be anywhere near the six-mile limit we originally set.'

'Unless something has already happened and her body has been hidden,' he replied.

Gaby raised her eyebrows at the typical, reality-check comment coming from Malachy Devine, which she should have been expecting. He'd proved himself to be an invaluable part of the team during the last case. The only thing stopping him from racing up through the ranks was his inability to edit whatever came out of his mouth, because stating the obvious to a room full of detectives was always going to be less than helpful. 'Yes. Well. Thank you for putting into words what we're all thinking but we have to stay positive.'

Picking up the red marker, she started writing bullet points on the board, her fingers clenched, fist tight. Malachy had annoyed her more than she realised. He was a good copper. Hard-working, committed and intelligent. He also had that little extra sprinkling of dedication that had kept him up all night roaming the hills. But that was irrelevant if he couldn't learn to curb his thoughts. Everyone on the team knew that the chance of finding Ellie alive was like looking at the final grains of sand disappearing through an egg timer.

With a nip at her lower lip, hard enough to make her flinch, she continued to speak. 'After we've interviewed Mrs Stevens, I'm going to have a little chat with Reverend Honeybun – we know that he's spent a great deal of time with Ronan. What's the likelihood that if we find the boy we find the girl?'

Gaby took a deep sighing breath, because of course Ellie Fry wasn't the only case on their books. 'Now over to Barbara Matthews, the elderly lady over in Deganwy who was reported missing yesterday afternoon by her bridge buddies when she failed to turn up for her own party.' She shifted her head at the sight of Jason strolling through the door, his hands tucked inside the pockets of his grey, houndstooth check trousers. 'Ah, just in time. Tell me again what you found over at Barbara Matthews'?'

'Blood. Not a lot but fresh and therefore worrying. After you left, we sprayed with luminal, which revealed an interesting array of splatter marks. I've sent off scrapings for DNA analysis. She doesn't have any living relatives that we can find but there's enough of her forensic fingerprinting at her home to make that fact irrelevant. I'm working on the report or I would be if you hadn't dragged me away from my desk. I hope to have it for you mid-morning at the latest.'

Gaby managed to hide a smile at the timbre of his voice. 'So, it is possible that we have a crime scene on our hands?'

He nodded, his face without a trace of his perpetual humour. 'Taking into account everything we know about the woman, it certainly seems that way. I have to say the impression we're getting is that something fatal happened in the hall and the perpetrator did a near-perfect job of covering it up.'

'But not perfect enough! Great, that's all we bloody need, excuse the pun.' She scanned the room, her gaze finally landing on Owen, the most senior officer on the MIT next to her. 'I appreciate that you're tied up with the funny business over at the crematorium but, in light of Jason's findings, this will have to take precedence as we have no guarantee that the prosthesis wasn't left over from a previous cremation.'

'Actually, that's not the case.'

'That's not the case?' she repeated, her expression hardening in an instant. 'Explain.'

'As you know, I went to see Doctor Mulholland yesterday. He's come up trumps with the hip joints and has confirmed that the largest two belonged to our very own Duncan Broome, which is what we were expecting. But you're not going to believe who the final prosthesis belongs to.' Owen paused a second for effect. 'None other than our missing person from last year, Katherine Jane.'

Gaby squeezed her eyes shut a moment, again regretting her lack of breakfast as her stomach lurched underneath her second favourite navy trouser suit, bought for a song in Zara's Christmas sale. To have to head up a possible murder inquiry on low blood sugar was bad enough. She couldn't believe her misfortune at having another complex case thrust into their laps. Most weeks were quiet, the odd arrest for B-class drugs and the issuing of ASBOs the sum total of their day-to-day activity. Now, in addition to having a missing girl and a missing OAP, they also had a murder inquiry on their plate.

Her eyes snapped open, instinctively searching and finding Amy's, her look of compassion and understanding clear underneath her overlong mousy fringe. Thrusting her shoulders back, Gaby returned her slight nod. Amy knew more than anybody Gaby's experience in managing multiple complex investigations. She'd manage all three cases, even if it killed her. Gaby was also experienced enough to know that it very well might.

'Right. It seems as if our workload has just trebled with Katherine Jane's body part turning up at the Welsh Hills Memorial Gardens in addition to Barbara Matthews' disappearance. However, Ellie Fry is our priority. Miss Jane, a year missing, is well past saving but, if the CSIs are to be believed, and I can't for a minute think that Jason has got it wrong, then with Mrs Matthews we have a murder inquiry on our hands.' She turned to Owen, making a rapid decision. 'I want you to put a task force together to concentrate on Katherine Jane and Barbara Matthews because I have a feeling that we're going to find out that they're linked. There can't be that many spinsters floating around Llandudno without a relative to their name and that's where I'd like you to start. If I'm wrong, I'll take full responsibility. I'll also have a word with the DCI to see if he's happy for Diane to stay with us a little longer but co-opt people in as you see fit, obviously running it by me first.'

Gaby had expected ructions and all she got was a grim smile, which was barely a smile at all – it certainly didn't reach his eyes. Owen liked to be at the centre of an investigation and had all of the skills needed for what was now an international hunt for the missing child. But the new lines around his eyes and a return to his previous pallor, despite the blistering sunshine, told her without him having to say a word that he still hadn't reached full equilibrium following the last case – a case that had put his whole family at risk. Being the boss was never tougher than in situations such as this, the right decision for the team often being the wrong one for at least one of its members. She'd have to make it up to him – she had no idea when or how.

With another deep sigh she swivelled on her low-heeled loafers. 'Come on, Marie. Here's betting that Janice Stevens has had the best of nights all topped off by a spa bath and a large bowl of the custodial sergeant's finest muesli! We'll meet back here at one unless something crops up to change that. I'll ask the canteen to provide sandwiches.'

Chapter 32

Jax

Tuesday 4 August, 8.40 a.m. St Asaph Police Station

Jax was the youngest member of the team. At twenty-six, he was resigned to being allocated the most menial of jobs like dog walking and the checking out of CCTV footage, which was all very well but they weren't the sort of tasks he'd anticipated when he'd started working towards his detective exams. They certainly didn't leave him with any feelings of contentment of a job well done. That was until Gaby had decided to shake things up and put him in charge of the air and sea rescue teams. Finally something he could wrap his teeth around.

Jax was also one of those people who if he wasn't doing, he didn't feel busy. But with leaders such as Dafydd Griffiths on the ground and the team over at Caernarfon coordinating the air search there was very little for him to do apart from check in with them on a regular basis.

Sitting at his desk with his refillable water bottle his constant companion, he pulled up the notebook App on his phone and started flicking back through the pages for inspiration on ways to shift the lacklustre investigation to the conclusion they all wanted. The safe return of Ellie Fry. He couldn't countenance any other outcome and he was young enough to still have youthful optimism on his side to drive away the negative thoughts that were currently eating away at his more experienced colleagues. No, what was needed was action but with no leads apart from an eighteen-year-old lad in the company of an instantly recognisable young girl …

Jax nearly tipped over his water bottle in his race to expand on the idea. It didn't take long for him to sit back in his chair with his drink cradled in his palms, barely registering the slight metallic taste from the water that was now an unsavoury lukewarm. If he was right – it didn't even cross his mind that he could be wrong – he was about to start a hunt for a very different set of clues.

Llandudno was heaving with holidaymakers, the beaches packed, and the ice-cream van – along North Parade – doing a roaring trade. Jax would like nothing better than to dip in the enticing, almost Caribbean-blue sea instead of taking advantage of the police station's car park and heading up towards the Great Orme, his long legs making short work of the distance.

He could have asked for assistance but, Jax being Jax, he decided not to pull any of the uniformed officers away from the search. With a street map downloaded onto his phone and a printout of the locations of all the public bins provided by the Conwy County Borough Council, he pulled on a pair of sturdy rubber gloves borrowed from the CSIs, much to the amusement of a giggling pair of teenage girls who were perched on the wall opposite, their tanned legs swinging in the air to the beat of their headphones.

They were easy to ignore. He had a job to do and the quicker he did it the quicker he could head back to St Asaph and to the nearest shower he could find. With his sleeves rolled up and his watch hidden away in his pocket, he followed a path from the last known sighting of Ellie near the Great Orme summit and back down Marine Drive towards Upper Mostyn Street, where the scent had gone cold.

Jax switched his mind off from the unsavoury task: the half-eaten take-outs, mingled with sweet wrappers, parking slips and even a broken bucket and spade. Apart from the list of clothes and belongings that Ellie's mother had provided, he didn't know what he was looking for as he mentally ticked off the next bin on his route to the train station. If he was unlucky with his choice of direction, he'd just have to follow an alternative route.

After the first hour, he could have written a thesis about the effects of recycling on modern-day North Wales. By the second, the rank scent of detritus had snuck up his nose and refused to budge. By the third he had a stained shirt, a perspiring brow and tomato pips running down his right trouser leg but he also had a carrier bag, the handle stained rust with the instantly recognisable mark of oxidised blood.

Chapter 33

Ronan

Tuesday 4 August, 8.40 a.m. Caernarfon

Ronan's day usually started a lot earlier than 8.40. If he wasn't up and about at six, there was a good chance one of the early morning dog walkers would catch him sneaking out of the cave – the very last thing he wanted. He wasn't so worried about the warden. Now that the caves were locked, there was no need for the man to check on whether someone had chosen one as an impromptu place to rest their head. So, unlike any other teenager he knew, he went to bed early. He was usually able to sneak back into the cave when the tea-time lull hit around 5.30 and most nights found him drifting off to sleep at eight, nine at the latest. The hard ground did little to prevent his weary muscles from relaxing after a day that included whatever back-breaking work the vicar had lined up for him interspersed with the hours he spent roaming the streets.

But today wasn't a usual day for Ronan. He'd found it impossible to settle after Ellie's outburst, his restless mind trying to puzzle out what it was that could have made her flee from everything she knew and everyone she loved. He must have eventually dropped off – his head hunched up in his neck, his legs stretched out in front of him – when the sun had started to shift the moon from its starlight perch.

He finally woke to the sound of clattering in the kitchen and cramp in every muscle possible. For an instant, just one, he missed the cave. The cave was his safe place, somewhere no one could touch him. It was his memories that were the problem. His memories that he was struggling with. The impossibility of sweeping away his past under the cloud of shame that both smothered his future and broke his resolve. If only he could forget ... but it was as impossible as reaching for the moon. He'd managed fine before the bullies had intervened. Now he had difficulty remembering what it felt like to have fun. To enjoy life.

In the dark of night when his defences were at their lowest, he dwelt on his reason for deserting the family home. It wasn't anything to do with his mother, not really. The truth was that he blamed himself for everything that had gone before. If only he'd tried harder at school, tried to fit in, he wouldn't have been targeted, taking away his dad's motive for that first attack.

Oddly enough finding Ellie had helped him reach acceptance, something that he wasn't proud of. The idea of a ten-year-old girl having an effect on him was ludicrous but while he was worrying about her, he didn't have any spare time to worry about himself – that made a strange sort of sense.

The clattering continued and, with a groan, he twisted onto his knees and levered up to his full height, one hand using the mattress for support, the other massaging the back of his neck where the biggest creak had decided to take up residence. He had no idea what she was up to but he'd best find out; after all, he was the only adult present. What a thought!

'Breakfast.'

He eyed the kitchen table, his heart tightening at the effort she'd gone to. His grandmother's moss-green dishes with the fluted edges, the same ones he'd eaten countless bowls of cereal from. The glasses filled with water. The spoons polished to a high sheen. She'd even managed to find a packet of cornflakes, the open cupboards evidence of her search and probably the reason for all that clattering and banging.

'Good for you. Well done,' he said, trying not to think about the expiry date on the packet or whether she'd had the sense to rinse the bowls under the tap before pouring the flakes into the bottom. There were probably worse things to die from than stale cereal, he thought, silently congratulating himself on remembering to buy a tin of powdered milk at the newsagent yesterday. Kids required calcium but there was no way that he could provide fresh milk for her, not that he intended to stay in the farmhouse for much longer. It was the first of the two decisions he'd made while he'd witnessed her meltdown. He had to find the courage from somewhere to carry out his plan. His age and purported wisdom should be more than a match for her obstinacy. His gaze rested on the stubborn tilt of her chin. She was as determined not to go back and face her fears as he was determined to make her.

'Have you washed your hands? How about you pop to the bathroom while I check through the rest of the cupboards to see if I can find something for us to drink other than water.' He turned away, listening to her fading footsteps as she strolled at a snail's pace down the hall. It looked like she wasn't going to mention last night, he mused, finding a box of unopened teabags in the back of the cupboard that were three months out of date and, using the tip of his fingernail, he broke the seal. He'd heard about the resilience of children from that child psychologist they'd made him go to see, along with his brothers, but he never would have believed it if he hadn't witnessed it for himself. Unless she'd forgotten all about the nightmare, something he couldn't imagine for a second.

His hand stilled, the box of teabags raised to right under his nose as he tried to decide whether they were okay to use or not but all he could smell was … tea. No. She remembered, all right. He'd brought her to a place of safety, providing the one thing she needed. Now he wanted to know why – the second of the two decisions he'd made earlier.

Within five minutes they were both sitting around the table, Ellie's legs tapping the bar of her chair as she relentlessly spooned in cornflakes, the sight of milk dribbling down her chin causing him to hide a smile. Apart from the hair, which was a raggedy mess, she reminded him of his younger brother even down to the untied shoelaces and grubby T-shirt – the fact that she was dressed in his brother's clothes only added weight to the thought.

What he wouldn't give to be at home right now, his brothers squabbling over whatever computer game they were playing, his mother silent and pale as she carried out the usual morning chores somewhere in the vicinity of the sink. He had to make amends to her; he'd known that for quite a while. The breakdown of their family unit hadn't been her fault but at the time he'd felt an unnecessary childish urge to blame somebody and she was the only one there. His father, the man he'd loved unreservedly, was too far out of his reach, his love and trust only a distant, bitter memory.

He returned his mug onto the coaster she'd found, pushing it slightly so that it was well away from the edge. He folded his arms in front of him as he leant forward. Their bowls were empty just like his mind but he had to start the conversation off somehow.

'How did you sleep after that … dream?'

'Fine.'

'Really! That's all you're going to say after nearly scaring the living daylights out of me?'

She clattered her spoon against the rim of the bowl. 'I said I'm fine.'

So fine that you burst into hysterics at some stupid nightmare!

'Okay, *fine*! We do need to talk about why we're here and what we're going to do next, Ellie. You do realise that staying long term

162

isn't an option? The police are probably scouring the whole of North Wales and it won't take long for somebody to put two and two together and come up with four.'

'I can't talk about it. I just can't.' He watched as she squeezed her hands into tight fists, her neck taut, a little pulse throbbing under the skin in rapid succession. She looked scared, terrified even, and he knew he had to be careful or she might decide to run away from him too.

'Ellie, we're friends right? Ellie and Ronan against the world. But for me to help, you need to be truthful.'

'As truthful as you've been?'

'Pardon?'

'Hiding away in that cave when you have a home to go to. What's that all about?'

His mouth formed a silent o at his naivety, because of course he should have seen it coming. He'd known she was intelligent; it took intelligence to do what she'd done but, up to now, he hadn't heard more than a couple of words stream from her mouth at a time. While he couldn't condone her actions at least she'd recognised when she was in need of help and the risks involved when seeking it. His thoughts returned to the vicious-looking dinner knife he'd found concealed in the bottom of her bag.

'You're right.' He sat back in his chair, his hands gripping the sides of his seat at the thought of sharing the reason behind his actions, a reason he'd never shared before.

'Like you, something happened,' he said, suddenly fascinated by the way the spots of milk she'd split were soaking into the wood. 'Something happened that I couldn't deal with. My mum became ill and then … my dad. I couldn't deal with it so I left.' He raised his head, meeting her eyes only to watch as she averted her gaze.

'I can't tell you. You can't make me and if you do, I'll run again.'

Chapter 34

Owen

Tuesday 4 August, 8.40 a.m. St Asaph

It took a lot to upset Owen Bates. He was the most mild-mannered of men who took life very much as it came. While it irked him not to be involved with the hunt for Ellie Fry, he knew that it was the most sensible option. He'd headed up the inquiry into the disappearance of Katherine Jane and, with his near-photographic memory, had one hundred per cent recall as to the facts of the case. It was nonsensical to be upset but he found that he had to make a conscious effort to arrange his muscles into a smile when he turned to speak to Diane. Within minutes, they were making for the stairs to the archives department, Diane matching his stride pace for pace as he filled her in on the details of last year's most mysterious of disappearances.

'Miss Jane, sixty-eight years of age, a spinster who'd lived in Llandudno since her retirement from teaching three years previously. She had a fixed routine of leaving her seafront apartment and going for an early morning walk along the promenade followed by a restorative drink at Providero, one of the coffee shops in the town. It's only by luck that the owner of the shop got worried when she didn't appear and, remembering a conversation about where she lived, decided to pop in to check up on her at the end of his shift. When he got no answer, he alerted the manager of the building, fearful that she'd be found collapsed or worse. When they opened the door they discovered the remains of her breakfast on the kitchen table, a book propped up against the teapot, her reading glasses, neatly folded beside her plate and a machine full of damp clothing.'

'But no trace of Miss Jane? I'm beginning to see a pattern,' Diane said, her forehead wrinkling.

'And that's the problem.' He pushed the door to the archives office open and gestured for her to go on ahead. 'She had no family apart from a distant great-nephew living in Canada who'd never even met her. The CSIs didn't come up with anything startling and, as Jason said, quite rightly at the time, if it had been a burglary gone wrong there would have been some evidence of a struggle. Originally we thought that she'd taken her own life, despite no evidence of ill health or depression. The only thing that made us think differently was an absence of any cash or jewellery found in the apartment. Her handbag was there but her purse was empty apart from a few coins.'

'Maybe she didn't have much on her and, as an unmarried woman, she might not have had any jewellery. Some women don't like the stuff, you know,' she added, spreading out her ringless fingers.

'Very true but, by the same token, most women have a watch or two knocking around,' he said, his attention fixed on the silver Seiko poking out the sleeve of her jacket. 'I think you're probably right in your assertion about her not having very much. It seems like she invested most of her money in her apartment and relied on her pension for the rest. She had set up standing orders for all her amenities so, apart from her food and day-to-day nonessentials like her morning coffee, she budgeted quite nicely.'

'But something still happened to her.'

'Exactly. Come on. Have you met Colin, our archives officer?' He nodded in the direction of the short, rotund, bespectacled man slouched in front of a computer terminal. 'He'll do anything for you if you remember to bring him back a coffee from the machine.'

'Duly noted,' she said with a grin. 'So, what are we doing down here then? I thought that most of the info would be on the system.'

'It is but I want to reacquaint myself with the scene of the crime photos – I'm old-fashioned enough to prefer to hold them in my hand instead of squinting down at a computer screen – not that there's much proof that a crime was ever committed.' He heaved a breath. 'The biggest breakthrough in the case so far is her metal hip being found among Duncan Broome's ashes and the similarities between her disappearance and that of Barbara Matthews.'

With the help of Colin, they located the correct stack of archive boxes and were soon ensconced in the string of photos that they spread out on the long span of tables at the back of the room.

The 360-views and blow-ups were a quick reminder as to the layout of the apartment, the cluttered walls and bookshelves an indication as to the type of woman that Miss Jane had been. Books took precedence, lining the walls from floor to ceiling, the occasional framed print interrupting the flow almost as an afterthought. The furniture was the type usually left over in auction rooms at the end of a busy day of sales, comfortable up to a point, the dusky gold brocade of a style that had barely been in fashion in the last century let alone the current one.

'She wasn't that mobile, was she?' Diane pointed out, her finger tapping a dark wooden walking stick propped up next to the door, 'So, if someone had attacked her, it's likely that she wouldn't have put up much of a struggle.'

'And taking into account that she barely made five foot in her shoes and weighed little more than a small child, it would have been easy to subdue her,' he replied, thinking back to the difference in the size of the prosthetics he'd examined with Rusty. 'Like taking a milk bottle from a baby.'

'There's something we're missing though, isn't there? A motive. If it was money, she was far from wealthy and it's unlikely her jewellery would have fetched that much.' Diane picked up the photos of the lounge, studying them in earnest.

'What is it you're looking for?'

'Something that isn't there.' She dropped the photos, lining them up beside each other, her buffed fingernail tapping on the top of an occasional table and the absence of any knickknacks. 'She reminds me of my late godmother. She was a teacher too and would have been from the same era, Sergeant.'

'Call me Owen. Everyone else does,' he interrupted with a smile.

'Owen then. So, where are her trinkets? Her photo frames? The *Art Nouveau* pot plant left to her by Great-Aunt Margaret not to mention the silver-backed hairbrushes that her father gave to her mother on their wedding day? Apart from the books, there's nothing personal to see other than her clothes and shoes, which wouldn't be worth fifty pence at a jumble. To my mind it seems as if someone has done a very clever job of taking what wouldn't normally be noticed as missing. Did we ever get any of her friends into the flat to have a gander? What about the place where she taught? It's probably a long shot considering that she was retired a few years prior to her disappearance but surely someone would have remembered the kind of stuff she used to own?'

Owen considered her with elevated eyebrows, on the one hand annoyed that he hadn't spotted it himself but, on the other, delighted that Gaby had decided to pair them together. He'd been to the apartment on more than one occasion along with the CSIs and not one person had observed what she had. 'Do you know what, Diane? I agree with the guv.'

'You agree with the guv?' She opened her eyes to the maximum, her mouth dropping open slightly. 'I don't understand?'

'Have you ever considered switching from PC to DC because, from where I'm sitting, you're exactly the type of candidate we need. Think about it.'

Chapter 35

Gaby

Tuesday 4 August, 8.40 a.m. St Asaph custodial suite

For the first time since she'd known her, Janice Stevens looked more than a little unkempt. Her usually immaculate hair was uncombed and her linen shift dress had more in common with a scrunched-up chip wrapper than the designer label embroidered on the pocket. But a night in the cells did that to people. It stripped them of all the modern essentials like their mobile along with their dignity before thrusting them into a barren room with a bed that was bolted to the floor, a mattress covered in thick, vomit-proof plastic and a metal toilet fixed in the corner. She'd have been offered a sketchy breakfast along with a whole night in which to think up answers to the questions currently marching around Gaby's head like soldiers on parade.

Walking into the interview room, Gaby had been puzzling over who Mrs Stevens would have chosen to represent her. As a lawyer, she'd know all the tricks but also the importance of someone on her side for the emotional as well as the legal support. The man standing to shake her hand was a shock and Gaby was hard-pressed to prepare a thin smile as she reached out to take his fingers in the briefest of clasps. After dumping Marie and moving his secretary into the family home, Ivo Morgan was one of the least welcome of people at the station and Gaby regretted with a sudden flare of annoyance who she'd chosen to accompany her. But with Marie following just seconds behind, there was very little she could do apart from hope that both parties would have the sense to bury their differences under a cloak of professionalism. She didn't have to worry.

'Ma'am, there's clearly going to be a conflict of interest if I stay,' Marie said, as soon as she entered, staring across at Gaby to the exclusion of the other people in the room. 'I'll get PC Carbone to take my place.' She pulled out her mobile and made for the door, only to stop at the sound of Ivo's voice.

'I'd like the opportunity to speak to you after the interview, if I may?'

Instead of offering a reply, Marie continued walking, her back ironing-board straight, which had Gaby's palms itching to break into a round of applause. She glanced across at Ivo's flushed cheeks, keeping her own expression devoid of emotion as she turned back to Janice.

'A little blip in the proceedings but PC Carbone will be down in a minute. While we're waiting, please can you confirm that you were read your rights yesterday and that your name is Janice Stevens? We will, of course, be recording the interview.' She reached out a hand, flicked on the switch of the wall-mounted microphone and spoke briefly into the receiver.

'Yes. Yes, of course you will,' Janice responded, her voice devoid of emotion.

It didn't take long for Diane to come rushing into the room and slip into the empty chair, her chest heaving at the effort to run down from the floor above.

'Right then, now that PC Carbone has joined us, please can you tell us your movements of yesterday and your explanation for the copious amounts of fresh blood found in your bathroom?'

Gaby didn't have time to spare on conversational niceties and, with a woman like Janice Stevens, she knew that pussyfooting around was the wrong way to go. By the pull of her brow, she could see that she'd struck a chord. All she had to do was ...

'Can I interject?' Ivo said, regaining some of the aplomb he was well known for.

'It seems like you just have, Mr Morgan.'

'How can you confirm that it is Elodie Fry's blood? Surely it takes a lot longer for DNA testing or is there some advancement in the field of forensic science that I'm not aware of?'

'Elodie Fry's blood, Mr Morgan? I don't remember labelling it in that fashion unless you know something that I don't?' She raised a finely arched brow, noting the sheen of moisture on his forehead with quiet satisfaction. 'Rest assured that as soon as the results are back you will be the first one to know. Is that all or can I continue questioning my witness?' Gaby waited a moment, her habitual bland expression hiding her dislike of the two-timing smarmy git. 'Mrs Stevens, do you have another explanation and, if so, what is it?'

'No.'

'For the record Mrs Stevens is confirming that she has no knowledge as to how blood was spilled on her bathroom floor,' Gaby said, her gaze meeting Janice's head on as she emphasised the point before abruptly changing the subject. 'What about your children? I believe you have three?'

'But only Jacob and Caleb are at home. As far as I'm aware, they haven't been into my bathroom recently – they wouldn't need to. They have a perfectly serviceable one of their own and if they'd had a nosebleed, or injured themselves, there's no way that they wouldn't have told me.'

'And what about your older son, Ronan?'

'Detective, do we really need to go through all this? You've already interviewed my client. She informed you then that her son is no longer a part of her household,' Ivo said on a long sigh, folding his arms across his chest, his diamond-studded cuff links peeking out from the sleeve of his navy pinstriped suit.

'Are you conducting this interview or me, Mr Morgan?' Instead of waiting for a response, she sat back and concentrated on Janice and the two bright patches of colour spotting her cheeks at her line of questioning.

'My son left home two months ago, Detective,' Janice said, her voice a hollow sound. 'As far as I'm aware, he's living rough in Llandudno. Reverend Honeybun is keeping an eye on him for me. It's been a difficult few months for us all, but particularly for my son who was very close to his father. But all that doesn't change the fact that I can't believe he would have kidnapped the girl and then murdered her in my en suite. What kind of a family do you think we are?'

'Can you tell me your movements since yesterday morning, from let's say 6 a.m.?'

Gaby decided to change her line of questioning simply because she knew that she wasn't getting anywhere. Part of her felt desperately sorry for Janice Stevens but sympathy wouldn't help her find the missing girl or explain the blood in her bathroom.

'Certainly. I was in bed until seven, which is when I normally get up to grab a quick shower. Getting up early is the only way I can have five minutes' peace,' she said, lifting a hand to her hair and brushing her fringe back off her forehead. 'After waking the boys, I made breakfast and pottered with lunchboxes and what have you while I encouraged them to hurry up. If we don't leave the house by eight at the latest, the traffic along the A470 is bumper to bumper and they'll be late.'

'Where were you taking them?'

'The sports centre, near Llanrwst. They run a summer school – anything to keep them off their computers for a few hours.'

Gaby made a quick note of the name on her phone. 'And what happened next? You dropped off the boys at …?'

'Eight-thirtyish after which I went to work, where I stayed all day. I even ended up having a sandwich at my desk. It was one of those days.'

'Yes. We have them here too, all the time,' Gaby said, managing a brief smile of understanding. 'And you can confirm all this?'

'Absolutely. The sports centre can with regards to the drop-off and pick-up of the boys and my PA at work can too. There'll also be computer records with regards to the hours I spent updating client files and the like.'

Gaby flicked a quick look across at Diane, who gave a little shake of her head in reply. There were no further questions to ask and no reason that she could think of to hold her any longer, not until they got the DNA back on the blood.

'I'll need to confirm everything you've told me then we should be able to release you.'

'Surely as Mrs Stevens is a respected member of the lawyer fraternity we can waive—'

'No, Mr Morgan. We can't and you should know better than to ask. Might I remind you that there is still the blood in the bathroom that hasn't been adequately explained in addition to a little girl missing, not to mention the unavailability of Ronan Stevens for questioning.' She turned back to Janice. 'If you could leave your full contact details with PC Carbone please – once we've confirmed everything with the respective parties, you'll be free to go. This interview is terminated at …' But before she could finish she felt a slight tug on her arm and, tilting her head, she glanced down at where Diane had scribbled something on the top of her pad.

'Okay, there is just one further question that my colleague has reminded me of,' Gaby said, her tone hiding the sudden excitement building. 'Did your son have a key to your property or, like ninety-nine per cent of the population, is it routine for you to leave a spare hidden in your garden for emergencies?'

She watched the colour fade from Janice's cheeks. 'He left his on his desk, along with a note, when he went. There's also a spare key hidden outside. I can't remember the last time we had to use it.'

'Right, thank you. It's something we'll follow up with you on your release.' Gaby finished the interview and depressed the microphone switch. 'Police Constable Carbone will accompany you to the cell. It shouldn't take more than a few minutes to check out your alibi. I take it you'll be heading back to the office in case we have any further questions?'

'Immediately after I've changed out of this lot,' she said, curling her lip at the state of her dress.

Gaby nodded, turning to the door.

'Detective Darin.'

She paused, one hand clutching on to her mobile, the other resting on her hip, her mouth barely registering a smile. 'Yes, Mr Morgan?'

'I'd like to have a quick word with my wife?'

I'll just bet you would! 'Well, as you can see, we're a little busy right now. All I can promise is that I'll pass on your message. Now, if you'll excuse me.'

Chapter 36

Owen

Tuesday 4 August, 8.50 a.m. St Asaph

Owen had started to run through the tasks planned for the day with Diane, only to have her whisked out from under his nose and a very unhappy Marie Morgan take her place. It didn't take her long to explain why, her speech interspersed with a couple of loud sniffs.

'I'm sorry, Owen, but I couldn't sit and face him.'

'No, of course not and no one would expect you to.' He pushed to his feet and grabbed his suit jacket from behind his chair. 'Come on. It's probably a good idea for us to get away from the office in case that erstwhile husband of yours decides that he can accost you at work. Diane and I have already arranged to meet up with Barbara Matthews' bosom pals over at her house to see if they can add anything now that the CSIs have finished with the property.' He picked up his pen and wrote a quick couple of lines on a Post-it Note. 'I'll leave this with the desk sergeant on the way out to let Diane know that I'll be working with you for the remainder of the shift. There's no point in swapping back halfway.'

Owen hated the complexities of people management, which was the main reason why he'd never decided to go further than detective constable, despite his crime-solving skills and excellent memory, which were a huge bonus to any team. He viewed himself as a backroom detective, quite happy to stay in the shadows and have the limelight diverted to those who relished the attention. The likes of CS Winters and DCI Sherlock were more than happy to leave him to it. It was only Gaby who was determined to see him shoot up the ladder, just as much as he was determined to stay glued to his current rung.

Having Marie along while he visited Barbara Matthews' home was his way out of a potentially awkward situation. With those three old biddies present, there would be very little opportunity for Marie to discuss anything that wasn't work-related – unlike the last time they were in the office together, he remembered. A win all round as far as he was concerned.

Owen found himself struggling not to laugh at the way Mildred Pennyworth and her friend Iris Farnsworth immediately accosted him at the front door, both vying for his attention and very much ignoring Doreen Frost, who had taken a step back and was clearly distressed at the whole situation. Once inside, it was Doreen who sat on the chair nearest to the door, her hands neatly folded in her lap, apparently quite happy for Mildred and Iris to take the lead. With her bright twinkling eyes and calm demeanour, Owen had already pegged Doreen as the more observant of the group. The other two would have been too busy asserting themselves to take much notice of anything else. He might be proved wrong but he very much doubted it.

With Marie taking notes, he led them through the lounge and across into the study while they argued between themselves as to what might be missing, Doreen trailing behind.

'There was a Georgian silver teapot,' Mildred said, 'and a collection of Royal Doulton Toby jugs. Three I think.'

175

'Edwardian, dear, and actually seven jugs,' Doreen interrupted in her quiet voice. 'Don't you remember her telling us that it was Henry VIII and his *six* wives?' She tilted her head towards Marie, a gentle smile holding a glimmer of the beautiful girl she'd once been. 'Barbara's father used to be a collector, you know. There were also some miniatures that she used to keep in that drawer over there.' She pointed to an apple wood desk with ornate brass handles. 'She rarely took them out as she hated the idea of paying her cleaner extra to dust them.'

'There's no sign of them now,' Marie said with a shake of her head as she stared down at the empty space.

'She employed a cleaner, did she?' Owen's brows knit together, trying to join the dots. If Ellie Fry's mother was Barbara Matthews' cleaner ...? He shook his head, unable to arrange them into a workable pattern.

'Two hours a week, rain, hail or shine,' Mildred said, darting a look of dislike at Doreen, presumably at the temerity of her hogging the conversation. 'Actually, that's a point.' She frowned. 'Someone's going to have to tell her to stop coming.'

'That's easily done. She's bound to have her details in that little red Radley address book she always kept in her handbag.' Doreen met Owen's gaze. 'She had a thing about Radley handbags.'

'So, basically what you're all saying,' Marie said, tapping away on her handheld, 'is that, in addition to Mrs Matthews' disappearance, there's an eclectic mix of potentially valuable antiques missing that no one, apart from her close friends, would necessarily have noticed unless they'd been itemised individually on her contents insurance?' She waved her hand towards the large, flat-screen TV and the top-of-the-range sound system.

'That's about it and as she didn't have any family, no one but us would have noticed,' Mildred said, rejoining the conversation, her narrow eyes sparkling but without a glimmer of compassion or kindness in their depths.

Owen ran his hand across his beard, disgusted with both her

behaviour and how he was letting her get to him, but he only had himself to blame. No. His hand paused as he remembered that it had been originally Diane's idea. If he hadn't worked with her earlier, he'd never have had the insight to arrange to meet up with the trio of supposed best friends.

'While you're here, can you tell me a little more about your friend so that we can get a better picture of the type of person she is? Is it correct that she used to run a shop in Llandudno?'

'Yes. Indeed. Bonbons, one of those old-fashioned sweetshops with everything stored away in those huge glass jars. It was situated next to *Marie et Cie*, which has also long since gone, more's the pity – used to buy all my children's clothes there,' Mildred said, again taking hold of the reins of the conversation and running with them. 'I don't know how she used to cope with all those horrible, sticky children fingering the shelves.'

'Actually I was born and bred in Llandudno,' Owen said, his brief smile confined to his lips. 'I remember it well. I used to be one of those – how did you put it – horrible, sticky children? Although now I come to think of it, I don't remember a woman … there was an old gent. Always wore the same blue bow tie?'

'That would have been her father. She only ran it for a short while following his death,' Doreen said, feasting her eyes on the blush staining Mildred's cheeks an unflattering cherry-red. 'Barbara wasn't really shop-owner material. She couldn't keep staff to save her life.'

'Why was that?'

'People have different expectations, Detective. I, for instance, expect very little from people and therefore am rarely disappointed,' she replied, her attention flickering between her two friends sitting opposite. 'However, Barbara is cut from a completely different cloth. She always has an opinion about everything and has no difficulty in sharing those sentiments, no matter how hurtful they are. While I'm sad she's missing, I'm not totally surprised that you're as concerned about her whereabouts as we are. Perhaps she said the wrong thing to the wrong person once too often?'

Chapter 37

Gaby

Tuesday 4 August, 10 a.m. The Vicarage, Llandudno

The last time Gaby had been anywhere near a church was when she'd been investigating the disappearance of Alys Grant – not her finest hour by any means and as memories went, one she preferred to tuck away in the back of her mind to never see the cold light of day again.

The manse was a tall, narrow building tucked down a side street. From the outside, it appeared to be a well-maintained Victorian property with a large garden bound by a groundsman-perfect lawn and a tidy hedge clipped to within an inch of its life. The forest-green door was opened by a well-rounded blonde with dark roots striving for freedom and a taste in shoes that would do any stilt-walker proud.

'Can I help you?'

Gaby quickly made introductions. 'We're here to see Reverend Albert Honeybun, if he has a minute?'

'Of course – I'm Mrs Honeybun.' She stretched out a hand, her grip firm, her fingernails talon long and fuchsia pink. 'Come this way,' she said, gesturing for them to follow down a long, dark hallway. The walls were panelled with wood and with a tiled floor in bold cream and red alternating squares that should have felt out of place but didn't. 'He's tinkering away in the study, keeping out from under my feet.'

Gaby managed to catch Diane's eye, her twitching lips reflecting her thoughts. If this was the wife, what would the husband be like?

Reverend Honeybun was nothing like his wife. For a start he was short and round with a head of wispy grey hair that looked as if it hadn't seen a brush let alone a hairdresser in months. But his kindly grey eyes and bellowing laugh, as he spoke to his wife, told Gaby more than any words coming out of his mouth that here was a man she could trust.

Gaby took in the book-lined study in one encompassing glance. The faded chintz furnishings and general air of impoverished gentility. The collection of pottery running the length of the mantelpiece, which included a fine display of lustreware teapots, the copper glaze reflecting the sunlight streaming through the mullioned windows. Unlike most of the homes she visited, it was a room she felt comfortable in. Her only query was that it didn't seem to fit in with Mrs Honeybun's glamorous persona, but who was she to judge, she thought, her mind swinging briefly to the state of her lounge and the two still-unopened cans of paint.

'Come in and take a seat. Tea, my love, and a few of those little Battenburg cakes, if it's not too much trouble. There's nothing like a little cake to help with sermon writing.' He patted his stomach, which hung over the belt of his dark brown trousers. 'Now, how can I be of help, officers?' he said, waiting a moment until the door had clicked closed behind his wife's retreating back.

'We're concerned as to the whereabouts of Ronan Stevens. Anything that you can tell us would be helpful.'

The happy-go-lucky, jovial face altered, the smile now a frown as muscles tightened to redistribute his features. 'Ah yes. There's a complex, troubled young man if ever there was one. The sins of the past lie heavily on his young shoulders.' He ran his hand over his neck, his speech paused at the sound of a trolley squeaking along the tiles outside the door. He only resumed the conversation when his wife had left the room for a second time after distributing an array of china. 'So, what exactly would you like to know?'

'Anything obvious that you can tell us.'

'There's not a lot. He came to me. No. That's not quite right,' he said, his frown deepening. 'I was in the Victorian Arcade, let me see now, it must have been about six weeks ago, when I saw this tall gangly lad sitting on one of the benches and I knew he was in trouble.' He raised his head, a muscle in his right cheek starting to twitch. 'It didn't take me long to realise how much.' He took a quick sip of his tea before clattering his cup back in the saucer, his fat fingers struggling with the dainty handle. 'There's always something about the eyes ... They aren't called the windows to the soul for nothing. His were dead, glazed over with the same stigma we find in kids who've seen far too much in their young lives. He couldn't have tried to save himself even if he'd wanted to.

'It was around about the same time that his mother came to see me – the work I do with society's less fortunates is common knowledge in the local community. I agreed to watch out for him and within days had put him to work in the garden. The church is surrounded on all sides and digging and the like is not my forte, shall we say,' he said, choosing a second cake and managing to pop it into his mouth whole with barely a pause in the conversation. 'I had thought that we were winning. The shell, once broken, is a fragile thing and so it was with Ronan. The general hubbub of church life was causing a hairline fracture through his emotions, the real Ronan seeping out through the cracks.'

'And what is he like?' Gaby asked, eyeing him over the rim of her bone china teacup, liking this unassuming man more and more and again wondering where he'd found such a wife.

'I'd say genuine and honest. Always keen to help and nice to be

180

around. Very quiet though, quiet and deep. There's a huge amount going on in that mind of his that rarely makes the surface.' He leant back in his chair, his cup now back on the tray, his hands neatly folded across his belly. 'Such a waste of a life but I did think that he was starting to get back on track, but it appears that that's not the case?'

Gaby was tempted to confide at least part of her concerns but something held her back; she had no idea what. It wasn't as if he'd break her confidence and they needed all the help they could get.

Instead of answering his implied question, she decided to ask one of her own. 'So, you have no idea where he might be? We need to speak to him urgently.'

'And he would know this, would he?'

Gaby met Diane's gaze as they both shared the same thought.

'As you say, he's an intelligent lad so, yes, he'd know.'

'Then I think you're in a lot of trouble because it's highly unlikely you'll find him until the time comes when he wants to be found.'

Chapter 38

Gaby

Tuesday 4 August, 11 a.m. St Asaph Police Station

Gaby and DCI Henry Sherlock had what could be termed a satisfactory relationship. He told her what to do and mostly she did it. They only fell out when she went *off piste* and, to be truthful, after the last occasion when she'd ended up in hospital attached to life support, she was trying to benefit from his wisdom and learn from her mistakes. Impulsivity in police work often ended with unexpected consequences, which she was reminded about each time her side ached as the wound in her left side continued to heal.

Being summoned to her boss's office was all she needed. But with her job application form in his inbox, in addition to three major investigations on the table, she couldn't really blame him.

'Take a seat and tell me how you're getting on with the search.'

Gaby lowered herself into the chair positioned directly in front of his desk, trying to marshal her thoughts as she pulled her jacket across her chest and linked her hands in her lap. There was a thing or two she'd like to ask him in return – like how Bill Davis's interview had gone. She'd seen him exiting the building in a brand-new suit and carefully arranged smile, which had the desired negative effect on her mood. But she was intelligent enough to appreciate that it was all for show. It wasn't in Sherlock's nature to make snap decisions. She was also wise enough to realise that if he did decide to appoint Davis, he'd only have himself to blame. The fallout on the team would be as immediate as it would be disastrous.

'Not as well as we would have hoped at this stage, thirty hours or so since her disappearance,' she finally said, managing a fleeting smile. 'Thoughts are that she's attached herself to Ronan Stevens, the son of Casper.' She leant forward, focusing briefly on his wire-framed spectacles, which were in their usual position on top of his forehead, before dropping her gaze to meet his. 'It's not something the press have managed to get hold of yet but, as we both know, it won't be long until somebody spills the beans and all hell breaks loose.'

DCI Sherlock rested his elbows on the desk and, steepling his fingers, propped his chin on the tips. 'Now, tell me some good news.'

There isn't any! But all she said was, 'We took Janice Stevens into custody because of blood found in her bathroom but we're going to have to release her if her alibi checks out and there's nothing to suppose that it won't. The facts all agree that, if Ronan took Ellie, there wasn't time for his mother to assist him. But she could still have helped him cover up his tracks following Ellie's disappearance. The blood is the most important thing. I've asked the CSIs to rush through the DNA analysis but until we can confirm or not that it belongs to Ellie Fry, there's not a lot we can do with the information.'

She paused to take a long breath. 'There's been no further sightings of Ronan Stevens and no suggestion as to where he would have taken Ellie, if indeed he has. But we've broadened the search with this in mind.' She lifted a hand up to tuck a stray curl back behind her ear. 'There's also the disappearance of

Barbara Matthews, sir, and a possible link with the disappearance of Katherine Jane. Bates is taking the lead.'

'Hmm. I received your application form earlier, Darin,' he said after a brief pause, shifting the conversation along with his glasses, which he dropped onto his nose. 'Cutting it a little fine, weren't we?'

'I wasn't sure if I had the necessary experience, sir.'

'What? Thirteen years isn't long enough? How much experience do you need?'

She refrained from answering, determined not to say anything she might regret. She had the makings of a good life, and one wrong move would end it in an instant.

'Okay. I can see you've taken an oath of silence,' he said, his eyes glinting. 'CS Winters has rearranged his calendar accordingly so back here in the office at five for your interview.'

'But—'

'No buts, Darin. We're already getting pressure from HR because of extending the submission date. The new DI will be announced 10 a.m. tomorrow morning whether we interview you or not. If you can't manage your workload then you're certainly not up to managing the team on a more formal footing.'

Back in the incident room, a coffee by her elbow, Gaby almost dropped her head into her hands in frustration at Sherlock's intransigent behaviour. He didn't seem to understand her workload, either that or he was unprepared to make allowances. But whatever the reason for his stance, she was far too busy to spend time thinking about it. The case had taken on a life of its own. It had so many loops and twists that she was struggling to stay focused. She recollected a conversation she'd had with one of her previous bosses about woods and trees but the forest was thick and the branches and foliage obstructed her view.

Her phone pinged and the first proper smile of the day touched her lips at the sight of Rusty's name filling the screen and the little x that ended the message. The thought of Conor having a sleepover and Rusty's plans to cook her tea around at his place broadened her smile into a grin until she remembered how unlikely it was that she'd be finished anywhere near the usual time afforded people in nine-to-five jobs.

With a quick tap of her fingers, she typed out a reply, which wasn't really a reply at all. *Busy. I'd love to but will phone you later.* Her finger hovered over the x briefly. It was a shift forward in their relationship and one he'd decided to initiate ... She depressed the key and hit send, her smile lingering as she returned her phone to the desk.

'Ma'am, can I have a word?'

She looked up as Diane made her way across the room.

'Certainly, take a seat.'

But Diane shook her head.

'It won't take long. I've been checking Janice Stevens's alibi and it doesn't quite pan out. She dropped the boys off at the sports centre just like she said at 8.30 but she didn't get into work until 9.15. I was speaking to her secretary and that's a good twenty minutes later than usual. Apparently she gave the excuse of a road accident along the A470. The thing is, I've checked with the traffic police and there was no such accident.'

'Silly woman thinking that we wouldn't spot that.' Gaby sat back in her chair, crossing one leg over the other, her fingers tapping a tattoo against the top of her thigh. 'So, what could Janice Stevens have been doing in those twenty minutes is the question – it's something I'm pretty sure she won't want to answer. Mmm.' She lifted her head from where she'd been studying her unvarnished fingernails. 'Where does she work again?'

'Gallard and Smithson of Deganwy.'

'Which is about seven minutes, give or take, from Llandudno. So she could have easily returned home to perhaps check she'd switched off the iron or to meet up with her desperate son and hide a body.'

'What would you like me to do?'

Gaby reached for her pen, swivelling it through her fingers a moment only to set it aside.

'What would you do, Diane?'

'What would I do?' she repeated, her jaw dropping slightly.

'Yes, you. We have two choices. Either trust it's nothing or question her again in the certainty that, if she's lied by omission once, it's likely she'll lie a second time, and bearing in mind that, as a lawyer, she'll know all the tricks of her trade.'

'Then there's little point in keeping her, is there? Statistically it's unlikely that she's involved in Ellie's disappearance. She wasn't spotted in any of the CCTV footage,' she added, qualifying her words. 'However, it is possible that her son contacted her and that she is involved now. I think we should release her but try and keep an eye on her movements.'

'A well-thought-out and reasoned argument. Right then, we'll let her go but alert our colleagues in blue to keep tabs on her.'

Chapter 39

Marie

Tuesday 4 August, 11.30 a.m. St Asaph Police Station

With a huge effort, which had more to do with her length of time as a serving police officer than any willingness to work after the shock of seeing Ivo, Marie forced herself to concentrate while she logged back in to her laptop. She had an ordered mind and liked nothing better than trying to solve a puzzle. Detecting was all about the discovery and manipulation of information. But to fit the pieces of the puzzle into the right place, she first needed to find out as much as she could about Ellie and the people around her. It was that or sit and mope and she'd spent far too long moping already.

She had yet to complete the background checks on Ellie's home life. Top of the list was a copy of her birth certificate, with the father's name left blank, something that they'd suspected but it still had to be confirmed. That didn't mean she wouldn't continue searching. The absence of the father's name could mean one of a few things. Ellie's mother might not have known who he was or she might not have wanted him to know about the child. There

187

was even the possibility that her conception had been via a sperm donor – nothing surprised Marie anymore.

Pausing to make a brief note on her A4 pad, she returned her attention to the mother and quickly confirmed that she was telling the truth about her single status. Anita didn't appear on their system apart from the odd parking ticket, which she'd paid within the recommended period. There was nothing to suggest that she was anything other than a hard-working mother trying to make ends meet. Moving on to the housing records, Marie discovered that Anita had arrived at the estate within weeks of the birth of her daughter and always paid her rent on time, which was all very well but didn't add anything to the reason why her daughter might have decided to up and run away.

After making another note on her pad, Marie rolled her shoulders, her attention shifting to Malachy as he flicked through a computer printout. So far his behaviour had been exemplary. To put her up, when she'd walked out of the marital home with only a couple of suitcases, was more than she'd ever expected from a fellow officer. At the start, she'd been reluctant to take him up on the offer, prey as she was to the very worst of thoughts as to his motives. While a good five years older, she only had to peer in the mirror to remind herself that she was still attractive despite the new lines that bracketed her eyes and pulled at her lips. But she needn't have worried. In fact, she was astounded at how well they got on. Apart from sharing the cooking, he kept very much to himself as did she, which was hardly surprising when funds were an issue until the end of the month when hopefully she'd have enough to manage on.

Staring back down at the list, she remembered that there had been something he'd wanted her to do for him with regards to keeping his mother off his back but, as he hadn't mentioned it in over a week, she'd conveniently forgotten about it.

'Do you want a top-up?'

She glanced up to find him pushing away from his desk and

stretching to his full height, his pale pink shirt stretched across his impressive array of muscles. Marie had always had an aversion to men wearing pink but he was rapidly changing her mind on the subject. Averting her gaze, she held up her mug with an outstretched hand.

'If there's any hot chocolate in the machine, please?'

He raised his eyebrows but instead of commenting strode out of the room. He was back within minutes, a couple of cups clutched in his hands, which he deposited on her desk before pulling up a chair.

'You all right? The desk sergeant's just told me that the delightful Ivo is downstairs in reception.'

'What! I thought he'd have left by now?'

'Nope. Not a bit of it. Clancy says he's glued to his seat for what looks like the duration.'

Marie managed to suppress a groan at the mention of her soon-to-be ex-husband – the one thing she'd been determined not to think about until she reached the privacy of her bedroom. She could just about cope with him moving his girlfriend, along with her couple of kids, into what was their home. What she couldn't cope with was him then deciding that he didn't want a family after all. He'd been hounding her to come back to him after just about throwing her out on the streets with only the clothes she'd been wearing and the emergency fifty quid she always kept in the side of her phone case. If it hadn't been for the support of Malachy and the rest of the team she'd have flung herself under the nearest train. In truth, the only thing stopping her had been the extra work it would have caused the emergency services having to scrape her remains off the tracks.

The problem was she didn't want to weaken. After ten years together, the last five married, she still had strong feelings for the man. One look into his storm-grey eyes and she felt her knees weaken along with her willpower despite knowing that he was one of the biggest tosspots around. To empty their joint bank account was something that she could never forgive or forget. Okay so he earned a lot more than her but that was no reason to be small-minded about the break-up. What had he expected her to do? Move back in with her parents, which he must have known was the only route open to her?

'He's even brought his laptop with him so that he can carry on working. It's a wonder you didn't see him on your return?'

'I came in the side entrance,' she said, not wanting to admit that she'd been afraid he'd stick around after she'd walked out of the interview. No one ever got the better of Ivo.

She shut her eyes, dimly aware that Malachy had picked up her hands and wrapped them around her mug.

'Go on, take a sip. It will make you feel better.'

He was wrong. Nothing would make her feel better except having Ivo out of her life. She still loved him, despite everything, but she wasn't prepared to trust him. If he could throw her over for a bimbo with two brats, who's to say that he wouldn't kick her out again? It had taken her weeks to get back on her feet and it was only now that she was starting to feel in any way normal. But her confidence and self-esteem remained at rock bottom despite moving into Malachy's spare room. The fun-loving party girl she'd once been seemed a thing of the past. What was worse than having your hopes trampled on by the person who was meant to love you the most? Nothing!

Washing down the bitter taste of regret with a swig of extra sweet chocolate, she managed to swallow back the tears starting to gather.

'Thank you. What did I do to deserve such a nice flatmate?'

He didn't answer. Instead he propped his hip against the desk and proceeded to change the subject.

'So, what are you up to?'

She tapped the next item on her list with her index finger, pleased that he'd turned the conversation back to the case. It was probably the threat of tears that had done it but, whatever the reason, she heaved a sighing breath of relief. She'd never found it easy to discuss her personal problems. Work was what she needed in order to keep her mind from wandering back to the one problem she couldn't solve.

'I'm about to phone St Gildas school to see if anyone remembers Miss Jane. It's likely she used to live in – that's the way it is with boarding schools. I'm hoping someone remembers if she had any trinkets that maybe we could get traced. All we need is the serial number, from a bicycle or similar, to break the case wide open.'

'Wouldn't it be better to head out that way with the original photos of her apartment taken after her disappearance?' he said after a moment. 'Seeing pictures is a sure-fire way of flexing someone's memory muscle.'

'Now that's a brilliant idea.' She managed a smile, which didn't make it as far as her eyes. 'Why didn't I think of that?'

'Because you're not me.'

'Ha, very funny.'

She threw him a fake punch at his arm, feeling tons better at the resumption of their usual banter. Malachy was a complex individual but they'd settled into an easy groove, which had nothing to do with sex and everything to do with friendship. She'd always thought that a platonic relationship wasn't possible between a man and a woman – she was pleased to find out that she was being proved wrong.

He leant forward, tweaking her ponytail in the same way a sibling might. 'Clancy and I have come up with a plan to smuggle you out from right under Ivo's nose, if you'd like to hear it?'

Marie grimaced at the abrupt return to the previous topic of conversation. She should have realised that he wasn't finished with trying to sort out her life. While she appreciated his thoughtfulness, it was about time she took ownership of her problems and stood up to her ex.

'You're both darlings but I need to sort this out, once and for

191

all. He's not going to go away otherwise. But thank you anyway.' She picked up her pen and clicked the end. 'So, how are you getting on?'

'Nearly finished. A few loose ends to tie up but I'm going to meet Amy around at Ellie's mother's shortly to fill in the gaps. There's only so much that can be done over the phone.' He stood, his long fingers hooked around his belt, a trace of his trademark, supercilious behaviour resurfacing. 'What hard and boring lives people lead. Ms Fry spends most of her life cleaning up other people's crap and the rest ferrying her daughter to and from ballet lessons, presumably while she sits in the car twiddling her thumbs.'

'But that doesn't mean she's unhappy, does it, Mal? We can't all be rocket scientists or brain surgeons. She knows how much money she has to live on and arranges her activities accordingly. That's more sensible than tragic. By all accounts, apart from the problems at school, Ellie's home life has been full of love and laughter. That's surely more important to a child than a pile of money?'

'Mmm.' He frowned. 'I'm struggling with that, Marie. If everything was so hunky-dory, why the need to run away?'

'Why indeed.'

'There is one thing though that may be of interest to Darin.'

'Go on then.' Marie placed her empty cup down beside her keyboard.

'I've been working through her list of cleaning jobs. Mostly local and within a five- or ten-minute car drive radius. You'll never guess who's on the list.'

Chapter 40

Ronan

Tuesday 4 August, 11.30 a.m. Caernarfon

Ronan always knew that he wasn't the most patient of individuals.
He wouldn't go so far as to call himself selfish although that was
a term that had been bandied about in the past by others when
discussing him, both to his face and, more than likely, behind his
back. He'd preferred the expression single-minded: someone who
didn't suffer fools. But whatever the term used to define him, he
was finding it increasingly difficult to keep ten-year-old Ellie Fry
entertained within the confines of the farmhouse.

He would have been quite happy grabbing a book from one
of the boxes piled up by the back door awaiting collection by
some charity or other. His grandfather had been a doctor and
had an eclectic collection of nonfiction that encompassed most
of the sciences. But Ellie wasn't having any of it. He'd tried to
interest her in the small pile of toys left over from their visits
but nothing appealed. In desperation, he took her into the hall
and, pulling down the loft ladder, followed her into the dark
and dusty attic, the musty stale air causing his nose to wrinkle

and his eyes to stream. It used to be his favourite place on rainy days. Now he could hardly bear to think about those happier times, let alone find the energy to follow her as she bounded up the vertical rungs.

There was a light, only a forty-watt bulb, hanging from an element in the middle of the ceiling but he left it switched off, instead choosing to use the narrow beam from his torch.

'Make sure you're careful where you put your feet,' he said, repeating the same mantra his grandfather had first told him all those years ago, his throat constricting at the thought.

'We do have an attic, you know.'

'Really? I should have remembered. After all, you have told me *all* about your home and the reason why you ran away,' he said, unable to keep the sarcasm from his voice.

But instead of replying, she turned to the largest of the tea chests and started to drag out random items of clothing, spraying dust particles into the thin band of light. In exasperation, he propped a hand against one of the roof supports and continued to watch as she tried on an old felt beret with a badge on the front.

'Very fetching. Why not try on the feather boa to match?'

'Feather what?'

'That long pink thing you're holding made of feathers! It used to belong to some aunt. I can't really remember her,' he said, his voice fading because now there would be no one to remind him of who she'd been, no one to pass on the memory. His mother had never been interested in that sort of stuff and his father had always had too many other things to do. It was only his grandfather who'd had the patience to share his stories: bright sparkling stories of intrigue and espionage that he must have embellished for little boys' eager ears. He clenched his fingers around the wood, the feel of the raw timber biting grooves into his soft skin a welcome diversion from where his mind was leading him.

'You're lucky having all this. Apart from my mum and me there's no one.'

'Believe me, you'll soon learn that the only one that you can rely on is yourself.'

'That's not very nice.'

'You think so? I would have thought that it's something you'd have realised already, having run away from home like you did.'

'That was different.' She replaced the feather boa, running her hand through the silky texture, a look of deep regret on her innocent face. 'I didn't have a choice because they would have ...' She shook her head, her bottom lip quivering under the weight of her thoughts.

'They would have what, Ellie?' he prompted gently. 'You can trust me, right? And who am I going to tell anyway?'

The colour leeched from her skin, turning it the colour of alabaster, her bright blue eyes almost hidden by the black pools of her pupils. If she had been one of his brothers, he'd have been tempted to draw her into a hug even though he wasn't that great with physical contact. But he didn't want to drive her away. He'd gained her trust and hopefully her confidence. One false move on his part and it would all come down like the houses of cards he'd used to spend his time perfecting in the quiet of his bedroom.

'They were staring at me. Those bloodshot eyes—' She blinked, a tear then two trembling on her lower lashes and dripping down her cheeks. 'I can't describe it. Please don't make me. If they ever find out ...'

'Ellie, you must. I know it's hard for you but I'm one of the good guys. Perhaps it isn't what you thought. You might even have made a mistake. I can't help unless you tell me.'

He watched her gulp, her throat working overtime, her fingers flexing and unflexing around the sides of the tea chest as if she suddenly didn't know what to do with them and, for the first time since waking, he regretted his decision to find out the truth. Not because of what it might do to her but, selfishly, of what it might mean to him and how he was going to handle it.

'There's a shed at the back of the house. I shouldn't have been there – Mum has always given me strict instructions – but I was bored and had nothing to do so I thought I'd see if I could find something to play with on one of the shelves. The key was in the lock so I––' She stretched out her hand, only to drop it like a hot brick at the sound of the front door slamming below followed by shoes slapping against the quarry-tiled floor.

They stared at each other, Ellie's horrified expression reflected in the widening of his gaze and the droop of his mouth as he banged his head gently against his hand.

He'd thought he'd been clever in taking her here, a place that no one wanted to remember. A house that his mother couldn't even give away at the current knockdown price. He'd been stupid or naive – most likely both. Someone knew and, with the person walking in their direction, they were completely trapped. There was nothing to defend themselves with apart from a pencil-thin torch and a pile of rags only fit for the bin.

'Quick, the ladder ...'

But it was too late. The noise had stopped along with what felt like his heart. He'd certainly stopped breathing. His fingers stretched to flick off the torch even as he pointed for Ellie to hide behind the tea chest. For all his careful planning someone must have either followed them or tracked them down. He couldn't imagine who or to what purpose. What next?

196

Chapter 41

Marie

Tuesday 4 August, 11.30 a.m. St Asaph Police Station

Marie searched in the bottom of her bag for her make-up and the tube of bright shimmering pink lip gloss that she rarely wore – certainly never to the office. With a slash of the brush, she coated her lips to maximum effect, taking an extra moment to fluff up her hair and straighten her jacket, her mind fixating on the need to make Ivo suffer for what he'd put her through. While she liked to look good, she rarely spent more than a couple of minutes getting ready in the morning. With an easy-to-manage haircut and a staple of coordinating separates hung in her wardrobe, she didn't need to. Now she thrust her shoulders back and rearranged her features into the semblance of a blinding smile. Ivo wouldn't know what had hit him.

'You wanted to see me?'

She didn't announce her arrival, instead tiptoeing across reception until she was standing right in front of him, her eyes travelling over his designer suit and conservative tie. Ivo, the man who'd begged her to date him in the early days of their acquaintance when she'd been too busy living it up with her friends to even think about a steady relationship. Ivo, the man she'd finally given her heart to only for him to mash it up along with any feelings of trust and respect. Marie could understand the devastation he'd felt at the thought of never being a parent – she felt the same devastation – but she would never be able to forgive him for the way he'd handled it.

Shoving his laptop on the chair beside him, Ivo jerked to his feet, his whole demeanour softening into the expression she knew of old, the same one he used for awkward clients. With that thought her heart hardened, the cracks merging into a consolidated mass of anger. The selfish bastard was in for a shock. The days were long gone when he'd been able to sway her with a pair of grey eyes and a fake smile. She knew him now, where before all she'd seen was what he'd wanted her to.

'Marie.' He lifted his arms, spreading them wide. 'What do I have to do to convince you of my mistake if coming to this place isn't enough? I'm all the fools rolled into one to think that another woman could ever give me what we had together. If you want me to crawl on bended knees …'

'Go on then.'

'What?' She watched his expression lose a little of its lawyerly patina, the hint of moisture above his top lip the only indication that being dressed in a three-piece suit wasn't the greatest of ideas with the temperature heading for the high seventies. Instead of focusing on his eyes – the most difficult part for her – she let her gaze drift to the knot on his Italian silk tie only to wonder if he'd worn it on purpose. Knowing him, probably. She'd bought it as part of last year's Christmas's gifts, the designer label costing her more than she'd wanted to spend. She'd thought him worth it; the biggest joke of all.

'If you'd like to go on bended knees there's nothing stopping you but I won't be around to pick up the pieces if you struggle to get back on your feet. You're not getting any younger, after all,' she added, allowing her attention to drift to his receding hairline. In the old days, the reality of which was less than two months ago, she'd never have dared refer to the state of his hair. Now she didn't care. He'd walked out on her within a week of finding out that the likelihood of them conceiving was an impossibility without medical intervention. At thirty-six, she could almost feel her eggs shrivelling at the thought of having to find another partner before it was too late. She wasn't stupid. It was already too late.

'You never used to be this hard.'

'No, well, perhaps that was part of the problem.' She shifted from one foot to the other, casting an overlong glance at her watch. 'I do have somewhere I need to be so, unless you have something to say – which isn't a repeat of asking me back – then I suggest you leave.'

'If only you'd see sense. It was a mistake all right, a stupid error of judgement.'

'And one you made with gusto, Ivo. You made your decision. Now you have to accept the consequences. I have. You'll be hearing from my lawyer. Sooner rather than later if you continue with this ridiculous behaviour.'

Marie was a snivelling mess by the time she reached the pool car that Gaby had kindly agreed to let her use, both in and outside of work. The only thing that helped to dry up her tears was the increasingly firm notion that Ivo was a complete arse – she was mad at herself for taking so long to realise it. By the time she'd arrived at St Gildas school in Beddgelert, she'd managed to swallow her tears over the bump of pain that had taken up permanent residence in the back of her throat. All that was left of the deluge was a slight pinkening around her eyes and nose, which could be easily explained away as a touch of hay fever to anyone who asked.

The imposing, gothic grey stone building came into view, the long sweeping drive bordered with hydrangeas in full bloom, their large balls of assorted mauves and blues bringing a glint to her eye for a completely different reason. She loved gardening. They'd had a little square of green behind their house where she'd spent most of her time planting and pruning. It was only the sight of the splendour in front of her that made her realise how much she missed it. Malachy's roof terrace was a sterile space with two designer chairs set around a wrought-iron table, a great bonus after a long day at work but hardly a replacement for the oasis she'd lost. It wouldn't take much to brighten it up. A planter or two and perhaps some winter-flowering pansies now that autumn was only around the corner. She'd discuss it with him as soon as she returned to the station and, if she had the nerve, she might pinch some hydrangea cuttings on her way back to the car.

The playground to the left was deserted as were the sports fields in the distance, hardly surprising as it was the height of the holidays. But schools like this never closed. Most of the teachers might be off enjoying their well-earned vacation but the headmaster lived on site as did the groundsman. She'd even learnt during her quick phone call that the clerical staff took it in turns to man the phones, working through the stream of paperwork that never seemed to reduce whatever the time of year.

Within minutes, she found herself sitting at an empty desk in the front office.

'Tell me again exactly what it is you need,' Mrs Newton said, her eyes sharp behind her tortoiseshell-framed glasses.

'It's a long shot really but a chat with anyone who would have known Katherine Jane prior to her retirement and move to Llandudno.'

'The old teacher who went missing last year? Poor soul. Well, not me for one. While I knew her, of course, we weren't by any means friendly. What exactly is it you want?'

'That's the problem.' Marie opened the envelope she'd been holding and, withdrawing some photos, handed them over. 'These were taken soon after her disappearance. Obviously we're aware that she worked at the school in the years up to her retirement. We were wondering if there were any of her friends still among the staff who would know if these images ring true as to the kind of possessions she'd have on display?'

'Isn't it a bit late to be asking?' she said, sitting back, her lips compressed. 'Surely …?'

'It's never too late to re-examine what happened. You may have read in the papers that it was a very unusual case? People of that age don't usually up and disappear into thin air like that. We're looking for closure.'

Mrs Newton picked up the first photo, studied it a moment and repeated the action with both the second and the third. 'Miss Jane was a bit of an oddity. As clever as you like, a Latin scholar with an Oxford degree, but a loner all the same who didn't tend to mix with the other teachers.' She glanced up briefly. 'And certainly not with the likes of the humble office staff. The students hated her *en masse* – not that she'd have bothered about that sort of thing. I think you'll be lucky to find any who would have been invited across to her flat except the students she used to take on privately to tutor up for their exams. There was a steady stream of those but, of course, as we don't keep records of any private arrangements between parents and teachers, that's not going to help you.' She returned to the first photograph, which featured the lounge and the wall-to-wall bookcases. 'As I said already, we weren't close but I did see the inside of her flat on one or two occasions when I had to gain access for the maintenance team.'

'And?'

'And I would have to say that she had a fine collection of silver frames, genuine at a guess. Also some crystal. Yes. I remember now, quite a nice collection.'

'What about jewellery?'

'I never saw her wear any, maybe a gold watch but I can't really remember and I don't think anyone else would.'

Marie stood, holding out a hand for the photos and returning them to the envelope.

'There is her leaving present, of course.'

'Her leaving present?'

'Yes, here. I happen to have one ready for the next presentation.' She pulled out the bottom drawer of her desk and removed a long slim box. 'These are quite a collector's item and nearly worth working at the school until retirement to get one.' She managed a laugh. 'I have a few years left until I get mine. Made especially by a firm in London.'

Marie focused on the gold pen, a flicker of interest flaring into a bright flame. 'What's that on the top?' she said, her fingernail pointing to the red and blue engraving.

'The college crest.'

Chapter 42

Ronan

Tuesday 4 August, 11.50 a.m. Caernarfon

'Mother, what the hell do you think you're doing here! You scared the sh—'

'Mind your language! You're not on the streets now, my boy. I could ask the very same thing about you and, believe me, I fully intend to.'

Peering down through the hole in the ceiling, Ronan felt as if he'd woken up from a nightmare. No. He hadn't woken up. The nightmare was still continuing just like his life. One big, long fucking nightmare with no end in sight.

He turned his head, suddenly remembering that it wasn't just the two of them. 'It's okay, Ellie. You can come out. There's no need to be scared, it's only my mum.'

Back in the kitchen with the kettle on – why adults always had to resort to hot drinks in times of crises was one step too far for his juvenile outlook – he asked the question that had been filling the gap in his mind.

'How did you find me?'

'I saw you yesterday morning in the *clos*. I knew then that something must be up but by the time I returned, after dropping the boys off, you'd disappeared. It didn't take me long to discover that the key to the farmhouse was missing out of the top drawer in your fa— in the office.'

She couldn't even mention his name now. That's what hurt the most. The man his father had been, wiped out of the memory banks. And Ronan's main problem? He couldn't forget.

Ronan didn't reply; he couldn't. Instead he sat in front of his unwanted drink and waited for her to continue. There was too much history between them. Now he wasn't sure if he knew how to put it right. Ellie remained silent by his side, her blank expression telling nothing of what she was thinking. She was his priority. If he could only discover why she'd run away, he might be able to protect her from whatever it was that had caused her to flee. He'd been so near to finding out the truth …

'So, I take it there's a reason why you've abducted a child, is there, Ronan? Because I'd very much like to know what it is.' His mother placed her empty mug back on the table, her elbows resting on the surface, her linen dress pulling at the shoulders. She had a wardrobe full of the things and rarely wore anything else unless she was either cleaning the bathroom or prepared for bed. He hated them nearly as much as he hated her hairstyle, the memory of how it had used to flow down her back something he'd relegated to the cupboard in his head with a *do not enter* sign firmly in place. Any more skeletons and he'd have to get planning permission for an extension, he mused, his expression as grim as his thoughts.

'You do know that there's an APB out for her, don't you, Ronan? The whole of the UK police are on high alert – she was even the top news item this morning on the BBC. There is no way that someone didn't see something.'

'She has a name, you know, Mother. Ellie. Ellie Fry.' He risked another quick glance at his mum, not that it would tell him anything. She was the master of containment. Nothing ever got past her set features and composed lips. The only time it had was the day his life had come tumbling down – the day they'd picked him up from St Gildas following his expulsion. He'd never forget her expression of disappointment; it was what he thought about last thing at night before sleep claimed him. That and … other things. Shifting his head, he stared across at Ellie. He couldn't tell much from her averted face. All that was visible was her ear and part of her jaw, but her jaw was rigid, her skin the palest he'd ever seen it. He wanted to reach out and take her perfectly formed clenched hand in his and tell her that it would be all right. But that would be a lie.

'Leave him alone.' The sound of Ellie's thread of a voice almost had him knock over his drink in surprise. She lifted her head, her eyes unwavering as she sought out his mother's face. 'He was only trying to help. I think—'

'Ellie, you don't have to—'

But his mother interrupted him, her hand on his arm, her fingers firm but gentle. 'Ignore my son, Ellie, and finish what you were going to say. No one is going to harm you, least of all me. You think …?'

Ellie dropped her head, all the fight suddenly draining away like an unblocking sink. 'I don't know what to do,' was all she said, her words coming out in a mumbled rush.

'And that's why I've parked Ronan's brothers with friends and taken the day off work – in order to help you to make the right decision. You must realise that the police will find you sooner rather than later. Let me help sort out what's wrong and we'll take it from there.'

The silence was intense, but only for a moment. Ellie sliced through the building tension with her next words.

'I want my mummy.'

She dropped her head onto her folded arms, the sound of muffled sobs the only thing to be heard apart from the dripping tap and his mother's deep sighing breath. Ronan felt as if someone had gained access through his chest wall and was even now attacking his heart with a shredder. It was finally his turn to meet his mother's steadfast gaze, his own as easy to read as someone flicking through a large print book with a magnifying glass.

Help her.

Chapter 43

Gaby

Tuesday 4 August, 12.30 p.m. St Asaph

Gaby dumped her bag under the desk she usually used in the incident room, the one nearest the coffee machine. She didn't even think about going up to her office; there would be little point. She needed to be where the action was and that meant the stale room with the window pushed open to the max in order to try and circulate the solid wall of hot air that seemed to have taken up residence.

After slipping off her jacket, she placed it on the back of her chair and settled behind her desk. She ignored her laptop for once, pushing it to one side and removing a thick A4 pad from the top drawer. Computers were all very well but she had some serious thinking to do and there was nothing better than paper and pencil to kick her brain into action. But instead of drawing up her usual timeline, she decided to try a different way of organising the information they had, to see if it would add something new to the mix. She wrote down the names of the detectives working the case as her starting point.

Jax hadn't turned up anything of use from the neighbours on the estate, which was a surprise but not as surprising as finding that he wasn't behind his desk. She picked up her phone to send him a quick text, her attention moving on to Marie and that unfortunate episode with Ivo Morgan. She would have preferred to have her sitting in on the interview with Janice Stevens but that couldn't be helped. Diane had done very well as a substitute, she thought, staring across at the top of her neat blonde bob just visible behind two large screens that they used when looking through reams of CCTV footage. Gaby would really have to do something about Diane Carbone, probably the only positive that would come out of this mess of a case.

With a shake of her head, she turned to Mal and what he'd had to contribute. He hadn't come up with anything from the small cohort of undesirables living locally, which had to be viewed in a positive light. She was interested in what he'd made of Ellie's timeline. If they could just find out why she'd run …

She only added Owen as an afterthought. The inquiry into the two missing women was a headache she didn't need right now but she had utter confidence in Owen's ability to manage the situation – she had more than enough to cope with.

A quick peep at her watch told her that it was time for their catch-up. But instead of gaining everyone's attention, she withdrew a twenty from her purse and made for the door without alerting anyone to her actions – they probably wouldn't notice anyway.

Within minutes she was back, a circular tin tray clasped between her fingers, which she placed on the table at the front of the room.

'Right then, while we're waiting for the kitchen to make our sandwiches out of some sliced ham that wouldn't recognise a pig even if it oinked, I thought you'd appreciate something cold. Sadly not beer,' she said, pulling the ring on a can of Diet Coke and taking a restorative sip.

She waited until everyone had a drink, her hand swapping the can for a black marker pen as she stood in front of the whiteboards.

'News from me, then we'll take it in turns. Diane and I have interviewed Janice Stevens and it's clear that she's hiding something, bearing in mind that I know the woman … well. On the face of it, she has no idea where her son is but I can't believe that for a minute. There was no hope in detaining her any longer – we were lucky that we managed to keep her overnight. There's still that outstanding blood to be addressed – Jason will be down shortly with an update. Diane, do you have anything to add?'

'Only that I've just come off the phone to Stevens's work. I wanted to speak to her about a query in her statement,' she replied, setting her mobile back on her desk.

'There's a query in her statement?' Gaby frowned.

'No. I was using it as an excuse to check up on her whereabouts,' she said, colour storming up her cheeks. 'I thought that with the pressure of the ongoing search, my colleagues might have overlooked the request we put in to keep track of her. After all she did say she was going back to the office. Did I do something wrong?'

'No. You did exactly what the rest of us would have … if only we'd thought of it. Carry on.'

'The upshot is that she's not there. Personal reasons.'

'And I take it that she's not at home and her car isn't in the driveway?' Gaby asked, her frown reappearing at the slight nod of Diane's head.

'Sorry, ma'am.'

'It's not your fault, Diane. Far from it. Check that there's an ANPR trace on her car ASAP.'

'I'm right on it,' she said, picking up the phone.

'Good.' Gaby lifted her head to find Jax racing down the corridor. He didn't need to tell her that he had news; his expression managed that all by itself. She was less impressed with his tracksuit bottoms and sweat-marked top but decided to wait until he'd settled behind his desk before pouncing.

'Am I right in thinking that you have something for us, Jax? If your choice of clothing is anything to go by, it had better be good.' She sent him a brief smile, angling her head in the direction of the depleted tray of cans. 'Never let it be said I overwork my staff so choose a drink.'

'Yes, ma'am. Sorry, ma'am. It was this or my suit, which is now only fit for the bin.' She watched him pop open a Fanta and take a long gulp, his Adam's apple working overtime. He only spoke when the can was empty. 'We've found Ellie Fry's clothes, well most of them at least, and there's blood on the T-shirt and jeans.' He drew the back of his hand across his mouth to mop up a drop of liquid. 'I know I was meant to be focusing on the train and bus station but I decided to take a little detour first and check all the bins on the way.'

'You had a hunch?' Gaby asked, trying and failing to identify his thought processes because nowhere in any of their catch-ups had anyone mentioned checking the bins. She wasn't in the game of jumping on her officers unless completely necessary but by the same token members of her team going off on a tangent wasn't how she liked to play things. This time he'd been successful. Next time he could have wasted valuable time they didn't have on a wild goose chase.

'I s-s-suppose you could call it that. I tried to work out how no one had seen them but we were all searching for a teenage lad and a ten-year-old girl. Then I remembered one of the train guards saying yesterday that he saw a young man in the company of his brother around Ellie's age. So, I thought what if she'd changed her appearance? They were in a bin halfway down Augusta Street, which is a stone's throw away from the station.'

'But it's only supposition that Stevens made her change her appearance. We don't know for sure why her clothes were dumped, do we?' she said, scanning his face.

The room went quiet, no one wanting to put into words what they were all thinking.

Gaby cleared her throat and, after picking up her drink, finished it in one. 'Okay, anything else?' she asked, scrunching up the can and aiming it at the nearest bin.

'Their CCTV didn't throw up anything so I've started pulling the footage from the surrounding train stations. Maybe he took her somewhere?'

'Maybe he did.' Gaby dropped her hip onto the edge of the table, only to stand at the sight of Jason walking through the door with a large tray clasped between his hands.

'Ah, Jason, and with our lunch too. Take a seat. Here.' She walked over to the desk he'd chosen and dropped a drink in front of him. 'Never say that I don't care.'

'You're all heart, Gaby.'

'And don't you forget it. So, what have you got for us?' She picked out a tuna and cucumber and took a huge bite.

'Not as much as you want,' he said, holding up his hand as if to ward off one of her snappy comments. Instead of opening the can straight away, he lifted it up and rested it against his forehead. 'It's far too early for the DNA results to be back from the blood found at both houses and on the clothes – you are keeping me busy – but I can confirm some matches. We already know that Elodie Fry is blood group AB and that this matches the stain found in Janice Stevens's bathroom.' He lifted his head. 'I can now confirm that this also matches the blood type found on the clothes Jax dropped off.'

'You know I can never remember how blood groups work. Remind me again how many of the population are AB?'

'Only about four per cent or thereabouts.'

'Okay, not what I want to hear but good work, thank you. What else?'

'There was also some hair, long blonde strands on the clothing, which will add additional proof one way or the other.' He opened the can and swallowed it down in one without pausing for breath. 'The clothes match the list supplied by the mother.'

Gaby aimed a look in Jax's direction, managing a small nod before returning her attention back to Jason, who was continuing to speak.

'With regards to the other case, Mrs Matthews. Again there'll be a hold-up with the DNA but the blood found in the hall is Group O, and therefore not as helpful as it's shared by half of the population, but it does match the records we have for her at the hospital.'

'Thank you. I'll fill Owen in …' She stopped, her attention on the corridor and the sight of Owen and Marie hurrying towards them. 'We can tell them now.' She jumped down and, walking towards them, held out the last of the cans. 'We didn't think you'd mind us starting without you. There's a lot to catch up on.'

'You're telling me. Thanks for the drink,' he said, flipping open the tab. 'Just what the doctor ordered. What have we missed?' He ambled across to his desk but instead of sitting, leant against the edge, his feet stretched out in front of him.

'Not a great deal. Mainly we think that Stevens may have disguised Ellie as a boy, which is good news in itself as it may mean that she's not dead.'

'Because there'd be no point in changing her appearance if he was going to do away with her straightaway,' Owen added, his face expressionless. 'There is that.'

'What about the Matthews case? We need some good news here,' she said, propping against the desk. 'And up to now the only positive is that she never had a hip replacement.'

'There is a bit of a breakthrough, thanks to Diane and Marie, not that it makes much sense. It looks like there's some stuff missing from her house, small items that could be easily transportable but probably not enough for it to be worth anyone's time and effort – as a motive for murder it's a paltry one. I did get the impression that Matthews wasn't liked. Her father had that old-fashioned sweetshop sited between what used to be *Marie et Cie* and the Take A Break Café in Gloddaeth Street. He was a real gent. It didn't last two minutes without him behind the till. It's the same story with items missing over at St Gildas, where Miss Jane taught up to her retirement. Anyway, we'll make as good a list as we can and do the usual rounds to see if anyone knows anything about the missing goods but it's likely that the stuff is probably out of Wales by now.'

'I can type up the list and ping it across if you like?' Marie offered with a smile.

Gaby nodded, pleased that she seemed back to her old self. 'Malachy, what about you? How are you getting on with the timeline?' Gaby said, feeling restless and unable to settle. Instead of continuing to swing her legs back and forward, she hopped down and started passing around the sandwiches.

'Nearly done, ma'am. Just typing it up. There is one thing that stands out though.'

'Oh?'

'Yes. Ms Fry mainly cleans for people in and around the Colwyn Bay area but this does include the staff toilets and public areas of the Welsh Hills Memorial Centre and—'

A phone rang, cutting him off. Everyone turned to stare across at Diane as she picked up her mobile and started to speak. It didn't take her long to turn back to the team.

'We have a lead, ma'am. They've spotted Janice Stevens's car over in Caernarfon.'

Gaby met Owen's gaze, a torrent of memories flooding her mind, as his hand hovered between a cheese on brown and a ham on white. It hadn't even occurred to her that Ronan would think to take her to the farmhouse. But it was ideal: isolated and remote. He could … Her thoughts lurched to a sudden halt, her brows drawn into a fierce line as she struggled to regain control.

'Here, take these.' She picked out a handful of sandwiches from out under Owen's nose and wrapped them in a serviette. 'No point in you missing your lunch. I'll meet you outside in two minutes with the engine running. Diane, continue tracking Stevens's car.

Jax and Marie, begin by checking through the CCTV footage from Caernarfon station and take it from there. Mal, print a copy of that timeline ASAP. I'll be able to work through it on the way.' She ran to her desk, ignoring her jacket, instead picking up her mobile, only waiting an extra second or two for Mal who was sprinting back from the printer, his arm outstretched.

214

Chapter 44

Janice

Tuesday 4 August, 12.30 p.m. Caernarfon

For Janice Stevens parenting didn't come easily. Following her degree, she'd been all set to become a barrister. She'd even managed to get called to the bar only to have her plans changed when she'd met and married Casper in a flurry of excitement after first love hit. Instead of a life in Chambers, she'd moved to Chester and then Llandudno and, instead of working lunches and late evenings ploughing through briefs, she spent her day assisting local businesses navigate through the minefield that was commercial law. In between her nine-to-five job, which was frequently eight to six, she ran the kids to and from their activities, managed a mountain of washing and produced an array of far from gourmet, kiddie-friendly meals. It was only when cancer hit that she realised burning the candle at both ends meant there wasn't much in the middle to fall back on.

For a woman to whom work had been everything, it was now only the vehicle to pay the bills, of which there were many. Having a husband on remand came with a host of unexpected costs, which drained her emotions along with her bank account. She was trying to hold on to the family home for the sake of the kids but everything else would have to go. Fate had thrown boulder-sized obstructions in her path, wrecking everything that was stable and turning them into dust. She'd picked herself up so many times that she didn't flinch at the next obstacle flung under her feet. As far as she was concerned, when you reached rock bottom there was only one way left to go.

Being a mother to three boys didn't come with any instructions and she quickly found that she had to hone her instincts and moderate her tongue when dealing with her sons. Ronan was the most difficult and any effort on her part to mould him into anything other than the Ronan-shaped box he filled to perfection rebounded with far-reaching consequences. He'd broken her heart in all the ways possible and he was still breaking it despite having reached an age where independence beckoned. Sitting around her parents-in-law's old table with a mug glued between her hands was the only thing stopping her from grabbing him into the deepest hug and never letting go.

She didn't take much notice of Ellie; all her focus was on her son. The girl was obviously hurting. She'd probably got herself into some sort of mischief at home and had struck on the idea of running away instead of facing the consequences. The only problem was that she'd chosen Ronan to save her. If he couldn't sort himself out then there was no way he'd be able to sort out anyone else.

Her mind pulled and stretched, trying to work a way out of her current dilemma. A way that would result in Ronan returning home instead of risking his future with his continued erratic behaviour. The problem was that she didn't know what he wanted anymore. There was a time when it was easy to meet his needs. She only had to glance in his direction to be able to work out what was going on in that head of his. Now it was like understanding a book on algebra. Impossible on all levels. Ideally she needed to drop the dratted girl off at the nearest police station, leaving Ronan in the car so that he couldn't get himself embroiled further in her little drama. He'd had far too much to do with coppers as it was.

'I want my mummy.'

It was like a blessing to hear those fateful words coming from the child's bow lips. If she wanted her mother then what could be the harm in returning her back into the bosom of her family?

Janice wasn't stupid, far from it. In her job, she'd come across all types of crooks trying to con the system and she prided herself in her ability to assess someone's worthiness from the outset. If she had any concerns when she arrived at the girl's home, she'd resort to plan B – the nearest police station. That way she'd placate both Ronan and her conscience at the same time.

217

Chapter 45

Gaby

Tuesday 4 August, 12.50 p.m. Caernarfon

Gaby recognised the road even though she hadn't been back. Caernarfon had been added to her reverse bucket list of places she never wanted to visit again. But here she was with the same man by her side, heading towards one of her worst nightmares. Her throat worked, trying to swallow when suddenly there wasn't enough spit in her mouth to do the job. A few sighing breaths didn't do much and clenching her hands only caused her muscles to ache. She relaxed her fingers, deliberately spreading them out across her trouser-covered thighs, the feel of the fabric slightly clammy to her touch. It was an insult to view a beautiful place like Caernarfon with such abhorrence but the brain was a funny thing. Just as she couldn't dissociate the smell of pasta with thoughts of home, every time the place was mentioned, her mind dragged up a pictorial image of that farmhouse from her memory banks.

'Do you need directions or do you remember the way?'

Owen didn't answer and she hadn't expected him to. It was

only something to break the silence as they reached the turning on the left that led to the dirt track circling the property.

The farmhouse was like she remembered, the long low building surrounded by mature bushes and trees that were thick with foliage, making it difficult to see. But it didn't take a genius to tell that the place was deserted if the empty driveway wasn't evidence enough.

Owen pulled to a stop and switched off the engine. 'What next?'

'Let's have a scout around to see if there's any sign that they were here,' Gaby said, climbing out of the car and heading for the front door, which remained closed under her touch.

'I could break it open if you like? There's a crowbar in the back.' Owen offered.

'I don't like! You take the left and I'll take the right. Meet you round the back in a mo.'

Peering through dusty windows was all part and parcel of being a police officer. But the last time she'd visited the farmhouse the door had been unlocked, the untold horrors within waiting to be found.

The back door opened under her touch, the hinges creaking under the weight of her hand.

'Do you want me to go first?'

She gave him a speaking glance instead of bothering to reply. Yes, she'd love him to. In fact, he could search the premises all by himself and she'd stand outside waiting for him like the spare part he was starting to make her feel.

The hall was dark with that musty smell that comes with houses left unoccupied for too long. She left Owen to check the last bedroom on the left – nothing good would come from her revisiting it. Instead she scanned the kitchen and bedrooms on the right only to meet Owen back in the hall, a small teddy bear clutched between her fingers.

'They were here.'

'I know. Where to next?'

Gaby's brows met in the middle, trying to see beyond the tragedy unfolding out in front of them. The Stevens family were well past breaking point, and a wrong move could push them over the edge. But one thing about Janice had always been her strength. She was living proof that forging some kind of a life following a disaster was possible. Even with Ronan's desertion, she'd managed to keep her head and keep her distance. An interfering mother was the last thing he'd needed, so watching from afar, while the local vicar kept a weather eye, was the very best of decisions.

Gaby knew instinctively that, if it had been her in the same position, she'd have struggled to cope with the thought of her child living on the streets. But she wasn't Janice Stevens. And with that thought, she knew that they were in trouble because there was no way she could ever think of herself in Janice's shoes. She had no idea what the woman had been thinking going to the farmhouse and couldn't begin to imagine where the trio were heading next. Instinct told her that Janice was a good person. After all, the judiciary was an unlikely profession for someone with criminal tendencies. In addition, if Ronan had broken the law, and that was a very big if, his mother would know all of the loopholes available to prevent him from serving a custodial sentence.

The truth was that Gaby had no idea what Ellie Fry was doing in the company of Janice and Ronan. She also had no idea why she'd run but she was determined to find out.

'Let's get back in the car and radio the station. The annoying thing is that we probably passed them on the way.'

Chapter 46

Ronan

Tuesday 4 August, 1 p.m. A55

The journey back from Caernarfon was quicker and far more comfortable than the journey out. It hadn't taken his mother long to convince them both that returning home was the right thing to do. Ellie wasn't talking, not that he could blame her. He knew of old that his mother was one of those people that had to take charge. In the battlefield she'd have been promoted up to the role of general and if politics had been her thing, she would have made prime minister, no question. As it was, she'd made partner in her firm within only a couple of years of joining the practice.

She wasn't a bad mum, he mused, tuning out of the relentless chatter she'd started up within seconds of putting her foot down on the accelerator. But he'd always had the feeling that having children was something else that she had to excel at, only to fail simply because she tried too hard. It hadn't mattered to him which school he'd gone to or that he didn't have the best bike or a designer label on his trainers but she couldn't see that even after everything that had happened to their small family.

He'd opted to sit in the back to keep Ellie company, not that it made any difference to her stony silence. After her brief outburst in the kitchen, Ellie hadn't said another word. She'd only nodded briefly when his mother had taken it upon herself to explain that it was better to hand themselves in before the police turned up on their doorstep and she'd waited silently in the hall while he'd gathered together their stuff. Ronan felt a deep pain beginning to form somewhere in the vicinity of his breastbone at the fruitlessness of her situation. There was nothing he could do to protect her. Whatever happened next was completely out of his hands.

Instead of spending the short journey going slowly mad, he decided to use the time to try and unravel what he wanted to do with his life. There had to be a next step because he'd come to the decision last night, when he'd sat and watched over Ellie, that his life had to change. The problem was he'd never known what he'd wanted to do at school. Choosing A levels was the worst kind of hell – he'd only ended up deciding on maths, further maths, biology and chemistry because that was what he was good at. But as for a job … He knew what he didn't want to be and that was either a pharmacist or a lawyer, like his parents, but that's as far as his thoughts had taken him.

Now, of course, with one A level to his name, and that only because he'd managed to sit maths in Year 12, university was out. The other option open to him – to move back home – held all the attraction of a faun in the presence of a starving lion, but he couldn't seem to think of what else to do. He could try for a job but who'd employ him and where would he live? The Great Orme was all very well but it would be winter in a few weeks. What then? Whatever his issues, he felt he had more to offer than being labelled a homeless social statistic.

The housing estate up ahead was a new experience for someone who had been protected for most of their life. Ronan had learnt a lot during his time on the streets, not least that most people lived very different lives to the privileged one afforded him by two parents in well-paid jobs. The sight of the disused shopping trolley, lying to rust in the corner, cemented this fact. He'd thought he'd seen it all – far from it.

Ellie reached out her hand across the seat between them, palm upwards, and with that gesture he knew that she was scared of what she might find inside. He squeezed her fingers gently, his gaze on the unassuming property, plain white net curtains pulled against neighbours' prying eyes. He couldn't offer her any assurances because he had none to give. But what he did offer her was a silent promise that, despite what his mother might say, he wouldn't leave her unless he was happy that this was the right place for her.

Chapter 47

Gaby

Tuesday 4 August, 1 p.m. A55

'The ANPR has just picked them up at Llanfairfechan, which means that we're not far behind. I still have no idea what they're up to.'

'Or if Ellie is even in the car, remember. Just because you found the toy and I noticed that the remaining water in the kettle was lukewarm means nothing,' Owen said, increasing his speed.

'Don't remind me but we have to do something.'

'What make did you say the car was again?' Owen said after a couple of minutes' silence.

'A grey Saab. Belonged to her husband. I thought you'd have remembered?'

Owen grunted. 'Like the one two cars ahead?'

Gaby squinted out of the window screen, excitement starting to build.

'Exactly like that one even down to the numberplate,' she said, checking her phone. 'Keep your distance. She'll recognise me in a heartbeat.'

'Do you want me to pull them over?'

'I'm not sure if I'm honest. We don't know for definite who's in the car, do we?' she said, staring at the one head she could see in the back seat.

'And the last time we went in without backup ...'

'Someone nearly died. You don't have to remind me. Okay, let me alert the team to what's happening and keep as we are.'

After calling it in, she picked up her bag and, rummaging down the bottom, pulled out a pair of large sunglasses.

'There's a sun hat in the glove compartment if you think it might help?'

'Bates, I've seen your taste in sunhats and I don't really think that ...' She pulled out the khaki safari hat with a grimace and, shaking out the sand, popped it on her head. 'There!'

Owen twisted away from the road a second, biting down on his lower lip. 'Very fetching. Even your own mother would pass you by in the street.'

'Ha-ha, very funny.' She flipped down the visor and stared at her reflection in the mirror only to slam it back into place with a deep shuddering breath. 'I barely recognise myself.'

'And it's unlikely they'll recognise me! Sadly amazingly handsome, bearded Welshmen aren't that uncommon while ...'

'While sexy Italian women are like gold dust? Is that what you were about to say?'

'Of course it is, dear.'

She slapped his arm. 'There speaks a man who has no idea of how to talk to women.'

'What? But ...' He threw her a second look. 'What's wrong with giving a woman a compliment?'

'Nothing, Owen. Nothing at all. Genuine compliments from genuine friends are very welcome. They raise a woman's self-esteem and make the world seem a much happier place. But when the aforesaid woman appears to be wearing' – she flicked a finger at the brim – 'something found among Tarzan's castoffs, that's a completely different animal.'

'I'll never understand women.'

'And that's your problem because you're not meant to.'

'Harrumph,' he said, bringing the conversation to a halt, which was so typical of him that she struggled not to pass comment.

They were in the middle of an escalating situation and yet the banter between them was the best it had ever been. Some coppers grew silent when situations reached danger point. Owen and Gaby cracked jokes. It was time to worry when the repartee stopped.

'Okay. If I'm not allowed to compliment you or question your decision-making, what about that timeline? What does it tell us?'

Gaby grinned, pulling out the folded paper from her trouser pocket. 'Darling, whatever would I do without you?'

'You can cut out the soft-soaping crap for a start.'

She smoothed out the creases and scrolled through the columns, taking a moment to frame a suitable reply. 'I have no idea how or even why Kate puts up with …' She paused, her fingers clenching and almost digging a hole in the paper, her attention on the car up ahead.

'What? What is it?'

'It's where this game gets very interesting, very interesting indeed.' Gaby positioned herself next to the window, all trace of their earlier banter forgotten. 'Tell me again about those interviews you carried out yesterday in relation to that problem over at the Memorial Gardens.'

'The interviews?' he said, adjusting his sun visor. 'Well, there was Martin Penrose first back at the station, but you know all about that and you were with me when I visited him again and met with the boss, Trevor Beeton. Now there's a right sleazeball if you ask me. Wouldn't trust him as far as I could throw him. I'll bet you a fiver that he gives Martin the boot for coming to see us.'

'Not a bet I'm prepared to pick up. Sadly there's no betting about it. Is that all?' She stared down at the list, her brow furrowed as she read the amendment at the bottom, which included all of Anita's cleaning jobs. 'And interestingly, thanks to Mal, we now know that Fry worked for Beeton at the Memorial Gardens but how does that link in with Ellie running away?'

'It doesn't unless she used to take Ellie there. She's on her school holidays so maybe she didn't have anyone to leave her with and abandoning her on that housing estate probably wasn't an option. I wouldn't like to be left there and I'm thirty-six!'

'But can you really see Beeton allowing a kid in while the mum's cleaning?' Gaby lifted her phone from her lap and within seconds was speaking to the man himself. It didn't take her long to settle her mobile back on her lap, her hands wrapped loosely around the case. 'It's as we thought, she asked and he turned her down flat which, if I'm honest, was the right thing to do. The thought of a child sitting so near all those dead bodies gives me the creeps.'

'But other employers might have been more amenable?'

'Or might not have even known if they were out at work.'

'So, are there any other interesting names on the list then?'

'Hold on a mo,' Gaby said, her attention on the sign up ahead for Colwyn Bay. 'I need to let the team know where we are.'

Chapter 48

Ronan

Tuesday 4 August, 1.30 p.m. Colwyn Bay

Ellie didn't have a key, which was hardly surprising. Ronan remembered his own rite of passage in that regard when he'd reached twelve and was allowed out on his own for the first time, not that he'd had anywhere to go. He still had the keyring it came with, the thought of the flashy Welsh dragon making him relax his facial muscles, but only briefly. For all Ellie's grown-up mannerisms, she was very much a child.

What was surprising was that no one answered the door. He watched his mother from the safety of the back seat, Ellie's hand clasped within his as they waited for what seemed like an indeterminate length of time, his worry levels skyrocketing. If his mother was to be believed, and he couldn't for a minute think that she had anything to lie about, then the whole of Wales was on high alert. So where was Ms Fry and, more to the point, where were the police? Surely she should be pinned to the sofa with the weight of her worry, her mobile making huge inroads into the tender flesh of her palm. That's what he'd be doing in her place.

'Do you think she's gone out, maybe to work or something?' Janice said, sliding back behind the wheel, drumming her long slender fingers against the dash. After numerous attempts of ringing Anita's mobile, her phone was now discarded on the passenger seat beside her.

'I don't know. Even if she's out she always has her phone with her.' Ellie's bottom lip trembled, something Ronan was starting to recognise with all the finesse of a new dad with a baby in possession of a full nappy.

'Okay, don't cry. It will be all right,' Ronan said when he was starting to suspect that it would be anything but. 'She's probably dropped off to sleep or something. What about a spare key?' he continued, remembering back to the one that lived under the third plant pot to the left of their back door. Not the most original of places but then Llandudno wasn't the crime capital of anywhere.

The key wasn't under a plant pot because there weren't any pots, or any plants, in Ellie's tiny front garden. Surrounded on three sides by a rickety fence that had seen better days, the straggly patch of green had far too many weeds to accept the term grass lightly. But they didn't have to waste time searching for the key because when Ronan tried the handle the door opened under his hand.

Chapter 49

Gaby

Tuesday 4 August, 1.30 p.m. Colwyn Bay

'What are we doing here again?' Owen said, staring out of the windscreen at Ellie Fry's house, his expression inscrutable.

'We're waiting.'

'But why?'

'Look, Owen, we've only been stopped all of five seconds. They certainly can't escape now you've blocked the entrance,' she added, suppressing a laugh at the way he'd slewed the Honda across the narrow road. 'It's a good job Jax is already here or he'd have had no chance of joining us. And anyway, the only reason that this would be the wrong thing to do is if Janice Stevens was involved in Ellie's original abduction. If that's the case why wasn't she on any of the CCTV footage? We'll give them another minute before we go in.'

'I still don't like it.'

'No. Well I didn't think that you would but softly, softly is how I want it played. Remember there isn't one but two traumatised children in there,' she said, focusing on the two heads that were now visible in the back of the car. 'Ronan might be eighteen and therefore legally an adult but a very immature one. Why don't you use the time to check if you have any messages?' she continued, flicking through her phone.

'Good idea. There's that list Marie was going to send me from St Gildas.' He pulled his mobile from his pocket and started searching. 'Ah, here it is. It doesn't look as if Katherine Jane was into jewellery but there's possibly some silver photo frames and a fine selection of crystal unaccounted for and all impossible to trace. Oh, this is more promising – her retirement gift. Not a clock this time, the stingy beggars. Only a slimline pen. Looks to be gold,' he said, squinting down at the photo that had accompanied the list.

'Engraved?'

Instead of replying, he shut off his phone and flung it on the dashboard.

Gaby glanced across, noting his stony glare and flared nostrils. 'What is it? Something about the pen you recognise?'

'Yes. How could I have been so bloody stupid—'

'Stop a mo. It will have to wait.' Gaby grabbed his arm, her gaze drawn to the scene unfolding across the road. 'Why doesn't Anita open the door?'

They both watched Janice return to the Saab before heading back to the house, this time with Ellie and Ronan by her side. Gaby jumped out of the car and started to run. She'd already reached the gate of the property by the time Ronan had pushed open the front door with the flat of his hand.

Gaby's home was her safe place but a locked door with the security chain fastened was the thing that made it secure. Ystâd golygfa'r môr estate was a world away from her little home in Rhos-on-Sea and for the Frys it must have felt frightening at times. As a parent, Anita had done everything possible to protect their safety, Gaby recollected, thinking about the industrial-sized Yale lock and thick security chain. There was no way she'd ever forget to lock her front door.

There hadn't been many times in Gaby's career when she'd felt in need of more protection than her brain, the only thing available to her right now apart from Owen's brawn. There was no reason for the sudden fear turning her belly to an ice-cold mass or for her bowels to rumble. She knew the science but understanding the role certain chemicals had on both her mental and physical state was of little help with her heart bounding underneath her Marks and Spencer's plain white blouse, her fingers starting to shake.

She raced up to the entrance, Owen matching her stride for stride, and was poised on the threshold when she heard the scream. But the scream didn't stop. It continued, one long, high, thin wail that ripped through the air, tearing her emotions to shreds and her muscles to blancmange. Had she got it wrong, yet again?

Chapter 50

Ronan

Tuesday 4 August, 1.40 p.m. Colwyn Bay

Ronan was the first to see the blood, the handprint positioned in the centre of the wall like some new art movement. Ellie, still clutching on to his fingers, was the second.

He pulled her towards him, his thin arms around her back, with no thought of how much he disliked being hugged. But no hug could stop the scream gathering momentum in the back of her throat just as no ear defenders were man enough to dim the piercing squeal by a single, solitary decibel.

The hall felt crowded all of a sudden and, glancing up from where he'd been awkwardly patting Ellie's back, he was almost glad to see that short detective, whatever her name, standing in the doorway, only partly obscured by his mother.

It took one look at the bloodied handprint on the wall and she'd taken charge. His sense of relief was intense as she passed them over to a colleague. There'd be questions that needed answering, lots of questions. But all he was bothered about was Ellie, who'd flopped in his arms as if the effort of standing

233

was suddenly too much, her scream changing to a low, heart-breaking moan.

'I'm Detective Owen Bates. Let's go sit in the car. If you'd like me to take her …?'

But Ellie, for all her inertia, clung on to Ronan with a grip far in excess of either her age or her size.

'No, I'm fine. We'll be fine, won't we, kid?' he said, trying to make light out of something that was deathly serious, and he was telling a blatant lie to boot. They'd never be fine again.

He huddled in the back of the Honda, ignoring his mother who'd slipped into the passenger seat. Ellie's sobs slowly subsided as she fell into a semi-comatose state.

It was only then that he met Owen's eye and whispered the question that had been tearing at his mind ever since he'd entered Ellie's home.

'Where's her mother?'

Chapter 51

Gaby

Tuesday 4 August, 2 p.m. Colwyn Bay

Anita Fry was nowhere to be found. There was blood in the kitchen, lots of blood, along with broken crockery and overturned chairs. Jason was on his way, along with a full complement of CSIs, but it would take time to puzzle out what had happened, and time was the one thing that they didn't have. Ellie was the key here, the little girl sitting in the back of the car with both Owen and Ronan watching over her.

Gaby, for all her calming presence and organised mind, was in shock. Not to the same level as Ellie but enough to start tearing herself up about what they could have done differently. No. What she should have done differently. If there was any blame to be apportioned, she knew she had to be the one to step forward. She should have worked it out sooner or even if she hadn't she could at least have listened to Owen's suggestion about flagging down the car. But what-ifs and maybes wouldn't help Ellie's mother, not now. Gaby had to make the girl talk. It wouldn't be that difficult, she reasoned, heading out to the car. After all, she had a fair idea as to what Ellie was going to say. As soon as she'd seen the full list of Anita's cleaning jobs a picture had started forming in her mind, the three cases converging. Katherine Jane and Barbara Matthews. One dead. One missing and presumed dead. And finally, Ellie. A little girl beside herself with grief.

The car was quiet, too quiet. Owen lifted his head from his phone and where he'd been most likely alerting the team back at the station as to what was happening. That's what Gaby would have done in his shoes.

She turned her attention to Ronan who looked worse than she'd ever seen him, his jaw covered in a straggly mess of what might pass for a beard in a few years. His eyes were red-rimmed, the whites bloodshot, his skin dry and coated in dark shadows. There was also a smell, the smell that accompanied the homeless whether they were aware of it or not. But underneath the grime, he was still the scared little boy she'd met all those months ago. A boy who'd had his world torn up into tiny shreds only to find it impossible to match up the pieces and all because of one vital missing part: his father.

'Hi Ronan.' She would have liked to add that it was good to see him. In truth, she meant the sentiment perhaps more than anything that had gone before. Instead all she said was, 'I need to speak to Ellie. You can stay if you like?'

He met her gaze, his own hardening, his meaning clear.

'I'll go easy, I promise.'

Ronan eased his arm out from behind Ellie's shoulders, rotating his own, which must have been aching from the time spent crushed under the weight of her body. 'Ellie, come on now. We need to find your mum. The detective here is going to help us but you do need to speak to her.'

Gaby crouched down beside the open car door, feeling the strain against the seam of her trousers and hoping against hope that she wouldn't be left with her knickers on show.

'Ellie, I know this is hard for you but we need your help. Will

I tell you what I think, then all you have to do is nod or shake?' she said, her voice continuing in a soft whisper at the slight incli- nation of Ellie's head. 'We think that, as it's the school holidays, your mum couldn't always find someone to mind you and that sometimes she took you with her when she went to work. Is that right, sweetheart?' She only continued when Ellie nodded a second time. 'We also think that during one of those times you saw something. It must have been boring trying to stay out of your mum's way?'

Gaby was no expert in the interview of child witnesses. The truth was, she knew she should wait for the assistance of a police social worker before even attempting any kind of questioning. But there wasn't time.

'I'd finished my book.'

'Exactly. You'd finished your book and wanted to find some- thing else to do?'

'There was a large shed in the back garden ...' Ellie stopped, her mouth quivering, her eyes filling with tears. Gaby noticed Ronan tense but all he did was place his hand over hers and squeeze gently, his face deathly pale under the grime.

'I thought I could sneak an ice cream as there were no toys, only rusty old tools. But when I pulled the door open to the freezer ...' She scrunched her eyes closed, a stream of tears pressing their way under her lids before starting a relentless trail down her cheeks.

'Go on, sweetheart, you're doing fine. There was something in the freezer that shouldn't have been there?'

'A row of heads. Their eyes open and bulging out through the plastic—'

237

Chapter 52

Gaby

Tuesday 4 August, 2.10 p.m. Colwyn Bay

The arrival of Amy on the scene was fortuitous. She quickly took charge of the sensitive dynamics between Ellie, Ronan and his mother and, within minutes, had them agreeing with her suggestion of accompanying them to the station to await news.

Gaby and Owen sat in the front of the car, where it only took a couple of minutes for Owen to shift the pieces in her mind into place. His hands clenched and unclenched as the story came out in fits and starts. A missing girl. A missing octogenarian. A handful of prosthetic hips when there should only have been a maximum of two. A distraught parent trying to scrabble together an existence by taking on cleaning jobs that paid well simply because of no one else wanting them. Three cases and one link: Anita Fry.

'That bloody pen. I should have known from the start that it was out of the ordinary. All shiny black and flashy gold – too good to be true just like her. It even had the f'ing school crest on the lid. If only I'd looked at the list before rather than after visiting the farmhouse, we might have been able to prevent ...'

'Now now, Owen. No good can come from blaming yourself. How were we to know that Ms Fry's main source of income came from providing a cleaning service to undertakers? It's more than likely that she got her clients word of mouth and who do undertakers talk to mainly? That's right. Other undertakers. It makes a strange sort of sense, as I'm betting it's not the most popular of places in which to work,' she added, restraining the shudder careening across her skin.

'Yes but I still can't in a million years think that Hayley Prince is involved.'

'Owen, you've been on the exact same courses as I have. You know the drill,' she said, buckling her seatbelt and adjusting the sun visor only to realise that she was still wearing his daft hat, which she flung in the back with far more force than was warranted. 'No matter how stupid and unlikely you might think the clues are, if they fit then you are duty-bound to follow their lead to the ultimate conclusion. Did you manage to get her home address?'

'Of course.'

'Hold on, ma'am. Wait up a second.'

The sight of Jax racing towards them had Owen shift the car out of gear and pull up the hand brake.

'What is it. We don't have time to ...'

'J-j-just that I questioned the next-door neighbour. She was peering out the lounge window waiting for her Tesco order and she saw Ms Fry being helped out to a car.'

'Helped?'

'That's the word she used.'

'What about the person with her?'

Jax shook his head. 'She didn't take any notice. A posh car though, James Bond like, she called it.'

'Okay, thank you. Carry on with the interviews and let me know if you come up with anything, even if you think it's not important.' She turned back to Owen. 'Put your foot down; we may be in time to save a life.'

He shifted into gear. 'I still don't reckon you're right about Hayley Prince. She couldn't have been more helpful when I met with her yesterday at the funeral home.'

'Because she's what? Young? Pretty? Dresses well? So what and who cares? Except you, it seems. You concentrate on driving and I'll see if I can find her on the system. While I'm searching her up, tell me everything you can remember.'

'Smartly dressed in a grey two-piece business suit, similar to yours but ...'

'But what?'

He cleared his throat. 'High-end.'

Gaby rolled her eyes. 'So she has money to burn, excuse the pun. What else?'

'Married.' He paused a second. 'That's right. Something about having a brother in the force. Whitstable, off the top of my head.'

'Okay, here she is,' Gaby said, peering down at the screen. 'No priors. Hayley Elizabeth Prince, widow. An only child.' She paused, sending him a look laden with sympathy. He wouldn't be the first man to be taken in by a pretty face but Owen would take the slip-up personally. 'Prince inherited the business from her husband five years ago,' she continued, tilting the phone in his direction briefly to share a photo of the grieving widow. 'There was a spread in the *Llandudno Chronicle*. Apparently she's done wonders in turning the funeral home into a flourishing business with her PAYG model, even so far as being nominated for North Wales businesswoman of the year on three separate occasions. Oh, this is interesting.' Her finger slid over the screen as she read further. 'Her father used to be headmaster of St Gildas, retired three years ago when presumably ...'

'Paul de Bertrand took over. A coincidence that consecutive headmasters are both tied up in murder inquiries.'

'And St Gildas is also the place Miss Jane worked as a teacher – you know how I feel about coincidences, Owen.'

'Have you heard anything from the de Bertrands, by the way?

Having your wife wake up beside the dead body of her flatmate appears to have been the glue needed to repair the fractures in their relationship. I was surprised that the school didn't offer him his job back in the end. After all, none of it was their fault.'

'They did,' Gaby said, checking her phone for messages only to return it to her lap, her fingers resting on top. 'I've had one or two postcards. They're travelling around Europe at the moment working from dig to dig. A middle-aged gap year is how she put it.'

'Lucky them!'

'As if you mean that. You're more than happy with your little family.' She scowled, unwilling to compare her own relationship failings to both Owen's and the de Bertrands'. No one, least of all her, knew what would happen between her and Rusty but, if history was to repeat itself, it was a disaster in the making.

'If it wasn't for the fact that Prince lied to you about having a brother,' she said, forcing the conversation back on its tracks, 'I'd have had to agree with you about her being an unlikely candidate for a double murder but she has so ...'

'She's played me for a complete fool,' he said, adding in a curse for good measure, which was so unlike him that Gaby's eyes widened in surprise.

'Oh, I wouldn't say that, Owen. Turning on the womanly charm in order to get what you want has been around since the very start of time. It would have taken a better man than you to suspect what she was up to but it was pretty stupid of her to make up a fictitious brother to put you off the scent, when you had no reason to suspect her in the first place.' She lifted her gaze from her phone, her brow lowering. 'Hey, where are you going? This isn't the way to her—'

'No but it's about time I used my head for once,' he interrupted. 'It makes no sense to take Ms Fry back to her house when she has a perfectly legitimate means to dispose of her body at her place of work.' He indicated right at the traffic lights up ahead before taking a sharp left and squeezing in between two cars with the expertise of someone who wasn't even thinking about what he was doing: a reverse parallel park of such precision that Gaby smiled, deciding to hold her tongue. No point in congratulating him on something she often struggled with, she thought, again blaming her lack of height for her inability to skilfully manoeuvre a car into any space that wasn't the length of a bus.

'What now?' She glanced across the road at the shiny plate-glass window featuring a tasteful display of headstones, a wreath of red and white flowers the only thing to offset the scene.

'You stay in the car while we wait for backup, bearing in mind that they currently think that we're going to Prince's home. In the meantime, I'll head round the rear.' He unclipped his seatbelt or at least tried to. Gaby's fingers suddenly appeared out of nowhere.

'Oh no you don't. And have all the fun while you leave me hanging around for the boys in blue?' She released his hand only to work on her own seatbelt, remembering to position the 'officer on duty' card in the window.

'Gaby!'

'Don't you "Gaby" me in that tone of voice, Owen,' she said, climbing out of the car. 'You need to remember that while I might be your boss, we're also a team and a bloody good one at that. We go in together or we wait for backup. It shouldn't be long.'

She watched him raise his eyes heavenward, his reluctant shrug of acquiescence telling her everything she wanted to know.

The back of the property was exactly how she imagined, her recent experience at the Memorial Gardens a sharp reminder that the glamorous frontage would only go so far – as far as the customer's inquisitive eye. The business end was a concreted forecourt hidden from view with three polished hearses and a bright red Porsche.

'Bingo. Not quite James Bond but near enough.'

Chapter 53

Owen

Tuesday 4 August, 2.25 p.m. H Prince and Sons

There was no one Owen liked to work with more than Gaby Darin. She had quite a few faults, more than a few. But she said it how it was, which meant that the team always knew where they stood with her. She also never asked her colleagues to do anything that she wouldn't gladly do herself if she had the time. Usually one of the first in the office in the morning and the last to leave, she had exacting standards, which she expected her team to live up to.

But – and there was a big 'but' coming – she was impulsive, an impulsivity that got her into tight corners and Owen, as her mainstay, got dragged along with her. She'd nearly died a few months ago … He squeezed his eyes tight not wanting to relive even for a second what had happened to Kate and the debt he owed Gaby for saving the life of both his wife and his child.

Owen didn't want to be here with Gaby simply because he didn't want to go into an unknown situation with a partner who had more guts than sense and a severe allergy to anything more energetic than turning the page of one of those romance novels he'd spotted in her glove compartment the last time he'd been rummaging for a packet of mints. He also didn't need to be reminded that, with a less-than-two-week-old baby at home, he wasn't on par. He was so below par as to feel sick with tiredness – trying to compensate with a mixture of caffeine and chocolate had only made his head buzz and his legs shake. But with Gaby marching towards the rear of the building, he had little choice but to follow.

'Hey, hold on a mo.' He ran to catch her up, the sound of his shoes against the concrete drive causing him to slow his stride. He couldn't do much, only try to contain her enthusiasm by touting a cautious note. 'How do you want to play this? Remember, she knows me but …'

'But not me. Good point.' Gaby stepped away from the door and back towards the gate and the street beyond. 'I'm going to head into the shop and see if I can't distract her while you sneak in the back and try and find Anita.'

Owen opened his mouth to reply but it would have been like speaking to a brick wall, which was the only thing he could see now she'd walked through the gate, around the corner and out of his line of vision.

Bloody women and bloody Darin in particular. One of these days …

His hand on the door, he tried to push on the wood only to lift it to his head instead and slap his forehead in disgust, his attention on the small keypad to the left of the frame.

Of frigging course it's locked. Security is bound to be high with all those dead bodies.

He looked over his shoulder and the direction Gaby had gone before turning back to face the door. There was nothing he could do other than follow her but that might mean putting her in danger.

The clock ticked, seconds passed while he considered his options, seconds that seemed to travel the same distance as minutes or even hours. The truth was he didn't have any choice. Decision made, he pulled out his phone and told the team that he was going in. He only hoped that it wouldn't be too late.

Chapter 54

Gaby

Tuesday 4 August, 2.25 p.m. H Prince and Sons

The front door was open but there was nobody at home, which set all the alarm bells ringing inside Gaby's skull as she took in the mahogany reception desk and mushroom-coloured carpet. Everything was coordinated with no expense spared. Her attention was drawn to the crystal vase of fresh cream lilies and small dish of mints that would have looked more in place in an upmarket beautician's than an undertaker's.

She hurried across the small expanse of floor and through an arch at the back of the room. The carpet carried on throughout, something she noticed without being aware of it, interior design not even making the list of her current concerns. There were two offices up ahead, both doors open and both empty, her breath leaving her body in a whoosh of relief that was quickly stemmed. The open front door worried her more now that she was in the heart of Prince and Sons. No one left a reception area unmanned unless there was a crisis and what better crisis than an unexpected dead body?

She continued on her journey, passing a long table littered with an artful array of leaflets, which barely registered. Instead she headed along the corridor on the left towards the plain dark wooden door that, by a process of elimination, had to lead to where all the action took place. Her footsteps were silent against the thick pile of the carpet, the only noise to be heard her heart drumming in her ears. The fear exploding in her chest was tangible. She could almost feel it creeping along her veins and setting to work on her muscles. Who knew that knocking knees was a thing! Most of her neurons and cells wanted to turn and run, her obdurate nature the only thing that kept the soles of her shoes fixed to the floor. Hayley Prince was not going to get the better of her, a mantra that Gaby repeated, over and over in the maelstrom of her mind.

With her hand on the brass knob, she listened a moment, her ear pressed up to the gap, before twisting the metal globe and inching the door open, millimetre by fatal millimetre, her eyes glued as the room revealed itself in short sharp bursts. The wall given over to stacked coffin-shaped fridges. The trolley angled against them as if someone had shoved it out of the way. The stainless-steel bench reflecting the light from the fluorescent strip that ran across the ceiling, a light that dazzled until her eyes adjusted to the brightness. The body of Anita Fry stretched out on top of the bench. Yes, body, because from where she was standing, there was little sign of life. The rhythmic movement of her chest absent, her pale hand dangling off the side, her fingers stretched out as if trying to touch the floor.

She checked the room again, taking her time as she examined every corner. But the room was empty, a fact that frightened her. Where was Owen and what was she missing because she had to be missing something?

Giving herself a little shake, she forced herself to man up and walk over to the trolley. If there was even a hair's breadth of a chance that Anita might be still alive, it was up to Gaby to try and save her. She pushed the thought of the bloody handprint down to the cellar of her mind. Blood wasn't her thing. It was so not her thing that it was the one fact about the job that nearly had her running for the hills each and every time she had to face it.

There was no blood that she could see. Her fingers reached out to feel for the carotid artery on the side of Anita's neck, the skin much warmer than she'd been expecting, her eyes widening in surprise as she felt the flicker of a pulse. Only a trace but a trace was all that was needed for her memories of the years working the beat in Liverpool to flood back, the countless Friday nights she'd spent toing and froing between the emergency department and the station. All those hours and evenings dealing with drunks, compounded by the annual mandatory course that drilled in, right down to the bone, the importance of first aid.

After ascertaining that Anita was still breathing, Gaby managed, with a bit of tugging and quite a lot of stretching, to roll her into the recovery position without rolling her off the edge of the narrow trolley. There had to be injuries. Gaby shivered at the thought as she remembered all that blood. But bodies could mend. Skin could be sutured. She'd seen time and again the way nature, aided and abetted by medicine, could heal the most horrendous of injuries …

Caught up in her musings, she neither saw nor heard Hayley Prince creeping out from behind the trolley and reach for the fire extinguisher, her hands clasping the cylinder between both hands and raising it aloft. All she felt was a sudden pain at the base of her skull then blackness swept away all thoughts, dispersing memories and feelings as her knees gave way and she slid to the floor.

She didn't see Owen arrive on the scene only a second too late to save her. She didn't hear the tortured scream rattle in his throat at the sight of what he wasn't able to prevent just as she was ignorant to his herculean jump across the room, which squashed Hayley Prince into a crumpled mass of raging woman.

The fire extinguisher bounced off the ground in an explosion of sound, the ensuing silence only interrupted by what looked to be an army of police bursting into the room.

Gaby, her head cradled in Owen's arms, heard none of it.

Chapter 55

Gaby

Tuesday 4 August, 5 p.m. St Asaph Hospital

Gaby was both cool and comfortable, the first time she'd felt cool in days. She had no idea where she was or why she was lying down with a fan aimed in her direction when there was a case to be solved but she'd take whatever she could get. A few minutes more was all she needed to recover enough to open her eyes and try and make sense of it all. Just a few minutes more ...

'She's a lucky son of a bitch, Rusty. If Prince hadn't been so short and slight and Gaby so solid, your girlfriend could have been in serious trouble. As it is, she'll have a headache for a couple of days. Nothing that rest and paracetamol can't sort.'

'Thanks, Doc. I'd better tell Owen.'

'You do that. I've never seen anyone in such a mess as him when he brought her in.' She heard what sounded like a back being slapped. 'If I didn't know any better, I'd say that you have competition.'

The words faded in and out but, like seeds on barren soil, gained no purchase, sleep again taking control of the situation.

When she woke again, it wasn't the sound of voices that roused her. There was something else. Something slightly outside of her field of vision. She frowned, trying to puzzle it out.

'At last! I thought you'd never regain consciousness.'

'Where am I?'

'Well, you're meant to be home with me while we make use of Conor's sleepover,' Rusty said, his blue eyes twinkling down at her, his fingers laced through hers. 'Instead we're at the hospital doing everything we can to wake you up.'

'Wake me up? I don't understand.' Gaby tried to move her head only to discover that movement meant pain. She sank further back into the pillows and asked the thing that was worrying her. 'Where's Owen?'

'Safe and well, back at the station probably cursing the life out of you for all the extra paperwork you've generated. You do know you're going to have to stop this Dirty Harry style of law enforcement or one day Owen won't be around to save you.'

'Not again.' She groaned, lifting her hand to her forehead and sweeping the hair away. 'I'm never going to hear the end of it, am I?'

'Nope but at least Hayley Prince is locked up and Anita, while not out of the woods, is holding her own.'

'I'm glad.' A wave of tiredness crept in from the side, trying to steal the question she wanted to ask.

'You said you did everything you could to wake me up? What worked?' she finally managed, her eyes flickering closed.

'This.' He bent his head, his lips grazing hers. 'Have a little rest. I'm not going anywhere, Gabriella.'

251

Chapter 56

Gaby

Friday 7 August, 10 a.m. St Asaph Police Station

Rusty and DCI Sherlock had wanted her to take the rest of the week off but, apart from an ache in her neck, she was back to normal, or as nearly normal as anyone could get after two serious attempts on her life in less than six months.

The incident room was humming with activity, which was how she liked it best. It meant that she could slip in behind her desk with no fuss. She'd managed to prop open the lid of her laptop before the sudden hush told her that she'd been spotted.

'Welcome back, ma'am.'

'Are you sure you're well enough to return?'

She smiled and nodded, feeling a fraud. If she'd only waited, she wouldn't have put extra strain on the emergency services with her overnight stay. They'd only approved her discharge when Rusty had piped up with an offer to act as her responsible adult. It was stay a second night in hospital or agree to his suggestion of his spare room. She had no idea why she'd accepted instead of ringing Amy and, the way Conor had treated her, part of her regretted that she had.

Owen was the last one to her desk, a welcome distraction from her thoughts.

'Thank you for the flowers, Owen, although I think I should have bought you some instead. What do you give the person who's saved their life twice?'

'A heart attack! Seriously, Gaby, if you ever try something like that again ...'

'I know. Lesson learnt big time.' She leant across the broad expanse of desk, her voice a conspiratorial whisper. 'So, we were right?'

'Well, you were. I don't think I've ever been more disappointed in anyone in my whole life as I am in Hayley Prince.'

'She certainly doesn't look like a mass murderer.' Gaby tilted her head to the front of the *Llandudno Chronicle* and the photo under the headline: *From Grave Digger to Grave Filler*.

'So, how are Jason and the CSIs getting on back at her house?'

'It's going to take a while of sorting but the freezer is packed with body parts. At least it will make IDing the bodies much easier.'

'Poor Ellie Fry.' Gaby felt her eyes fill and struggled to sniff the tears back where they belonged, which was as far away from a detective's cheeks as possible.

'I think she'll be fine now that she knows that her mum is on the mend.'

'I still don't get why Prince attacked her? What had she to gain?'

'I think that's partly my fault. I must have rattled her cage when I went to see her and later, when she heard about Ellie's disappearance, she must have put two and two together and worked out what must have happened. It seems as if she visited Anita on Tuesday afternoon on some pretext or other and when she didn't get the answers she was looking for, with regards to Ellie's whereabouts, she went berserk, if the state of the kitchen is anything to go by. But we won't know for sure until Anita is well enough to be interviewed properly.'

'But what about her motive? The paltry bits and bobs she

took wouldn't have brought in much and the business, by all accounts, is booming.'

'Not now it's not. The council have closed it down. She's not speaking either, which is a pain but we've come up with a motive. Whether it's the right one or not remains to be seen.'

'Go on, I'm listening,' she said, resting her elbows on the desk and cupping her chin in her hands.

'We've managed to find out that she's had run-ins with both Katherine Jane and Barbara Matthews in the past. When Prince's dad was headmaster of St Gildas, Jane on one occasion accused her of theft. The same thing happened when Prince got a Saturday job working at Bon Bons sweetshop. Rumour has it that, if it wasn't nailed down, it would end up in Prince's pocket. When she got older, she thought up the ultimate revenge for anyone she didn't like.'

'That's another thing you haven't explained.' Gaby stole a hand to her neck, kneading the tense flesh. 'How did Katherine's prosthetic hip manage to find its way into the cremator when Duncan Broome had an open coffin?'

'You'll have to thank your boyfriend for that.'

'Owen,' she warned, flicking her eyes to check that no one was within hearing distance.

'It's all right, Gaby. If you think you can keep it a secret, with the enormous bunch of red roses I just spotted arriving in reception, you're a lot dumber than I ever imagined.' He grinned, obviously enjoying her discomfort. 'Hayley Prince is a piece of work. Not only did she chop up the bodies, using a junior hacksaw would you believe, and store them in the freezer, she then waited for a body to turn up for cremation and slit them apart, sewing the body parts back inside. It wouldn't have been too difficult especially if she chose the ones that had already been sutured following autopsy. The only problem was the heads.'

'The heads?' Gaby said, her voice faint.

'Too large. Someone would have noticed the size and smashing up all that brain tissue. It would have gotten terribly messy even for someone with her – let's say unusual – skill set.' Owen shook his head. 'They've found five, Gaby.'

'Five,' she repeated, not quite believing that she'd heard him correctly.

'That's right. Five heads. And the one funny thing about all this is the pen,' he continued as if she hadn't interrupted.

'The pen?' she whispered, her mind still thinking about all those heads.

'Yes. The pen that led me to think that it might be her in the first place. It was a gift for Prince's father when he retired from St Gildas. It even had his initials engraved on the rim of the cap. Miss Jane's great-nephew has confirmed that her pen, from her days as Latin teacher, was among the few items forwarded on to him when the apartment was cleared. A lucky break.'

'Very lucky.'

'Oh, by the way, I have a gift for you.' Owen put his hand in his pocket, withdrawing a small blue bottle with a matching bow tied around its neck, the word *d'Orage* etched across in gold lettering. He nudged it across the desk. 'Don't get any ideas. I bought it for Kate but it's a scent I find I cannot like.'

'Ah, our little hero. Take a seat, Darin. This won't take long.'

Gaby settled in the chair opposite DCI Sherlock, her hands neatly folded on her lap, her attention wandering between Sherlock's bent head and CS Murdock Winters' composed smile. It was like trying to read a lump of cheese for all the clues they were giving her as to the reason for her summons. She'd missed the interview and had very nearly missed a whole lot more but at least the newspapers had been kind.

'Right then. The super and I don't know what to do with you, Darin. What have you got to say about that, hmm?'

Gaby decided the best option was to maintain a dignified silence. After all, it had worked the last time.

He carried on after a moment. 'As you are aware, we would have chosen a new DI on Tuesday if it hadn't been for that little stunt you pulled.'

So they hadn't appointed Bill Davis in her absence. At least that was something.

'Yes, sir.'

'Basically you have a proven track record and the way your team have been moping about since Tuesday, you'd think that someone in the office had died. So, if you want the appointment to be formalised, we've both decided that there's only one question we need you to answer.'

Gaby didn't know what to say. She didn't even know if she wanted the additional pressure and she certainly couldn't begin to second-guess what question they felt they had to ask or indeed what her reply should be.

'Sir?'

'In hindsight, Detective, faced with the same situation that you were in on Tuesday, what would your actions be?'

She let the air seep up her chest and out through her mouth in a silent sigh. That was easy because she wasn't about to start lying for the sake of a job she wasn't sure she wanted.

'My actions wouldn't change, sir. I'd do exactly the same thing again.'

Epilogue

Ronan

Monday 10 August, 5 p.m. Llandudno

Having a mother who was a lawyer had its advantages – who better to entrust your child to? With no friends or relatives on the scene, Ellie had been heading for emergency fostering by the social services until Ronan's mum had stepped forward with a calm smile and the generous offer of accommodation until Anita was back on her feet.

Ronan set the table for supper, the smell of lasagne bubbling gently in the oven making his stomach rumble in anticipation. Having a mum who was also an excellent cook was something he'd used to think about long into the night when the sound of pattering hooves outside his cave disturbed his sleep and heightened his anxiety. Common sense told him it was only the Llandudno goats going for a stroll but in the damp, dark, isolated cave common sense didn't have a look-in.

He smiled at the shouts coming from the playroom, his facial muscles getting used to shifting in an almost forgotten direction. Caleb was giving Ellie and Heather a run for their money on whichever computer game they were playing. Ronan's smile broadened at his brother even thinking he had a chance of winning against them. He'd soon learn.

Picking up his rucksack, he headed into the lounge. There was still two weeks until he joined upper sixth at St Michaels. He had a plan finally, which started with sitting his A levels. He didn't know where his plan would take him but that was one of the things he'd learnt over the last few months. He could and would adapt to whatever life chose to fling at him next. Living on the Great Orme, he'd felt his life was over. Now he knew that it was only just beginning.

Acknowledgements

Another book. Another year as I sit writing this on the first of January in the hope that 2021 will draw a line through the previous twelve months. *Lost Souls* will be my fourth book published with HQ Digital and the fourth during lockdown. Here's hoping for a better fate for book five.

Writing is an isolated profession but I couldn't have continued to develop the character of Gaby Darin without help. Firstly a huge thank you to my outstanding editor, Abi Fenton, for her support and faith in my work. I probably wouldn't still be writing if she hadn't found me lurking in her slush pile! Also thanks to Dushi Horti, who has helped pick up the reins at HQ Digital and keep me on track. I'd also like to thank editor Helena Newton, editorial assistant Audrey Linton, and narrator Janine Cooper-Marshall. Writer Valerie Keogh also deserves an early mention. Her daily chats are a huge incentive for me to carry on tapping away on my keyboard.

While the characters here are fictitious there are a few who aren't. Amy Potter, my friend and colleague, appears again as do swimming pals, Barbara Matthews and Katherine Jane, neither of whom resemble their characters and were happy to be murdered off, at least in print! Albert Honeybun is a wonderful name. It belonged to the father-in-law of a crime fiction reader over at the UK Crime Book Club. Thank you to Andrea Delene for giving me permission to use it.

My books are set in Wales and I can't speak the language but Rhian Jones, over on Twitter, can and helped me enormously with the Welsh translations needed for the school and housing estate, so thank you.

I also like to use local businesses for authenticity. Castell Gwyn's award-winning cracked black pepper cream cheese exists. Thanks to Jackie Whittaker for allowing me to use it. I look forward to sampling it next time I visit Wales. Nathan Jones is a very talented Welsh artist who creates the most amazing paintings, which are available online (@NathanJArt) and to view at The Life: Full Colour art gallery in Caernarfon. It was an honour to include one of his paintings on Amy's lounge wall.

My mum used to live in Llandudno. Take a Break Café was one of her favourite places and so gets a mention as does Providero Café.

Much of the book centres around hip prosthetics, an idea that stemmed from a conversation I had with local jeweller, Paul Paint. The idea was expanded on with help from orthopaedic surgeon Ben Burgess, who very kindly met up with me to cement the idea and how it might work in my story. Also thanks to Julie Dunk for information on prosthetics following cremation. As a nurse, my knowledge of UK policing is limited to what I read so any mistakes are my own. I've researched everything that I've written about but errors are bound to creep in so apologies in advance if I've missed something.

I have a wonderful street team, a group of fans who are right beside me every step of the way. A huge thank you for all the support. Also thank you to all the book bloggers and book reviewers for helping my work find their audience. I continue to be in your debt for all the work you do behind the scenes. Never underestimate your worth.

Finally, as ever, thanks to my tribe of four who are always on my side with offers of mugs of tea and who get to hear first-hand how my writing is going, or not as the case may be. Buns for tea.

If you enjoyed *Lost Souls*, please think of leaving a review. The next in the series will be out in November.

Thanks,

Jenny x

Keep reading for an excerpt from

Silent Cry ...

Prologue

Izzy

Five years ago

'Be careful. It's the first time you've been out with her by yourself.'

'Give over nagging, Izzy. We'll be fine, won't we, gorgeous?' Charlie said, bending on his haunches and gently running his finger down his daughter's plump cheek, her dark blue eyes staring back at him. 'We're going to let your mammy have some rest while we go to the shops. It's time we got better acquainted. I can tell you all about football and which team to support.'

'You will not. Don't listen, Alys. There's only one football team worth supporting and it's not his,' Izzy teased, feeling redundant now that Charlie had stolen her attention.

This would be the first time she'd be apart from her since the birth and already she could feel the bonds of motherhood straining at the thought of Alys being out of her sight, even if it was only for half an hour. It had only taken a week for her world to shrink to the boundary walls of the house. But she'd never been happier. Her eyes grazed the pair of them, and love filled every corner. But Charlie and Alys needed this time, both of them, and a few minutes alone after another interrupted night's sleep would be like a gift from the gods. Izzy had never felt so bone-achingly weary and, while she dreaded being apart, a rest would make all the difference.

'Now, what about a goodbye kiss from your pretty mam then?' Charlie said.

Pushing himself to standing, the car seat in the crook of his arm, he leant in for a kiss reminiscent of the best Hollywood romances.

'You daft thing,' she laughed. But secretly she was pleased, more than pleased.

She watched as he reversed the Mini into the road and continued watching until they were out of sight before returning to the warmth of the house. She slipped off her shoes by the front door and, fumbling into her slippers, headed for the kitchen. There was washing and ironing, not to mention food to prepare. There were so many things she knew she should be doing but she felt sick with tiredness. With a mug of tea in her hand, she returned to the sofa and, feet propped up on the end, rested back, allowing the silence to envelop her.

There was always noise in the cottage. It wasn't Charlie's fault that he was one of those men you could hear long before you could see them: Charlie, her one-night stand, who seemed to have taken up root in both her house and her heart. He was always clomping around the place with a heavy tread and if it wasn't him, it was one of his mates he'd invited back for her to feed. The house suddenly felt empty with the pervading sound of silence.

She'd close her eyes, just for five minutes … they'd be back soon.

The fire had died back to nothing, the embers just a pale glow in the grate. She turned her head towards the window, her hand instinctively pulling the woollen blanket around her shoulders, a shiver snaking its way across her spine. The last time she'd looked out, the sun had been streaming in through the pane but all that was visible now was the dense grey of twilight. The phone rang, slicing through her sudden fear. She struggled to sit, her neck stiff from the arm of the sofa. A million excuses chased through her mind.

They've been delayed, maybe had a puncture … or knowing Charlie, he's run out of petrol.

Her hand lifted the receiver to her ear before gently replacing it. She'd learnt the best way to treat cold callers was by doing exactly that. No comment. No words. Nothing.

She pulled the throw tighter over her shoulders, her eyes now on the clock on the mantelpiece, her mind in a tangle.

Two hours? How the hell could she have slept for so long? This was quickly followed by the worst thought of all: *He must have had an accident. Even now, he's in some anonymous hospital bed and as for Alys …*

Her stomach clenched when there was no need – she'd just ring his mobile. Reaching out a hand, she quickly tapped in his number.

The person you are trying to reach is currently unavailable. Please leave a message after the tone.

She was scared now, really scared. He never left his phone switched off even if it was only to check on the football scores. They'd been gone hours. She had no idea where the hell he could have taken her. Alys would need a feed and a nappy change. There was nowhere he'd go, not with a newborn.

Izzy heaved a sigh at her foolishness and, for one long moment, relished the feel of wool against skin as she tried to laugh her fears off. She wasn't his keeper. They'd got held up. Something had happened, something silly that she couldn't guess at and, in a minute, she'd hear the creak of the gate and the turn of the key.

The moment passed. The minutes continued ticking and her sliver of calm disintegrated.

In a sudden burst of movement, she leapt from the chair and

ran up the stairs.

That's it. They came in earlier, hours earlier and even now they're both curled up in their beds, not wanting to wake me.

But Alys's cot was empty, apart from the pale-yellow blanket folded neatly over the end, just the way she'd left it that morning. Their bed was empty too, the duvet flung back any old how, the sheets cold, wrinkled, uninviting.

Outside. Maybe he pulled up and decided to close his eyes. Maybe it's like the last time when he forgot his keys and, if Alys has fallen asleep in the car, he might have decided not to wake me.

She remembered the last time. His sheepish grin when she shook him back into the land of the living, which developed into their first big row and ended in a swift coupling against the back of the sofa.

There was post on the mat but she just stepped over it. She wasn't in the mood for bills and flyers. She just needed to know that Alys was safe.

The air was cold, wiping the smile from her face. There was barely a glimmer of light as twilight switched to dusk. They were far enough away from everyone for darkness, when it hit, to mean exactly that. There wasn't even a visible moon or any stars to light the way. She took a second to drag air into her lungs, the smell from the winter-flowering jasmine around the door filling her senses, but there was no joy to be had from the scent. Her eyes adjusted enough to see the outline of the gate and the telegraph pole next to it. There was no car, no indication that he'd returned. There was nothing apart from the empty track leading up to the house.

Izzy stayed a while. Something was wrong, dreadfully wrong – something that she had no way of putting right.

She finally wandered back into the hall, the post in her hand, the throw trailing in her wake. She was cold down to the bone, but it wasn't the type of cold that the warmth from wool was going to solve. Her hand stretched towards the phone for a third time, her arm brushing against her breasts, now heavy with milk. She hesitated, her gaze lingering on the mail and the postcard on top. Was she overreacting? Was this the paranoid response of a new mum? Maybe. Possibly. Hopefully.

The card was plain white and, with no name or address scrawled on the front, must have been hand delivered. She flipped it over and all thoughts of a simple explanation died along with any hope in her heart.

I've got Alys. Don't try to find us, Charlie

Chapter 1

Izzy

Monday 23 December, 5.10 p.m. Swansea

It took one look, just one, for Izzy's world to shatter a second time.

To anyone else it was only a flicker, a face in the crowd but to her it was a face so intrinsically linked to her past that she paused in her fur-lined boots, unable to do more than stare at the woman disappearing across the street. It was all there in the angle of her head, the sway of her hips, the colour of her jet-black hair. It had been five years and yet it still felt just like yesterday.

Grace. Grace Madden.

A wave of ice-cold worked its way across her shoulders and down her spine, pinning her to the spot. She couldn't move even if her life depended on it. Instead, she watched, transfixed as Grace clambered into a waiting taxi before zooming into the distance. She was too late and yet what could she have done? Shout? Scream? Surely she could have done something instead of just standing there? The tears came in a sudden deluge. Tears for the opportunity she'd just lost.

'Are you all right, love? All this Christmas cheer getting to you?'

271

The stranger's soft Welsh accent was a welcome interruption.

Izzy wiped a hand over her cheeks before scooping up her bags.

'I'm fine, just a little overcome,' she said, jolted out of her reverie. She was standing outside Costa, her gaze still lingering on the spot where she'd last seen her. Stepping out of his way with a brief smile, she headed inside to buy a coffee she didn't want simply because the tremors running up her legs made sitting an urgent necessity.

Costa was busy but she managed to secure a table right at the back and, pushing her coffee to one side, rested her head in her hands.

Was it even Grace? It certainly looked like her with her distinctive black hair sweeping her shoulders in sharp contrast to her pale face and razor cheekbones. But now, as the seconds ticked into minutes, she wasn't so sure. Bottle black was such a popular look these days and it wasn't as if she was that unique.

Squashing back tears, she reached for her cup with an unsteady hand and took tentative sips until the cup was drained. But still she sat, clenching it between her hands, trying to drag the strength up from somewhere to think about someone she hadn't thought of in a very long time. Grace, the woman she'd thought her best friend. A great friend she'd turned out to be, leaving town at a time when she'd needed her the most – the weekend Alys disappeared. She hadn't even bothered to get in touch since. But now she was back.

Izzy frowned, trying to remember but suddenly the only thing she could think about was the glaring fact that Grace had chosen to leave the area at the same time Charlie had taken Alys. Now it seemed a little too convenient and, if she hadn't been on fistfuls of tranquilisers at the time, surely, she'd have forced the police to investigate this aspect of the case further.

She didn't know how long she sat, staring into the past. Time was irrelevant to someone like her. Time was irrelevant to someone who'd had the whole world in the palm of her hand only to lose it in an instant. She didn't know what pulled her out of her fugue. A rattle of cups? The door being pushed? The happy family of two-plus-two at the next table making more noise than sense?

In a spurt of energy, she picked up her scarf and wrapped it loosely around her neck, a quick look at her watch confirming that she'd spent far too long thinking about the past. She couldn't do happy families, not now. Now she had to leave, if only to catch the last train home. Spending the night in Swansea weighed down with shopping was the very last thing she wanted to face just before Christmas.

The local supermarket was packed, but it was always going to be at this time of the evening. Her mind was still buzzing with thoughts of Grace but she clamped them down under an iron lid. She would think about her but not now. Not here. Not yet. She'd get all her jobs out of the way before letting her creep back inside.

Head down, she avoided anyone and everyone. She wanted to buy what she needed before journeying home and slamming the door. Only then would she allow her thoughts to drift back into the past.

'Hello, Izzy, long time no see.'

She looked up into the face of DI Rhys Walker, brother of Rebecca, an old friend from her school days, and the lead detective in the search for Alys. St David's wasn't the largest place in the world and she was always bumping into people she knew but not in Rhys's case. He was right when he said he hadn't seen her around but that was only because she'd managed to avoid him by ducking into whichever bar, shop or restaurant she'd happened to be standing outside.

She'd dealt with Rhys. She'd spent what felt like a lifetime holed up in Swansea Police Station going over the case. It was just her luck that he'd decided to commute when he'd been promoted rather than move out of St David's altogether. Every time she

273

caught a glimpse of his burly frame around town, she had to shove her heart back down her throat with a thump. She'd had no choice but to deal with him then but now? Now she chose to avoid him and, if it hadn't been for spotting Grace, she'd have managed to avoid him again.

It wasn't that he was bad-looking, far from it. He wasn't that tall, probably five-ten but his well-muscled, powerful build made up for what he lacked in height. His dark brown hair used to be collar-length before police regulations dictated the short crop he was currently sporting. All in all, he was your boy-next-door type. A boy she'd grown up with through the years, despite him being six years older. They'd gone to the same school. They'd frequented the same cinemas and social venues. But he was a copper, only that.

She hopped from one foot to the other, her gaze flicking from her trolley to his and back again before landing on his ringless left hand. The last time she'd spoken to him he'd been single. But, by the state of his trolley, nearly overflowing with Christmas cheer, there was now bound to be a bride and a bundle of babies to complete his happiness. Well, bully for him. However, instead of passing the time of day, all she wanted was to hide under her duvet and think about the implications of seeing Grace again because, despite her misgivings, she was now one hundred per cent sure it was her.

He wasn't going anywhere. She could see it in the way his gaze drilled down through layers of skin, flesh and bone right to her heart, if indeed she still had that organ thumping inside her chest.

His hand fastened around the wire rim of her trolley before leaning in to inspect the contents. 'Not having turkey and all the trimmings?' he said, a frown replacing his smile.

Her gaze followed his and she saw what he saw: four rolls of wrapping paper nudged up beside two bottles of plonk and one of whiskey, all topped off with a ready meal and a tub of chocolate ice cream. It was a lonely basket for a lonely woman, and it was also none of his bloody business.

'Yes, well. I'm not home for Christmas.'

'No? Where are you off to then?' His smile was back and she remembered again just what a nice bloke he was. 'I hope it's somewhere exciting?'

'Hardly! Only to my parents. And you? Do you have an exciting time planned?'

'Not really, although I do have Christmas off for a change.'

She held his gaze for a second before turning her attention back to the contents of his trolley and the large bag of Maris Pipers on top. Meeting him hadn't been as bad as she'd feared and the questions far less intrusive. But that wasn't surprising being as they were standing next to an old woman in a purple hat as she picked over the sprouts with a slow deliberation. She knew she should bat back a question about what he was up to with his full trolley. He certainly wasn't the only solitary man wandering around with a bemused look on his face while they searched for the cranberry sauce, but he was the only one she didn't want to get drawn into a conversation with. There was no way she was going to continue talking about turkey and the like. In truth, she didn't give a damn where he was spending his Christmas or with whom. She didn't give a damn whether he was planning to gorge himself silly on turkey or a plate of nut-roast with deep-fried falafel on the side. She just didn't care.

They'd given up. They'd given up searching after the first few weeks, but it wasn't something she'd ever be able to do. Charlie had stolen her child and then had the arrogance to post a card through her letter box boasting what he'd done. What kind of man would be so cruel? Certainly not the kindly man hovering in front of her. She felt rejuvenated suddenly. Seeing Grace had rejuvenated her and changed something. Where before she'd been prepared to let it ride, now she couldn't. For the first time in what felt like a very long time she was going to get off her behind and do something. The only question was what.

Her gaze shifted back to his face, an idea hovering. Should she tell him about seeing Grace in Swansea? Would he be interested after all this time? And finally, what good would it do? Before common sense interfered and stopped her, she leant forward, lowering her voice to a thin whisper.

'Actually, I'm pleased I've bumped into you. There's something I need to tell you.'

Dear Reader,

We hope you enjoyed reading this book. If you did, we'd be so appreciative if you left a review. It really helps us and the author to bring more books like this to you.

Here at HQ Digital we are dedicated to publishing fiction that will keep you turning the pages into the early hours. Don't want to miss a thing? To find out more about our books, promotions, discover exclusive content and enter competitions you can keep in touch in the following ways:

JOIN OUR COMMUNITY:
Sign up to our new email newsletter: http://smarturl.it/SignUpHQ
Read our new blog www.hqstories.co.uk
🐦 : https://twitter.com/HQStories
🅵 : www.facebook.com/HQStories

BUDDING WRITER?
We're also looking for authors to join the HQ Digital family!
Find out more here:
https://www.hqstories.co.uk/want-to-write-for-us/
Thanks for reading, from the HQ Digital team

ONE PLACE. MANY STORIES

ONE PLACE. MANY STORIES

If you enjoyed *Lost Souls*, then why not try another utterly gripping crime thriller from HQ Digital?